ANGELA D. SHELTON

Echoes of the Imperium

The Y Chronicles Book Two

*To my readers—thank you for your grace and patience as I
brought this second book in The Y Chronicles to life.
And in memory of my parents—your unwavering encouragement
and support made this journey possible. This book is for you.*

Contents

Acknowledgments

To my readers, thank you for your grace and patience as I worked through this second book in *The Y Chronicles* series. As I launched book one, my siblings and I walked alongside our mother through hospice. And as I wrote this book, we gathered once more to ease my father's passing.

Grief wove itself through every stage of this book—writing, editing, and revising—making the process both painful and slow. If you have lost a loved one, I pray you give yourself grace and time. Healing doesn't follow a schedule, and our hearts and minds need space to process such deep loss.

My parents were my biggest encouragers, always believing in my writing and cheering me on. I was truly blessed to have them in my life. To those who have supported me through this journey, I am deeply grateful.

If you have experienced loss and would like to connect, feel free to reach out at **angeladshelton@outlook.com**. Let's share our stories and find strength together.

I'd also like to thank my critique partners for enduring my early drafts with patience and grace. Your encouragement means the world to me.

Special thanks to the **ACFW Critique Loop**, especially **Rich Goodwin, Carrie Hachadurian, Lynne G., Kathy McKinsey, and Susan Sloan**, as well as my **ACFW YA critique group: Shanna Heath, Suzie McKaig, and Lauren**

Thell.

A special appreciation to my sisters, **Amanda Bentley and Carrie Lofquist**, who are always there for me, ready to listen, encourage, and be my sounding boards when I get stuck.

Now, on to part two and the conclusion of Lexi's story.

Chapter 1

Lexi's eyelids popped open as an arm snaked around her and yanked her across the bed. *They found me.*

With a growl, she pulled back her elbow, then used all her might to ram it backward into her captor's ribs. A satisfying grunt preceded the release of her assailant's grip. She jumped out of bed and ran to the door to escape.

A moan stopped her from turning the doorknob. "What'd you do that for?"

Reeves. She spun to the bed. There, her husband of less than a week gripped his ribs, his head bandage askew. She rushed back. "I'm so sorry. I thought..." Her cheeks burned as his pain-filled eyes gleamed. Dark smudges under them testified to their exhausting week. "I thought you were a Freedom Force fighter."

Still gripping his side with one hand, he shoved himself up and dropped his feet over the bedside. He laced her fingers with his free ones. "You pack a wallop, Lex. From now on, I'll remember you don't like morning snuggles."

The heat moved from her face to her neck. Did all young brides suffer this sort of embarrassment, or was it reserved for those on the run from the Imperium? She tried to pull away. "I'll go look for an ice pack or something."

His chuckle calmed her, as did the swirl of his thumb against her palm. "If I can handle a bullet, then I can survive a gouge to the rib cage."

Her heartbeat, having slowed from her initial fright, ticked up once more. Their hands fit together perfectly, like puzzle pieces set into place. This must be how it felt to be a new bride. He leaned toward her and drew her in. Their lips touched, and the awkwardness evaporated. She deepened the kiss and reveled in her new reality—he belonged to her and she to him.

A knock stopped her from taking the next step to cement their bond. They broke apart, breathless, and eyes locked on each other.

Reeves scrubbed a hand across the back of his neck, huffed, then rose. She straightened her clothes as he strode to the door and opened it.

Her mom stood in the hallway. "Glad to see you're up early. We've got a lot to do today. I'll see you downstairs in fifteen?"

Lexi's shoulders slumped until she remembered her father. How could she be so selfish as to want to play honeymoon games while the man who'd risked his life for her remained a prisoner? And the retirees they'd planned to save. What about them? "We'll be there."

After Reeves shut the door, he returned to the bed and snuggled Lexi into his arms. "This conversation can wait for tonight, but we definitely need to finish it."

The chaste peck on her nose when he released her left her unsatisfied. "Definitely." The memory of her father's face on the vis sluiced cold water over her heart. Now wasn't the time. "I need to run to the bathroom. I'll meet you downstairs."

She made her way down the hall, but as she raised her fist

to knock on the door, a sob echoed from inside. It had to be Rumi, her father's new young wife. Figured she'd fall apart when they'd reached safety. Everything about the girl seemed too fragile for the harshness of this life.

Should she knock and offer help? If Lexi had been the one sobbing her eyes out, she'd prefer to be left alone. Probably best to find another bathroom.

She hadn't taken five steps away before the bathroom door opened.

Rumi called out. "Lexi?"

Great. Pretend everything is fine. Lexi set her face to a neutral expression and turned. Rumi's eyes blinked red, but the rest of her pallid face could have been that of a ghost.

Lexi sighed. "Are you okay?"

Rumi shook her head and sucked her lips into her mouth. Then her eyes brimmed, and tears trekked down her cheeks.

Lexi swallowed back another sigh. Why must it be her responsibility to take care of this girl? How fair was that? She nudged Rumi back into the bathroom. A washcloth lay folded on a shelf, so she ran it under cool water, wrung it out, and handed it to the girl. "You okay?"

Her response came through hiccupped sobs. "I'm fine."

Lexi's heart stuttered. *Give the girl a break. She's got nobody.* "You're welcome to hang out with me and Reeves today. We'll figure this all out."

"Thanks." Rumi handed the washcloth back. "But I know you'd rather spend time with anyone besides me. You must be excited to catch up with your mom. I can find someplace else to be."

Lexi couldn't recall the last time she'd seen eyes so weighed down. She ground her teeth over this impossible position, but she unclamped them as the girl's shoulders slumped and her quiet sniffles escaped. "I'm sorry you're stuck with us." She patted Rumi's back, the girl's ebony hair slipping over her hand. "This can't be easy—especially now that we know my mom is alive."

A bitter laugh rang out. Rumi shrugged. "It's not exactly what they taught us to expect in marriage classes, is it?"

Understatement of the year. Nothing Lexi experienced in the last weeks had been topics in the Imperium school curriculum. If only they'd offered Rebellion 101. Mom would have been an excellent instructor. Scratch that. Mom's talents would have been better used to teach Deception 101. "I'll see you downstairs?"

Rumi wobbled a weak smile. "Sure."

Within minutes, Lexi met Reeves, Ms. Becky, and Fletcher in the living room. When Rumi arrived but hovered in the doorway, Lexi held back an eye roll and motioned her over.

Mom entered. "Let's get started."

She led them to a set of wooden pocket doors. Guards on either side slid them apart, and the group walked into a high-ceilinged space. Lexi's mouth dropped open at its magnitude. Wall-to-wall monitors and computer equipment flickered and hummed. Men sat in a row of chairs, sporting gloves with sensors running from a central source in their palms to their fingertips. Vis displays allowed observers to follow the drones they controlled. The aircrafts' speed coupled with sharp turns and dips over the outdoor terrain made watching the monitors nauseating.

Thrym stood in the center, surveying his kingdom while monitors displayed camera feeds from all over the Imperium. Including what looked like the headquarters conference chamber.

Fletcher harrumphed. He sidled up behind a vis projecting a drone above a farmhouse. "I'm assuming this is where we are now?"

Mom nodded. "We've got full squads watching the compound. The Imperium can't get within miles of this place without us knowing." She waved at the banks of monitors. "Our technicians have also tapped every feed we can manage inside the Imperium. Just brought one online yesterday with a view outside of Reclamation, which is how we knew you needed a hand."

Ms. Becky's gaze flitted from screen to screen. "This is amazing. We could save every retiree if you've got access to their systems."

The label Retiree grated. The Imperium had coined the term for those deemed no longer useful and claimed they moved to Solitude for rest and relaxation. Instead, the Imperium executed anyone they considered too old or frail to serve their purpose.

"Saving the retirees isn't our end goal." Mom's lips thinned. "We're tearing it down. All of it."

Reeves frowned at Lexi, then her mom. "Are you crazy? You're going to war against the Imperium? You can't possibly have enough soldiers or technology to win."

Fletcher pointed to the aerial property view. "Look at the number of tents. Not sure how many of these hold retirees, but I doubt half the occupants are able-bodied fighters. Even if you had the tech to back them up, there still isn't enough."

Mom bristled. "I know what I'm doing. We've got the tech, and the people will come with our recruiting plan. We've been stealing weapons, medical supplies, and food, usually from sympathetic workers at the plants—easier to cover up the theft. Add trained soldiers, and the Imperium is going down."

Ms. Becky grabbed Fletcher's arm. "No. We won't be a part of any war. Y is a peaceful movement."

Fletcher's eyes flashed at his mentor before he let out a huff, nodded, and placed his hand over hers.

A vis came to life. The first of the Imperium's mottos scrolled across it. *Unity above all else.*

Lexi's stomach knotted. Whatever the coming announcement was wouldn't be good.

Thrym grumbled. "We keep up with the propaganda. Technicians we recruited spliced into their network, so we see everything the Imperium does."

Tempest Malachy, the Imperium's mouthpiece, looked smart wearing a Freedom Force dress uniform as if newly recruited. She timed her first words for the moment the final motto scrolled off the display. *One marriage—many children.* "We have new information about the identities of rebel spies. All citizens should be on the lookout for dangerous members of the rebel group known as Y. Any sympathizers will be treated as combatants."

Three images flashed in the upper right-hand corner—Lexi's school ID photo wedged between pictures of Rumi and Reeves.

Tempest continued. "I recently interviewed a former friend of this renegade family."

The scene changed to a video of Tempest standing beside Courtney Blakeslee, Lexi's nosy neighbor. The girl's smug smile beamed at the camera. "I knew something was suspicious about the Verity family. I told my parents, but of course, they wouldn't listen. Too trusting," she gushed, at ease with her moment of fame. "I especially worried about their daughter, Lexi. She never fit in."

The knot in Lexi's stomach tightened. If she could get her hands around Courtney's neck through the monitor, the girl wouldn't utter another syllable. Instead, she prattled on until Lexi couldn't take in another word. "I need some air." She headed toward the door.

Reeves followed. "Wait up. I'll come with."

She spun and held up a palm. "No, it's okay. I just need a minute." She waved toward the walls of video and data feed. "You can figure this out."

His wince brought an ache to her chest, but he stayed put as she walked away. She paced to the front of the house, out the door, and flopped onto soft green grass. The sensation of plants under her palms soothed her tattered soul. If her plan had worked on testing day, she'd be with the growers now. Maybe she'd never have found her mom's diary. Her father would be safe, and she'd be elbow-deep in the hydroponics.

It was a lie, but she'd rather believe that than think about her mom's betrayal.

"Lexi?" Mom hunched beside her. "Walk with me, will you?"

Since the initial shock of seeing Mom and Nana and Gramps alive had worn off, Mom's deceit took center stage. How could she have left Lexi behind? Left her to the Imperium's whims and thinking they'd all died horrible deaths? She needed to confront her. For that, they needed privacy. She rose and followed.

They walked around an open area where men and women, dressed in black from head to toe, practiced hand-to-hand combat. A petite woman performed a leg sweep that took down a man who stood a foot and a half taller than her.

Whoa. Lexi wouldn't mind a lesson or two herself. Though, if it resulted in more dangerous attacks on Reeves in the early morning hours, it might be a bad idea.

"I've got something to show you." Mom rested a hand on the small of Lexi's back. "You'll like this."

They passed several tents, ranging from small ones, probably sleeping quarters, to larger ones with open flaps revealing medical beds and equipment. Other tents held tables and chairs for meetings, and one narrow tent housed gray-haired adults resting in beds or sitting in wheelchairs.

The moment they passed the infirmary, their destination came into view. Even if Mom hadn't pointed it out, it would've been Lexi's stopping point as soon as she sighted it.

The greenhouse overflowing with plants stood in an open field. Her heart melted, and she ran to the building's doors. As she stepped inside, heat and moisture enveloped her. She closed her eyes and inhaled the scents of earth—of life. Her ears drank in the water's trickle through the hydroponic tubes, like a brook running through a forest, green with life.

It'll take the entire Freedom Force to pull me out of here. Never. Leaving.

A hand on her shoulder brought her out of her reverie. Sadness flattened her mom's smile. "I've been dying to share this with you. It's been so hard to be away."

The words jolted Lexi back to reality, dragging with them the searing memory of the explosion and the heartache that consumed her as she mourned. The anger she'd been holding back surged, spilling over in an unstoppable wave. "How could you let me believe you were all dead? You know people really died in that explosion, right? I was in the hospital."

Her mom's flinch said Lexi hit home.

Good. She needed to hurt too.

Then Mom's slight nod offered an unspoken acknowledgment of the pain she caused. "I had to choose a different path from your father. If I'd brought you with me, I'd have chosen for you as well. I couldn't steal your options."

"But you left the diary and the necklace on purpose." Lexi's hand went to the locket, warm from her skin. "Did Father know what was in them?"

Mom motioned for Lexi to follow her down the first aisle between rows of bean plants heavy with pods. "For years, I tried to accept the teachings of Yeshua. I snuck food into the Favela. Wormed information out of your father whenever I could to rescue retirees without him knowing." She plucked a pod from a plant and broke it in two. "It wasn't enough. People suffered from hunger and died of diseases we could have cured. I couldn't accept the way we treated our grandparents. When it was Nana and Gramps's turn to 'retire,' something inside me broke. I couldn't run fast enough to join the rebels who'd had enough of Y's peaceful movement. The Imperium declared war on older adults right from the beginning. It was time to fight back."

Lexi froze. "You could have told me." Her voice trebled, her emotions scarcely restrained. "You could have given me the choice back then. Instead, you let me believe I'd lost everyone I loved. You left me with a father who cared more about his status than he ever cared about me—only about how my career could boost his own."

A fire ignited in Mom's eyes. "Don't you get it? I can never go back to safety. Now that you're with me, you can't either. We either fight to live—fight to free the Imperium's people— or we die. I wanted you to choose this rebellion of your own free will. The government has looked the other way when Y rescued retirees. They ignored our trips into the Favela to feed the homeless. They aren't ignoring this new movement, this offshoot of the passive Y."

Lexi gulped, but the truth was hard to swallow. "I need some time alone. Time to think."

Did Mom's eyes glisten before Mom spun on her heels and strode down the aisle and out the door?

* * *

The sun began its descent while Lexi helped with the bean harvest. When Reeves strode into the greenhouse, she held a basket belted to her waist so she could use both hands to pluck the ripened pods. The opportunity to sample fresh vegetables proved to be a bonus of working the harvest. If not for the confrontation and the looming threat of the Imperium, this would have been the best day in her seventeen years of life.

Reeves's face was haggard, as if he'd aged in the hours they'd been apart. His ruffled mop of blond hair stuck straight up through the crooked bandage that protected his wound. "You, okay? Your mom said you needed time alone, but I didn't expect you'd stay away this long."

"Sorry." She waved to her surroundings. "This is my happy place. I've wanted to work in the greenhouses since I was little."

He nodded. "It shows. You're all lit up—even more stunning than usual." His face reddened as if he'd said something he shouldn't have. Then he ducked his head and plucked a bean from her basket and munched the end off. "It's getting late, though, and they've assigned us to a tent. Ready to see our new home?"

Their new home… Maybe that's why she'd lingered here so late, a part of her uncertain what he might expect tonight. She dropped her basket of beans on the counter for the cooks to process, then followed her husband out. After the greenhouse's heat and moisture, the cool and dry outside air stung her exposed arms and face. She slid her arm through his, taking in his spicy scent. "What have you been up to today?"

"I've been learning about the plan of attack against the Imperium. It could work if they can finish their training and find enough recruits before the government finds us." He hugged her arm closer. "I want to be a part of it. Now that I know what they're doing to older citizens, I can't stand by and let them keep killing."

She shivered. Must they talk about the Imperium or any rebellion? "It's peaceful here. Green grass. Plants thriving and producing. There seems to be enough to eat. Can't we just hang out, help with the harvests, and take a break?"

He squeezed her tight, then stopped at a tent, and zipped open a flap. "Here we are. Home sweet home."

Inside, two cots each held a folded blanket and a thin square pillow. No way could they sleep together in one of those. Should she be relieved or disappointed? Snuggling might've been nice, but was she ready for more? Maybe the cots were a good thing… for now.

She grasped her husband's hands, savoring the connection. "I don't want to fight forever, but if we could rescue my father and sneak him to safety, then we could have a real life out here. Maybe we could convince the others to let the Imperium be. If we leave them alone, maybe they'll return the favor."

He shook his head. "It'll never work. Even if the Imperium ignored us, could you live with yourself, knowing they kill people just because they're old or sick?" He wrapped her in a hug, his breath warm against the top of her head. "I've already made my decision. I'm joining the fight to take down the system. You need to make your own choice, though."

She nodded, but couldn't form her thoughts into a sentence, even for her internal narrative. Reeves had a point. But the thought of hurting another human...

Later, she lay awake, listening to her husband's quiet snores. They'd pulled the cots together, but the rod frames separated them, preventing them from cuddling. It didn't matter, anyway. He'd fallen asleep within minutes of his head hitting the pillow.

In the weeks she'd known him, he'd been the decisive one, so his mind seemed to sleep soundly while her indecisive thoughts swirled. She'd never given Reeves an answer—hadn't wanted to choose. What the Imperium was doing was wrong. But Ms. Becky had a point as well. They could continue to rescue people and bring them to this new city. There didn't have to be a war, at least not one the rebels started.

Could she convince her mom and the rest of the leadership that war wasn't the answer? Or would they sway her to their opinion? Battles meant more loss of life, perhaps even Reeves's. She pressed a cold hand against the lump in her gut.

Her father invaded her mind as well. In the dark, with no greenhouse to distract her, the guilt ate at her like a rodent gnawing at a protein bar. Her father broke the rules for her. Yes, he'd probably done it for selfish reasons, but he'd done what *she* asked him to do and landed in prison for it.

Now she had a choice to make, and his life may depend on

her decision.

Chapter 2

Every inch of Lexi ached as she sat on a hard bench, her elbows on the matching bamboo table. She'd left Reeves to sleep as long as he could, but the cot had been less than compassionate on her back. Thoughts of stiff muscles evaporated amidst the aroma of fresh vegetables in the chow tent. Steam rose from the fragrant cooked greens, and she drew in the aroma of garlic mixed with—were those collards? The tiny black specks in the dish looked like bugs had invaded the kitchen. The server said they were chia seeds. According to her studies, they provided protein to a vegetarian diet. There had been no sight of any chickens so far, but who knew what the rebels might have tucked away on their camp's outskirts?

Unappetizing as the speckles were, she wouldn't waste a single bite. After she'd eaten mostly protein bars her entire life, anything fresh was welcome. The first bite titillated her taste buds. She wasn't certain how, but she could taste the green in the leaves, a bitter bite beneath the notes of garlic. With eyes closed, she savored each forkful until nothing but an empty bowl with a smatter of the miniature seeds remained. Did the rules permit a second serving? A tap on her shoulder jarred her.

Mom joined her on the bench. "Good morning. I hope you slept well."

That her mother slumbered in a proper house on a comfortable mattress while Lexi slept on a cot under a canvas roof niggled at her. But no reason to stir up any arguments. "Well enough."

"You'll be expected to train with the rest of the recruits. All able-bodied Solitude residents are required. I'll pull some strings to get you an extra rotation or two in the greenhouse, but you're going to learn how to fight."

Whoa. Hold up. Her spine stiffened. "Fight? As in *war?*"

"Yes. Being my daughter doesn't excuse you. It's a responsibility we all carry. In fact, our relationship means people will look to you to set a good example. You'll be under the microscope, so to speak."

"I thought we had freedom of choice in Solitude. If I'm obliged to become a soldier, it's no different from the Imperium." A queasiness unrelated to breakfast climbed up her throat. "What about Ms. Becky and Fletcher and the other peaceful Y members? Are you going to force them against their will?"

Mom sighed. "Ms. Becky is too old to fight. It won't take much to convince Fletcher or the rest of her protection team. Something tells me they've been itching to get their hands dirty."

The big guy towering over Ms. Becky filled Lexi's mind. More than once, Fletcher's eyes had given away that he didn't agree with his boss. That didn't mean Lexi liked the thought. "But they've always been peaceful."

"Now that we saved her men, Ms. Becky expects *my* team to

help rescue the retirees." Mom rolled her eyes. "But that's not my mission. I've had enough of saving a few here and there. It's time to save them all."

It was hard to disagree. The Imperium's control had to stop, but were they trading one form of manipulation for another? People had bullied, deceived, and pushed Lexi around long enough. "What if I refuse?"

"I don't think you understand the situation. Ms. Becky and her Y volunteers have been saving people from the Imperium's disposal program her entire life. Do you know how many she *doesn't* save? Hundreds." Mom rubbed the back of her neck before stretching it side to side. "Those who get rescued land in the Favela, where they often succumb to hunger or illness. Or simple infections the Imperium's doctors could cure without blinking an eye. If we're going to stop that, I need weapons, bullets, medical supplies, food, and the most important resource—troops."

Lexi's chest tightened. She'd never forget the lump of rags she'd seen the first time she'd entered the Favela. The man underneath had nothing while she'd eaten eggs and bacon to celebrate her birthday that morning. She couldn't go back to the innocent life she'd lived, but could she be a warrior? The tightness further constricted her breathing. In the battle at Y's headquarters, a man died within her arm's reach. "I'm willing to defend and rescue, but I can't kill."

Placing her hand on Lexi's, Mom nodded. "I felt that way when I was younger, but the more death I saw under Imperium rule, the more I realized I needed to change." She squeezed Lexi's fingers. "You can change too. Become a person who fights for hundreds of lives by taking the dozen who control the city."

Resources. That was all Lexi was to her mother—a tool. The person sitting beside her had morphed from the one who'd penned the diary and cooked breakfast for her nervous daughter and given warm hugs every day before school. She was unrecognizable now. Perhaps the happy homemaker had been a façade, and the leader inside had been the reality all along. "I won't kill another human."

Her mother stood and brushed unseen dirt from her black pants, eyes flashing. "You'll do as I say. Report to the training tent this morning and do your part, or you may never see your father free again."

Color drained from Lexi's hands as she gripped the bench and held in the words she wanted to scream at her mother's retreating form. This couldn't be happening. Every curse word she'd ever heard teased her tongue. Cussing wouldn't change anything, though. Someday soon, they needed a long discussion where she could have her say.

Fighting back hot tears, she scrambled for positive thoughts to combat the fury. Nana and Gramps were safe. Reeves was in her life. She'd get extra time in the greenhouse. That was something, small as it was. Maybe her mother cared, at least a smidgen. Or Lexi could see it for what it was—a bribe.

Time to get moving. Yesterday, she'd passed by the training tent where she needed to be, but Mom hadn't said *when* this morning she had to be there. Hurrying out of the tent, Lexi headed to the farmhouse. Gramps hadn't looked so good the last time she'd seen him, and he might not be around much longer. She'd take every opportunity to be with him while she could.

Men with terrifyingly hefty rifles patrolled the wraparound porch, and drones buzzed overhead. One man blocked the front door and stopped her before she reached the top porch step. "This building is out-of-bounds."

Giving her brightest smile, she froze in place. "I'm Lexi Verity. My mother and grandparents live here. I'm just popping in to see Gramps." Using her maiden name had to have some perks to counterbalance the scrutiny, didn't it?

The scowl deepened. "It's off-limits. I have no orders to permit any visitors."

She let her shoulders droop, and a frown pulled her lips. "But I don't know how much longer Gramps will be with us. I'm sure you've seen him? The older guy in the wheelchair?"

His eyes softened, and he cleared his throat. Looking to his right, then left, he whispered just loud enough for her to hear. "Your grandma works in the infirmary. Takes your grandfather with her most days to get him out of the house. Third tent behind this building. She's probably there now."

Her smile became genuine. "Thanks."

Wasting no time, she hurried to the canvas structure. They'd tied open the entrance flaps, and no one stopped her from entering. Although the exterior looked large, her steps slowed at the number of people packed inside. They had connected dozens of smaller tents to form the space, but they could draw flaps to section it off when needed.

The first area she passed through must be for people who needed minor treatments. A guy a year or two older than Lexi sat on a stool while a woman wearing a red jumpsuit sewed a gash on his arm. He frowned at Lexi as she passed by, probably because she couldn't look away from the scars crisscrossing his shoulder and biceps.

In the next area, beds lined up as if waiting for people with more serious injuries. One held a sleeping man. Bruises covered his face. His leg hung suspended in a series of straps and pulleys, held in place to keep it still while it healed. Another baby-faced teenager let out a moan. She paused, uncertain whether to offer help or keep going.

The call of her name drew her to the next section. Nana stood in the aisle, a mug in one hand and a metal bowl in the other. "Lexi, it's so good to see you. I need to take care of this gentleman, but if you keep going to the end, you'll find Gramps visiting one of his buddies. He'd love to see you."

Nana set the mug and bowl on the man's bedside table. "Let me sit you up a bit, son. I've got something for the pain."

A groan, followed by an agonized cry, came from the bed as Lexi hurried further into the structure, as much to escape the misery as to find her grandfather. The chemical aroma grew stronger, and soon older adults, either dozing or sitting up, occupied the beds lining the edges, their eyes fixed on someone in the center of the room. A group had gathered in a loose circle—some standing with walkers or canes, others seated in wheelchairs. A woman guided their exercises. Ms. Becky?

Hands raised toward the ceiling, she encouraged her audience. "Now stretch as high as you can. Go slow. We don't want anyone getting dizzy. Daily stretching is so important for your stability."

Ms. Becky appeared ten years younger in the clean black jumpsuit the rebels provided. With her face washed and her frizzy hair tamed into a ponytail, she could have been another person entirely, but her authoritative voice as she cajoled the group into action was all her.

Ms. Becky's gaze lit on Lexi. "Good morning. I assume you're here to visit. Last bed on the end."

Every eye in the room followed Lexi past the exercisers.

Ms. Becky leaned in to whisper. "We need to talk about the retirees. There's still time to save them. I'll find you."

The last thing I need is to be caught between Mom and Ms. Becky. But what about the retirees? Who'd save them if Ms. Becky didn't? Although what could Lexi possibly do to help?

She entered the final tent. The open flaps allowed a breeze to flow through. Grateful for the fresh air, she moved to the last bed. She struggled not to stare at a man asleep on the mattress. His wrinkled skin appeared painfully dry, and his short white hair stuck straight up in defiance. Growing old looked terrifying.

In a wheelchair nearby, his visitor dozed. The bald spot on the back of the visitor's head gave him away—the man she'd longed to spend time with since the explosion changed her life forever. She slid an arm around his shoulders and pecked his cheek. His startled reaction made her chuckle. "Morning, Gramps."

He turned in slow motion like a turtle peeking out of its shell. Perhaps she should encourage him to join the group as they limbered up. His smile relaxed her from the inside out and lifted the weight she'd carried in her gut since Mom's demands. "How's my favorite grandchild?"

A giggle escaped like it did every time he used the line on her. "I'm your *only* grandchild."

He grasped her hand, his skin cool and dry. "That doesn't mean you aren't special." He gestured to the man in the bed. "This scoundrel here is a cousin of mine. Ernie, meet my grandbaby, Lexi."

She nodded. "Nice to meet you, sir."

"Sir?" The man laughed. "I'm no fancy administration

worker. Of course, none of that matters here." He broke into a coughing fit.

Lexi rounded her grandfather and picked up a glass of cloudy water on the bedside. When Ernie struggled to sit up, she lifted his head and tilted the glass to his lips for a sip. Once she'd settled him back into the bed, she set the glass down and hugged her grandfather. "I have to go, Gramps. Mom's putting me to work, but I'll come back here to visit as much as I can."

His smile faded. "You be safe. I keep telling your mother she's insane to think they can take down the Imperium."

No response came to mind, so she grinned, kissed his cheek again, and headed toward the training tent. But aphids! Why'd Mom think they could take on the Imperium and win? How many lives would she sacrifice?

Thumps emanated from the structure sheltering the trainees. Guards stood outside the closed flaps, black rifles at the ready. The man on the right stepped aside, opening the way for her to enter. He'd been posted at the farmhouse the night they arrived. Inside, the scent of unwashed and overworked bodies enveloped her. Men and women stood in multiple semicircles around instructors.

The group closest to her took turns at a kick bag hanging from a beam. Their instructor held it from behind. A young guy twice Lexi's size went next. *Thump, thump, thump.*

"Come on." The instructor spat. "You hit like a baby."

The trainee's skin blotched and his lips contorted. *Thump, thump, thump.*

"Good, keep your feet moving."

Hitting a bag didn't look all that terrifying, but a group further in wielded knives while the instructor demonstrated proper handholds, slices, and jabs. A shudder ran down her spine. She hurried past the group, certain the instructor's eyes followed her. Definitely not a good starting point. They could force her to train, but the Imperium would be desolate before she'd jam a knife between another human's ribs.

A squeak slipped out when a hand grabbed her shoulder. She twisted to see Reeves, his skin red against the white of his brilliant smile. Sweat beaded his brow, then joined the stream running into his soaked shirt. A small bandage had replaced his head wrap. Warmth radiated from her chest at his touch. Perhaps he'd decided to join her. They could work out together.

"Isn't this place fantastic? I learned more in my first hour here yesterday, than I did in my entire semester of war education back in school." His words came out breathy like he'd run to catch her. His eyes shone. "After we finish the hand-to-hand training, they're going to teach us how to shoot the big guns. Rumor is they might even train some of us in explosives."

He's enjoying this. Her heart twisted. At a vision of his dead body on some battlefield, she struggled to breathe past the grip on her chest. "I stopped by the medical tent to see Nana and Gramps." She glanced around. Everyone seemed absorbed in their lessons. "Soldiers are there, injured men and women. We… you need to be careful. This is serious."

His brow crinkled. "Of course it's serious. We're preparing for war." He grasped her hand. "You need to learn this stuff too. I won't always be around to protect you."

She gasped in a stuttered breath at the thought of him using any of these skills, much less using them herself. "I know we need to help rescue my father and the retirees. Sweet seedlings, maybe we can sneak in and out without having to hurt anyone."

He rolled his eyes. "Don't be naïve. This isn't only about rescuing a few citizens. It's about freeing them all." He poked her arm. "It wouldn't hurt for you to get some self-defense moves."

She raised her chin. "I'm not naïve—I'm worried *you* might be. No matter how much you train, they could kill you. We could all end up dead. Look around. We're no match for the Imperium."

He huffed. "Don't count us out yet. I've heard some talk about weapons we might get our hands on, weapons that haven't been used since the Great War." His lips quirked up into a crooked smile. "That'd shut 'em down. Make them listen to us and our demands."

She pulled her hand out of his. How could this be the same guy who'd tried to snuggle with her? This place changed people, perhaps even more than the Imperium. She searched his eyes for the man she'd married. One day past their official honeymoon, and he'd morphed into a soldier-in-the-making.

All sounds quieted as everyone paused their exercises and conversation and faced the entryway. Her mother entered behind two armed soldiers, scanned the crowd until her gaze stopped at Lexi, and nodded in approval. After a brief pause, Mom focused on the crowd. "I didn't mean to interrupt. Keep up the good work." Then she pivoted and exited the tent.

The trainees returned to their tasks, but Lexi could still feel the stares drilling into her. Heat pooled on her face and neck. If only the ground would open beneath her and suck her in. Being the leader's daughter would have some challenges. She cleared her throat. "I guess we'd better get to our lessons, then."

He pointed out a group of young girls in a far corner. "Start over there. That group is learning how to defend when faced with a larger enemy."

She leaned in to kiss him goodbye, but he spun and walked away before she could land her lips on his. The heat on her face flamed even hotter. Certain the entire tent had seen the moment, she rushed to join the group he'd indicated.

Rumi stood, arms crossed on the end. When Lexi joined her and whispered a hey, Rumi acknowledged her with a nod, then redirected her attention to the woman at the center.

The instructor stood no taller than five feet, and her wiry frame and ponytailed hair resembled a teenager's. But the faint frown lines etched on her face betrayed the passage of years and hinted at a life well beyond her youth.

Her voice commanded attention. "When coming against someone taller and heavier, mobility is key. You need to stay out of reach. Look for vulnerabilities where you can strike. Knees, shins, throat, and eyes are excellent targets, but only if you can hit with speed and strength."

Lexi could run, but could she strike first?

Determined concentration hardened every face except Rumi's. The girl held her bottom lip between her teeth, and worry-filled eyes blinked in a pale face. She bounced on the balls of her feet as if ready to take off in a sprint at any hint of danger. Rumi was no warrior. Instead of forcing her into an army, someone needed to protect this frail waif.

"Miss Verity?" The instructor captured Lexi's attention. "Do you mind?"

The entire group stared at Lexi as if expecting something. She stepped toward the instructor. "It's Mrs. Scheffer. I'm

married."

The instructor smirked. "Congratulations, but I doubt your name change will have any effect on the Imperium's desire to make an example of you. Care to learn how to protect yourself?"

A fire ignited in her gut. Rumi didn't need to be thrown into a fight—she needed protection. More than that, Lexi's father needed rescuing, and retirees' lives hung in the balance, desperate for someone to step in. Taking another person's life was out of the question, but that didn't mean she couldn't make a difference. If her mother was determined for her to learn to fight, then Lexi would do it—but on her own terms. "Teach me how to defend others."

"Huh. I guess the rumors are true." The instructor's smirk curved into a knowing smile. "You *are* like your mother."

Spreading her feet into a fighting stance, Lexi lifted her hands to defend herself as others had done. "We'll see about that."

Chapter 3

Lexi limped out of the training tent. Not only had her last attempt at an oblique kick been an utter failure but now her shoe grew tighter with every hobble. It was the sixth grade all over again. Back then, the instructor called her father to take his daughter to the infirmary right after physical training ended. Of course, Mom showed up instead.

Not today. Today, the trainer bellowed at her. "I said with your *shin*, Scheffer, not your *foot!*"

Summoning every ounce of fortitude, she'd ignored the pain until the lesson ended and she could escape the curious eyes. Everyone who watched evaluated her performance. Would their leader's daughter have her mother's tough exterior?

She took another step and winced. *Nope.* Not even close.

The sun dipped low, most of the day wasted in training. So much for the greenhouse. Though she'd promised herself a visit to the hydroponics after the last lesson, no way could she make it all the way across the campus.

She leaned against a wooden light pole, thankful the beam's angle pointed outward to provide a shadow to rest in. Not too much farther to her tent. Maybe Reeves would be waiting and could help her to the infirmary to get something for the swelling. She dragged up her pant leg to examine the injury. The medical team might even have to cut her shoe off if she didn't get some ice on her ankle soon.

A sob pulled her attention away from her misery. Rumi hugged her waist, her tears flowing. The instructor had an arm across the girl's shoulders as they headed toward Lexi.

Watching Rumi had been painful. Her half-hearted punches were more like love taps than any sort of aggression. Whenever a trainer tried to push her, she'd shrivel into herself, and the waterworks began. Why couldn't these people see not everyone could fight?

As the two drew closer, the instructor's words became audible. "I know it's been a rough day for you, but one of our physicians has been working on some new medications that can help. It's still experimental, but you'd be an excellent candidate for his regimen. It'll help you conquer your fears." Her gentle shake jostled Rumi's shoulder. "You'd like that, wouldn't you? To feel invincible?"

Rumi shrugged. "I don't think I can do this. Any of it. I hate the thought of hurting people, especially myself."

The woman laughed. "That's what I like about you, kiddo. You're honest. We can work with that. Will you trust me and try to let the doctor help?"

As if giving up all hope of escaping the inevitable, the girl deflated like a balloon with a slow leak. "I guess so?"

"That's my girl." The instructor thumped Rumi on the back. "I'm willing to bet the doctor has time right now."

They moved out of Lexi's hearing range toward the medical tent.

Something seemed off. How could anything the doctor gave

Rumi get her past her fears? That girl could barely walk past a shadow without trembling, but they thought they could turn her into a fighter. And with a pill, nonetheless.

Pain spiked up Lexi's shin. She'd set her weight on the injured foot. Rumi's problems would have to wait another day. Lexi needed to get herself treated, or she'd never get a wink of sleep. "Shake it off, buttercup." Though she hated the instructor's insult, it motivated her. "One step at a time."

Two halting steps and she had to pause once more. Her entire leg throbbed, and the shoe had tightened until it felt like a vise on her toes.

An arm snaked around her waist. "Let me help you." Lexi's breath caught as she whipped around. Ms. Becky's eyes locked onto hers, their edges creased in worry.

Lexi allowed herself to lean into the other woman. "Oblique kick gone wrong. I used my foot instead of my shin."

"Hmm. They're moving too quickly in your training." She snugged Lexi closer to her. "Let's get you to the infirmary."

Progress was slow as they walked like contestants in a three-legged race. Each step brought fresh waves of agony. "Stop. Please. Just for a minute." Lexi eased the pressure off her injured appendage.

Ms. Becky tsked. "Perhaps I should get a wheelchair?"

Wouldn't that make for a fun bit of gossip? The big boss's daughter couldn't even make it through the first day of training. "No. I can make it. I just need to rest for a second."

"Well, I've been meaning to talk to you, anyway." Ms. Becky draped Lexi's arm across her shoulders, giving Lexi extra stability. "We need to get to those retirees. Your mother won't listen. I was hoping she'd hear *you*, though."

Ms. Becky's eyes pleaded. Trusting the daughter could

influence the mother.

"You realize Mom never told me what she was doing, right?" Heat smoldered in the words. "She let me believe she was dead—that my grandparents were gone. Why would you think I'd be able to sway her?"

"Your mother loves you." Ms. Becky's soothing tone drifted over Lexi's fiery emotions, softening them like a cool mist. "I saw her relief when she first laid eyes on you after they saved us."

It had been a wonderful moment—the moment Mom pretty much came back from the dead. The pain of her betrayal hadn't hit, and all Lexi had was happy tears over having her family back. Now she had time to process it all. Time to realize what her mother had done to her, to Dad. The man lived behind bars because he tried to help his daughter, even though he didn't believe in Lexi's methods.

The heat flared through her again. Mom should have been honest.

"Let's try a few more steps." Somehow, the fury distracted her from the pain, and they made progress toward the tent. "I'll try to convince her, but I can't promise anything."

Ms. Becky's response came out barely above a whisper. "Thank you."

The infirmary technician gave Lexi a shot that kicked in within seconds and left her almost pain free. A boot that alternated between icing and warming reduced the swelling by the time she reached her tent. Darkness had set in, and the tent was pitch black when she closed the flap behind herself.

Where was Reeves? She'd seen him a few times in the training tent. Near the end of the day, he'd nodded at her before walking out with Thrym and Fletcher. Looking like a dwarf between two giants, he sauntered away, deep in conversation.

He shouldn't be away too much longer. After all, they'd just finished their honeymoon. Even though she hadn't met the guy until the day before the wedding, he'd grown on her. *No.* It was more than that. She'd given in the day the Freedom Force shot him. Though they'd barely done more than kiss, he'd more than earned her trust. She'd come to care about him—even, she'd begun to suspect, love him. And when he held her, she believed he was beginning to love her too. She'd never had anyone follow her and fight for her as unconditionally as he had. Now, more than anything, she wanted to get to know him, to let him know her, the her even her parents had never really known.

It wouldn't be much longer, and he'd be home, pitiful as their tent was. She needed someone to talk to—a sounding board to help untangle the day's chaos. Someone to hear about the strange offer made to Rumi and Ms. Becky's overwhelming request. He'd know how to help her figure out the best way to approach Mom.

Then, after they'd talked out their day, they'd have time to be together. Weariness pulled her down like a weighted blanket. Perhaps she'd rest while she waited. She lay on her cot, elevating her foot, per the technician's instructions, by positioning it on the bar holding the canvas. It wouldn't hurt to close her eyes for a minute.

Troubled visions fogged her mind. Rumi, with eyes that glowed red, ready to attack on command. Reeves, covered in blood, eyes shut and breaths shallow. Her father, standing opposite a line of soldiers, guns aimed at his chest. Lexi powerless to protect any of them.

Daylight shone through a crack in the flap and straight into her eyes. She squinted at the cot beside her. Reeves slept on his back with his arm over his face as if he'd known the sunlight would wake him. She hadn't heard him come in. They'd lost the entire day, kept apart by responsibilities, and the night as well.

Some marriage this was turning out to be.

She sat up and swung her legs to the floor. The boot clunked against her uninjured leg, but her foot didn't complain when she stood on it. Could it have healed overnight? She loosened the straps holding the boot on and freed her foot. The swelling had all but disappeared. She tested a tentative step. Wow, between the shot and the boot, her foot had no residual pain.

They hadn't had this type of technology in the Imperium. How could these rebels have better drugs out here in the middle of nowhere? She gazed at Reeves as his soft snores rumbled. Who cared how they did it? She had a healthy foot and wanted time with her man. There was so much to tell him.

Leaning over, she brushed her lips against his cheek. His hand shot into the air, smacking her on the chin. Then his eyes went wide. Confusion morphed into compassion, and he sat up. "I'm so sorry. Did I hurt you?"

She rubbed at the spot. "Not really. Sorry to wake you." Backing away, she tamped down the disappointment of another failed romance attempt. "I didn't hear you come in last night. You must be exhausted."

He sprang out of bed like someone had set it ablaze beneath him. "What time is it?"

"Early. Only 0700. We've got plenty of time before we report for training." Time for a chat at the minimum, but perhaps an opportunity to replay the morning kiss, only without the rude awakening. She moved in again, this time with her eyes fixed on his. "Before breakfast even."

He flopped back down and pulled a boot on. "You don't understand. I've been invited to join the planning team. If I work it right, I'll be on the next mission back to the Imperium." He tightened the lace of the second boot and stood to face her. "I need to get going."

The peck he placed on her cheek was so chaste and brief that it barely warmed her skin.

So much for wedded bliss. Abandoned again. Would there ever be a person in her life who cared for her without reservation or ulterior motives?

On her way to the meal tent, antiseptic drifted from the infirmary. She wrinkled her nose. The smell made her think of Gramps. How much longer would she have him in her life? Every time she laid eyes on him, he seemed less vibrant, more shrunken. Soon he'd fade away. Was it better to spend every minute she could with him so not a moment got wasted? Or would it be better to avoid him and make the pain less intense when he left this world?

"Morning, Lexi." Rumi, dressed in her black uniform, stood as tall as her five-foot-nothing frame would allow. A spark flashed in her eyes, and confidence widened her stance.

Whoa. "Looks like you slept well. Not sore from yesterday?"

Rumi bounced on her toes like a kid waiting to open her birthday presents. "A little, but nothing like before I got that shot at the infirmary. They've got quite the cocktail going on with those drugs. Not sure what's in 'em, but sign me up for another dose."

True, the medications were powerful. Lexi's healed foot

was proof. But something more than pain relief was going on here. "I heard you talking to the instructor last night. She said something about seeing a doctor for help with your fear?"

Rumi's face lit like a neon bulb. "Dr. Ichtacka. He's the GOAT."

How could she think a doctor was the greatest of all time after one visit? "Did he give you something to help?"

"Did he ever! Of course, the pain injection was amazing, but he also gave me some pills to take last night and again this morning. Just twice a day." She wriggled a receptacle from her pocket and flicked open the lid. Two earpieces rested benignly inside. "These are the best part, though. He said to sleep with them in. I've never slept better, and I had the *best* dreams. I conquered every obstacle I ran into—all night long." She jabbed at the air as if striking at an opponent. "Like I'm some sort of superhero. I can't wait to get back to the sparring ring."

The hair on Lexi's neck rose. Who was this girl, and what had she done with Rumi?

Something ten shades of wrong was going on here. "That's great you're feeling better. Aren't you afraid of getting hit? You seemed a little put off by the whole idea of hand-to-hand combat yesterday."

Rumi squinched her eyes before she shrugged. "Dunno. I was nervous at first, but I feel like I could conquer the world today. You know?"

Lexi searched Rumi's face for a telltale sign this person was an imposter. Other than the new attitude and improved posture, nothing contradicted what the girl had said. "Not really, but—go you."

Rumi giggled, then skipped toward the food tent.

Lexi remained rooted to the ground. Maybe the girl was having some sort of reaction to the pain medications. There had to be a logical explanation for the about-face. Before she could follow, someone tapped her.

Mom stood watching, flanked by armed guards on either side. "I heard you'd been injured during training. Looks like they patched you up all right."

"Good as new." Would her mother be honest if Lexi asked? "I just met up with Rumi, who also got medical attention last night, but she doesn't seem herself. Any clue what the doctor gave her?"

Mom gave a dismissive wave. "Who knows? That girl's kind of flaky, if you ask me." She stepped forward and grasped Lexi's shoulder. "I thought you'd like to take a day off from training. Go have a rotation in the greenhouse, like I promised."

Her heart's tempo ratcheted up. *Finally*. She squealed and hugged her mother, crushing her into an embrace. Then she remembered her father and the retirees. She released her grip and eased back. "Thank you so much. I can't wait to get back to the greenhouse, but about the plan to rescue the people we left behind… When are we going back for them?"

Mom's face clouded over, and her lips flattened into a thin line. "We don't yet have the resources we need to take on the Imperium or rescue your father. The prisons are too well guarded. After your escape, they've grown more vigilant about the retiree trains. It's unlikely we'd succeed in saving anyone."

A weight settled in Lexi's stomach, pushing her emotions down along with it. "So we're not going to do anything? We're going to leave them to die?"

"You're going to have to grow up and realize you can't save

everyone. Sometimes not even those you love the most." Mom jammed her hands into her pockets and said the next words as if to herself. "*I* learned that lesson the hard way."

How could Lexi argue the point? It wasn't as if she knew how to free her father or anyone else. She couldn't even land a simple kick without self-injury. "Maybe I should keep training instead of visiting the greenhouse. You need every able-bodied person, right?"

Mom's shoulders slumped. "That probably would be best." Her words sounded more like resignation than agreement. "I'll expect you in training, then." She looked at her guards, then continued into the food tent as if there was nothing left to discuss.

"I must be insane." Lexi kicked a pebble against the tent. "Exchanging a chance to work in the greenhouse for getting myself beaten to a pulp."

She skipped breakfast for a brief visit with Gramps and Nana. Nana's warm hug set the world to right again. Gramps snored lightly and didn't wake when Lexi placed her hand on the cool skin of his arm. It was as if his body didn't have the will to hold heat. He looked too fragile, his connection to life more tenuous.

Nana's face wrinkled. "He's the love of my life. I don't know what I'll do without him."

Her words knifed into Lexi's heart. "I love you, Nana."

Nana's sad smile didn't help. "He fought your mother when he heard the plan to get him out of the Imperium. He hated the thought of leaving you behind."

At least *one* of them had. "I still can't understand how Mom left me so easily."

A far-off look came into Nana's eyes. "I had a sister, much

younger than me. She used to play with your mother all the time. They acted like sisters." Her eyes gleamed. "They had this signal for each other. I figured it out eventually. If one of them tugged on their earlobe, they were letting the other know they were lying. Once I figured that out, the jig was up."

So Mom learned deception early on? She'd prepared for her role as a rebel leader her entire life. Even if she hadn't known it.

Unable to process anything more, Lexi kissed Nana and then Gramps's forehead and headed off to face her day. When she exited the infirmary, the greenhouse at the compound's far end beckoned. The vise squeezing her heart tightened as she headed in the opposite direction. She wasn't certain what she'd done wrong in life, but somehow, she didn't deserve the right to enjoy a career of her choosing. For the foreseeable future, she was a fighter. Not a grower.

Chapter 4

A sweaty scent mingled with rubber assaulted Lexi's nose when she entered the training tent. Though she wasn't late, a group had already formed around a blue mat in the far corner. *Just get through today without breaking anything or looking like an idiot.*

While an instructor yelled to be heard above the trainees' catcalls, two combatants battled to take the other down. Grilled helmets protected their heads and faces, and thick rubber shields covered their cores, but the match wasn't equal. The combatant with the blue-padded four-foot pole stood more than a foot taller than the combatant who wielded a red one.

"Protect your head." The female instructor who'd walked Rumi out the previous evening hollered at the taller combatant after his opponent landed a vicious blow to the chin. "You going to let that little pipsqueak take you down?"

The verbal jab coaxed a growl out of the blue warrior. He swung his pole wild, but the red opponent dodged it with ease. Set off-balance by the missed attack, he neglected self-protection. A second blow to the chin landed him flat on his back.

Lexi froze, her breath catching in her throat as the winner pulled off her helmet.

Rumi's face emerged, flushed with triumph, her eyes gleaming like polished steel. A chaotic symphony of cheers and applause sent a shiver through the air. Rumi stepped back and tossed her gear to the next challenger in line, her movements fluid and unhurried as if this kind of victory was just another day for her.

Lexi's mouth hung open. She clamped it shut, only to find it opened again, unable to stop the words from spilling out. "No way." Her fists clenched at her sides, and her eyebrows knit together. Rumi's fierce strikes replayed in Lexi's mind, raw and undeniable. It didn't compute. The timid woman who once jumped at a door slam now stood there basking in glory, a lioness fresh from the hunt.

A grin quirked Rumi's lips, sharp and full of intrigue. She caught Lexi's attention and tipped her chin in recognition. Not only had Rumi morphed into a warrior overnight—she was happy about it. Self-confidence practically oozed from her pores.

Maybe those earbuds weren't just a gimmick after all.

After the joy for Rumi's success ran its course, nervous tension jittered through Lexi. If they could mold a fighter overnight, why hadn't they given everyone the same treatment? What had they said in that overheard conversation? Experimental? How many people had they tested the regimen on? The transformation seemed too complete and too rapid.

Winning was great, but could Rumi's petite body withstand the strain? Was she sacrificing herself? Utter joy radiated from Lexi's stepmother's face as she cheered on the next two opponents. Her confidence seemed to belie any imminent danger.

Well, no reason to make mountains out of molehills. Lexi refocused on the scene and the trainer's bellowed instructions. She'd be ready for her turn.

A tap on her shoulder drew her attention away from the next round.

Reeves stood behind her. His lips twitched upward before he schooled his face and straightened like a soldier returning to attention. "Your mother wants you at the main house."

Her heart jumped at the glimpse of the man she'd married, but it pounded at the mention of her mother. What could she want? "Do you know what for?"

Reeves pointed toward the exit. "Let's find out."

She followed close on his heels, out into the sunlight and down an alley between two tents. The moment the tents hid them from view, he gathered her into his arms. His lips were on hers before she understood his intentions.

Shock and excitement stole her thoughts, and she allowed her body to melt into his, deepening the kiss she'd yearned for since their morning mishap. His soft lips contrasted with the muscled arms that flattened her against him. A rush of adrenaline sent her heart racing, and she rose to reach her arms around his neck. Her hand slid into his tangled blond hair and pulled him closer.

This was what it meant to be married. She wanted to be one with him. The kiss deepened until she thought she might drown for lack of air—what a beautiful way to go.

A shout shattered the moment. Reeves yanked himself away and pushed her out to arm's length. *No.* She wanted more. His eyes, brimming with desire, told her he craved the same.

He closed his eyes and shook his head like a dog ridding

itself of raindrops. When they opened again, the storm had passed, and the soldier returned. "Sorry. We don't have time. I… just needed to comfort… my wife. You looked so stressed."

The hammering of her heart slowed, and she grasped his hands and caressed his knuckles. Eager for more, she pressed in closer, but he'd moved past the moment. His eyes hardened.

With a shake of his head, he strode down the alley, tugging her along behind. "We need to get to headquarters. Your mom…"

How could Lexi have forgotten? She needed to get her hormones under check.

Her shoulders fell. Nana always said there was a time and a place for everything. Reeves was right. This wasn't the time or the place, but sweet seedlings, surely it would come soon.

When they reached the meeting room, Mom stood in a circle of people that included Thrym, Fletcher, and Ms. Becky. From Mom's red face and hands-on-hips stance, Lexi and Reeves had walked in on an argument. "We don't have the resources." Mom's voice rose. "If we go too soon, our odds of getting out alive are slim, much less saving anyone else."

Ms. Becky's eyes flashed, and she jabbed a finger at the ground as if staking a claim. "They don't have any time left. What good is it to have a resistance if we don't, well, *resist?*"

Reeves cleared his throat and broke into the circle, dragging Lexi to his side. "Found her."

Mom's mouth snapped shut, her eyes softened, and she touched Lexi's shoulder. "A scout returned from the Imperium with a message from your father. One of his guards is a silent supporter of the rebellion. Your father said not to come after him. They're waiting for us if we try." Her eyes pleaded for understanding. "His trial date has been set."

The room dimmed. It could have been just the two of them here. Lexi was five again, asking for a unicorn for her birthday, her mother explaining why it was an impossible request.

Her spine stiffened. Getting her father *wasn't* hopeless. "But we're not going to stop. Right? We're going to rescue him, anyway? We have to."

Mom drew in a breath and winced as if Lexi had struck her. "I was explaining to Ms. Becky—we don't have the resources. Not yet. But we're trying."

Fletcher's grumble reminded Lexi they weren't alone. "Not every attack has to be obvious. We've snuck retirees into and out of the Favela for years, sometimes right under the noses of the Freedom Force."

Thrym growled, his face stony. "And if we continue to do nothing but sneak around in the shadows, people will continue to die. It's time we fought for the citizens' rights to return to the freedoms we had before the war." He smacked one fist into the opposite palm. "The right to choose our mates and careers and the right to live into our old age in peace." His set jaw and beefy arms crossed over his barrel chest dared any further argument.

Fists balled into miniature bowling balls, Fletcher stepped toward Thrym, mouth opening to return fire in the verbal war. Ms. Becky blocked the giant's access to his rival. "Gentlemen. We're on the same side. The fact that we have different opinions on our next move needn't prevent us from working together." She angled her head toward Mom. "Tora, help me out here."

Lexi itched to jump into the conversation and agree with Ms. Becky's plea. Before she could get a word in, her mother squeezed Lexi's shoulder and barked at Thrym. "Stand down.

We're not going to tear each other apart. Ms. Becky's right. We have a common enemy."

Both men mumbled under their breath, but Fletcher returned to his place in the circle, as did Ms. Becky. Mom nodded her approval, then scrubbed a hand over the back of her neck. "We all know we need more resources, especially fighters. The only way to get more of those is to continue to have conversations with the people we've been working to recruit." Both men nodded as she continued. "I'd hoped our people would have more time to connect with others who are dissatisfied enough to join the fight. Perhaps when they hear the movement is underway, it'll light a fire whispered conversations can't."

Mom's gaze assessed Reeves. "Now that you're a married man, you'll have more in common with those who've been forced into similar situations. Especially those who are less than satisfied with their assigned spouses. We need young, strong, stubborn soldiers. Thrym will be your connection to our network of recruiters."

Reeves's eyes glinted, and Lexi's stomach lurched. He couldn't wait to get into the fight, any way he could, could he?

Well, no way was he going without her. "I can help with recruiting."

Mom shook her head. "Your face is too well-known. You'd be more of a liability than an asset to a team trying to sneak in and out unnoticed."

Lexi raised her hands. "You think Reeves isn't recognizable? He was at my side when we were running from the Freedom Force."

"You're Gunner Verity's daughter—he's the biggest traitor the Imperium has captured. *Ever*." Mom paced away from the group, then back. "If they catch you, they'll no longer need to keep your father alive as bait."

Her mother's overprotective stance wouldn't keep Lexi on the sidelines. She stepped into Mom's path, joining the inner circle. "That's why I need to get involved. I could be a diversion while another team is busy with the rescue."

"Absolutely not." Reeves hauled Lexi away from the group, his jaw clenched. "You'd be more of a hindrance than a help. We'd have to assign at least two guards to you, and we need every person we can get to connect with recruits." He leaned in and whispered. "I can't risk losing you."

She pushed him away. Heat rushed through her veins as she glared. "And I sit back here twiddling my thumbs while you take all the risks?" The laugh that bubbled up sounded like she'd lost it. Perhaps she had. "That's not okay with me. If you don't take me with you, I'll find a way to get there myself."

"Thrym…" Mom raised her eyebrows at her right-hand man and indicated her daughter.

Before Lexi could blink, the giant had a viselike grip on her biceps. Nodding to her mother, Thrym stood ramrod straight. "Ma'am."

"If my daughter sets so much as a toe outside this compound without my permission, your men are to hunt her down and drag her back, kicking and screaming if need be." Mom jabbed a finger at her. "And you *don't* have my permission."

Lexi's heart hammered in her chest, her breaths rapid. How had she escaped the Imperium only to end up a prisoner of the rebellion? She looked to her husband, imploring him with her eyes. "Reeves?"

At his terse headshake, her heartbeat slowed. An ache settled in, the pain of betrayal overwhelming. How could he?

Almost every eye in the room glared at her as if she were wasting precious time. Only Ms. Becky's guilt-filled eyes looked away. Lexi wrenched her arm to free it, only to have the grip tightened like a tourniquet.

"Enough." Mom's nostrils flared, and she moved to the door. "Lexi—with me."

After a last squeeze, Thrym released her. She stormed after her mother, jogging to catch up.

Mom stopped in the entryway of the old home. "Why can't you behave yourself and act like an adult?"

The heat in Lexi's veins surged to boiling. "How can I act like an adult when you treat me like a child? You claimed you abandoned me instead of forcing me to choose. Now you're leaving me behind again, even though I've made my decision. I'm your daughter, but I'm not a kid anymore. Stop treating me like one."

Her mother winced, and her shoulders slumped. "You're right. It *is* your choice to make. But it's also my responsibility to ensure I've prepared my troops before they enter battle."

"And...?" Lexi let her words trail for fear of losing progress.

The leader of the rebellion stared as if she were any other fighter. "Can you truthfully say you're ready for war?"

Lexi shivered and swallowed beneath an assessment meant to wither her will into submission.

Visions of Rumi taking down her opponent flashed one after another. Her improvement proved how far Lexi had to go.

"Well?" her mother goaded. "Are you fully prepared?"

"No," Lexi squeaked. "Not yet." She unfurled her fists by force of will. Though she didn't want to wait, she couldn't deny she'd be a burden, not an asset. "But I *will* be."

The next few hours were a blur. Hand-to-hand combat drills, then an hour-long group-training session. For one lesson, she joined a team of four tasked to evade capture while moving from one end of the compound to the other. Thrips and aphids. They'd failed the mission because one woman, as timid as Rumi used to be, gave up and revealed her location, ending the exercise.

The trainer insisted they ensure all team members made it to the goal—even if they had to treat one of their own as an enemy to do it. If they couldn't control their own, they were as good as captured or worse. Dead. Just like Mom's argument.

Lexi sagged when the lunch break arrived. If Gramps's time on earth was short, she wanted every moment she could have with him. After she grabbed a handful of carrots from the mess hall, she hurried to the medical tent. The cool air blew divinely against her sweat-soaked skin, a refreshing balm after the workout. She could only hope she didn't reek of body odor.

Gramps had parked his wheelchair beside the same bed, just inside the end flap. Both Gramps and his cousin were sound asleep.

She pulled up a nearby stool and munched on her meager meal, wondering if she should wake him. Before she could decide, Ms. Becky came through the tent and stopped when she saw Lexi.

Ms. Becky laid a gentle hand on the older man's forehead. "His fever hasn't resolved, but he's not as hot as he was last night." She patted Ernie's arm before turning to Lexi. "I'm sorry to have caused a quarrel between you and your mom. It wasn't my intention."

Lexi waved her words away. "Not your fault. I can't seem to get along with anyone these days. Not even Reeves." Her heart sank at her husband's betrayal. Perhaps, like her mother, he'd been right. She wanted him to support her, regardless. "I've been so angry. First with my father, now Mom and Reeves. I'm thinking the common denominator is the problem—me."

The older woman's understanding smile calmed Lexi's racing thoughts. Ms. Becky took a blanket from a nearby bed and draped it over Gramps's lap. "Nothing's wrong with you. If the amount of upheaval you've experienced happened to me, I'd be curled up in a sniveling ball of fear." She sat on the end of the bed, facing Lexi. "Not you, though. You've got the warrior strength of the archangel Michael when he fought the devil."

That sounded like a fairy tale. Not one Lexi had heard before. "What's an archangel?"

"One of God's head angels."

It'd been a while since that ancient history class she'd taken as a student. "Is this part of Greek mythology? Zeus was the top god, wasn't he?"

Ms. Becky tsked. "Hasn't your family taught you anything about the Bible? Christianity? Jesus? Nothing?" She raised her eyes to the sky. "I guess your mother walked away from more than a peaceful movement."

She huffed out a breath. "Before the war, the Imperium was one of the largest cities in the country. The founders of the nation built their rules based on the idea of freedom to choose. Liberty, self-determination—all who came here from distant lands craved these rights."

Lexi pictured having latitude to choose the direction of her life, regardless of whether it served the greater good. "That would've been a beautiful place to live. I wish I'd been born in those times. Maybe then I'd be busy planting and harvesting in my own greenhouse instead of stuck in this camp training for battle."

A grin spread across Ms. Becky's face. "An entrepreneur, huh? They were everywhere back before it all fell apart."

Entrepreneurs. "I heard about them during a history lesson." The Imperium's education system painted them as selfish rogues, but she'd found the concept fascinating. Did Ms. Becky's opinion agree with the official Imperium stance? "Do you think that's why it fell apart? Entrepreneurs got too greedy? Or did it have to do with the religious people?"

Ms. Becky's mouth twitched as if something smelly had landed under her nose. "Religious people. Hmm. Never heard them called that before." She cleared her throat. "There was already a lot of trouble floating around in the world before the last Great War. Vast swarms of people walked away from faith altogether. Those who maintained their beliefs became targets of those who'd been hurt by religion in some form or fashion. It grew messy, and the country stood on the precipice of civil war for the second time in our history."

"Like now?"

The patient in the bed moaned.

Ms. Becky smoothed her palm across his forehead again, soothing his brow until he relaxed in his sleep. "No. What we have now is a government dictating to its people while rebels try to wrestle control away from them. Back then, there were so many factions it would have been hard to count them all."

Having only known the Imperium's mandates, Lexi couldn't imagine so many differing opinions. "If the Imperium falls, what will keep us from fracturing again? There's barely anything left for us to live on as it is. Another war would lead to extinction."

Ms. Becky shook her head. "Perhaps your mother has a point. I've pandered to the Imperium for a long time. But one saying's always stuck with me. 'Those who live by the sword will die by the sword.'"

Perhaps Lexi shouldn't have brought up the possibility of a life-ending battle. "I'd better get back to training." She rose, padded over to Gramps, and kissed the top of his head. So as not to wake him, she whispered, "Before the day ends, I'll stop back to see you. I love you, Gramps."

"Lexi." Ms. Becky reached out to Lexi, who clasped the proffered hand. "I'm going to pray for you."

"Oh, um, thanks." Lexi detached herself from the older woman's grasp. Ms. Becky was losing it. Perhaps already had. There had been rumors among her classmates of people who talked to invisible beings and called it praying. Lexi looked around, half expecting a phantom to rise from the dirt floor. Mom needed to know the leader of Y no longer had a grasp on reality.

Chapter 5

The warmth of human exertion wafted over Lexi when she entered the training tent.

"Lexi!" Rumi hollered and waved from the far end. "Over here."

Lexi suppressed the temptation to ignore her. It was time to let her anger go. Rumi's role equated more to being an Imperium pawn than a home-wrecker. The fault lay with Mom, who abandoned her family and played dead.

Lexi trotted over to join one of the few people she knew in the classes. Rumi's eyes shone, but her dilated pupils seemed odd—the tent was well lit. The afternoon's training had been exhausting. Perhaps the hard work wore on her more than on others? "What's on the agenda for this afternoon's training?"

"Oooh, you're going to love it." Rumi shifted her weight to her toes and back down again like a child expecting a gift. "Ms. D. said we're going to the firing range. I hope I get an enormous gun." She held her arms wide like she cradled a bazooka.

Lexi thought back to the firefight at the barn. The weight of the pistol. The coppery scent of blood streaming down Reeves's face. The terror of losing him. "Who's Ms. D.?"

Rumi crossed her arms. "Seriously? You don't know the name of the best trainer in the Imperium? Ms. Draven's as wicked as they come and taught me everything I know—and then some. Even let me call her Ms. D." She tipped her head toward the end of the tent. The female instructor who'd walked Rumi to the infirmary stood in the opening, pistol in hand, pointing out its features to a trainee. "Let's hurry. I don't want to get stuck watching when they run out of today's bullet allotment."

In a rush to keep up, Lexi followed Rumi out of the back flaps. Fifty yards away, someone had set targets against a dirt mound backstop. A waist-high wooden bench presented a hodgepodge of rifles, pistols, and even a malicious-looking grenade launcher. At the far left, a podium held a drone with four propellers that must have weighed as much as a ten-year-old child.

The guns—and the memories attached to them—sent a shiver up Lexi's spine, but the quadcopter might be fun to work. She leaned toward Rumi. "Who gets to fly the drone?"

Rumi shrugged. "Dunno. But who'd want to when they can hold one of these?" She lifted an assault rifle and peered through the scope.

"Patience, ladies." Ms. Draven walked up behind them and stole the rifle from Rumi. "We're limited on ammunition, so we'll only fire off a few rounds. Don't want to waste ammo before you've had formal training. Right?"

Rumi beamed, and her eyes sparkled. "Yes, ma'am. I'm ready."

Ms. Draven laid the rifle back on the bench and her hand on Rumi's shoulder. "You feel stronger this afternoon?"

Rumi's spine stiffened to attention. "Yes, ma'am. Every

day brings more confidence. Feels like I could tear my way through an entire platoon today, taking them out one at a time."

"That's my girl. Today will be fun."

The woman walked the length of the row, chatting with the young adults lined up. Rumi didn't pick the weapon up again but inspected it as if it were a rare seed pod and she was marveling at its potential, studying every curve and crack with care.

Lexi eased toward the podium. Sweet seedlings, maybe her proximity would grant her access to the less terrifying option. After all, how much damage could a drone do?

A pistol lay on the bench between her and Rumi. A guy a couple years older than they were stomped up like his mission for the day was to possess the gun. He picked up the pistol, jammed the magazine into it, and aimed downrange. His hands vibrated, causing the gun to waver. He had earbuds in—duplicates of the ones Rumi wore at night. Why was he still wearing them?

Rumi turned to him. "We're not allowed to shoot until we've gotten our instructions."

A shoulder twitch was his only response, like he'd shrugged off a pest. He pulled the trigger in rapid succession. Three bullets went wild, missing his mark and kicking up dirt in front and behind the targets.

"Kempton!" Ms. D. bellowed as she strode toward the guy. "Weapon down. *Now.*"

He gave his trainer a sideways glance, then refocused downrange. The quiver of his hands seemed to crawl up his arms, and his head twitched like a nervous tic. He didn't seem to fully register his trainer's order.

He's out of control. Something's wrong. He acted like a sleepwalker—not fully aware of his surroundings.

As Lexi edged toward him, she kept her hands at her sides and her voice low. "Hey, Kempton. I'm Lexi." When he flicked his head to the side and blinked, she continued. "Is Kempton your first or last name?"

His eyes snapped to face her, and his aim followed, the handgun leveled at her chest. Her breath caught, and her heart stuttered. A flash of memory—blood flowing down Reeves's face—turned her vision red. She could smell the acrid residue from spent shells.

This couldn't be happening. She raised her hands, palms out, to show her lack of weapons and swallowed the lump of terror threatening to choke her. "It's okay. *You're* fine. It's safe here."

Besides his bloodshot eyes and dilated pupils, sweat trickled down his unshaven face. His left eye twitched, but he focused on her face. "At war... kill... enemy... must..." Though his lips continued to move, she couldn't hear the words. His eyes lost focus. In some kind of trance, he seemed to stare at an unseen apparition between them.

"Kempton." Ms. D. rushed the final yards between herself and the standoff. "Lower your weapon." She motioned to Lexi to move out of the line of fire, raised her pistol toward his back, and took sideward steps into his peripheral.

Lexi slid to the side in slow motion, giddy with relief when the gun trained on her didn't follow. Since he could retarget her in the blink of an eye, she continued her measured paces toward the armed instructor. The pistol aimed at the young man appeared to grow larger by the second, and her racing thoughts settled on one theme she repeated over and over, willing her protector to hear the unspoken words. *Don't shoot. Please don't shoot.*

Ms. D. stepped between Lexi and Kempton, acting as a human shield. Her voice dropped into the soothing tones of a mother to a hurt child. "David. Put the gun down. You're in training. There's no enemy here." She edged closer to him, within arm's reach. "Let's go see Dr. Ichtacka. He can help."

Rumi slid her hand over the rifle on the bench and motioned for Lexi to join her.

If only Lexi could disarm all three of them. They were allies, not enemies. The moment she reached Rumi's side, Rumi lifted the rifle and aimed at Kempton. Lexi's blood ran cold at the gleam in Rumi's eye when she set her sights level on her fellow trainee.

Reflux burned in Lexi's throat. If he didn't back down soon, he'd force the instructor to act. *Please don't kill him.*

"David. Are you with me, son?" Ms. D. reached one hand toward Kempton while the other kept the pistol aimed. "I'm going to help you get to the medical tent. You're going to be fine." She flicked the earbud away on one side, causing him to flinch. "Put down the gun, David." Her voice grew firm— once again the military leader. "Report to Dr. Ichtacka ASAP, soldier."

He lowered the weapon to his side and stretched ramrod tall. "Yes, ma'am." With mechanical motions, he placed the gun on the range bench, pivoted, and paced toward the medical tent.

Ms. D. blew out a breath as she reholstered her pistol and bent to pick up the earbud. She held it out to Rumi. "Return your weapon and make sure Kempton reports as instructed. Give the good doctor the earbud along with a detailed report of this occurrence and let him know I'll be there within the hour."

What had happened? Shakes set in to Lexi's legs while Rumi accepted the tiny device, clattered her weapon onto the bench, and jogged after Kempton. What sort of experiment made recruits mindless automatons? Lexi edged closer to Ms. D. "Are you certain Dr. Ichtacka knows what he's doing?"

Ms. D.'s eyes flashed. She picked up Kempton's pistol, checked the clip, and rammed it back into place. "He's the most brilliant researcher the Imperium has ever seen, and we're lucky to have his brain focused on our side." She set the pistol back down and motioned to those gathered at the firing line. "Listen up, people. Today we're going to talk about gun safety, maintenance, and, of course, accuracy. Which of you have at least held a weapon in the past?"

So that was it. Discussion over. How could Ms. D. trust the doctor after what they'd witnessed? What if Kempton didn't snap out of it next time? What were the earbuds doing to their brains at night? Or were the drugs turning their brains to mush?

Rumi had changed so much, so fast. Too fast. How many others were part of the experiment? Lexi peered down the line of young recruits. Had she seen a twitching shoulder near the end? The air grew thick and lay heavy in her lungs while her knees wobbled.

"Ms. Draven, may I borrow two of your trainees for an hour?" Ms. Becky strode toward them. "I've got an assignment Lexi and Rumi would be perfect for." She glanced down the firing line. "Where's Rumi?"

"I can get her." Lexi awaited Ms. D.'s approval.

A wave of dismissal released her into Ms. Becky's control, and Ms. Becky nodded. "Once you've gathered Rumi, meet me at my tent to discuss the plan. Fletcher is waiting for us."

Lexi sprinted to the medical tent, half afraid of what she'd find when she got there. Her imagination ran rampant with images of probes and wires coming out of Kempton's head. Instead, she found Rumi standing just outside a curtained bed, listening to a conversation on the opposite side. She lifted one finger to her lips to silence Lexi.

A woman's voice followed the tear of a Velcro blood pressure cuff. "BP 160/100, heart rate 120, respirations 25."

The male voice that came next had to be Dr. Ichtacka. "Why didn't you remove the earbuds when you got up as instructed?"

"I… I don't know. I don't remember getting up. Thought I was on a mission." Though she'd only heard his voice once, it had to be Kempton. His confusion was clear, even to her untrained ear.

Dr. Ichtacka cleared his throat. "Let's run some more blood tests. Could be the dose is too high or the nightly instructions ran too long—past the REM cycle."

"Yes, Doctor." The female exited the curtain and glared at Lexi and Rumi. "Ladies, I don't believe your services are required any longer. You may return to training."

Rumi's cheeks flushed red. "Yes, ma'am." She started toward the exit.

Lexi jogged after Rumi, her brain ticking away. She caught up to her the moment they exited the tent. "We're supposed to meet Ms. Becky at her place. She's pulling us from training for some task."

They switched their trajectory and headed to the meetup, but Lexi couldn't let what she'd heard go. "Are you sure this experiment is a good idea? I mean, you've changed so much since you joined it. Look what happened to Kempton today.

What if that had been you?"

Not missing a stride, Rumi huffed. "You're kidding me, right? There's no way you miss the sniveling wimp you had to drag out of the Imperium."

Well, Rumi had a point. "I'm not saying you didn't have some improvements to make, but you've gone from fainting at the sight of a gun to worshiping the stupid things. In days—not years or months or even weeks—*days*. That's not right."

A few yards away from Ms. Becky's tent, Rumi pivoted and froze, arms out to keep Lexi from plowing into her. "You know what's not right? All of this." Rumi gestured to the tent city they now called home. "We're on the run because the Imperium's rules imprison or execute those we love if they slide even one toe out of line. I won't put up with it one more day. Maybe you need to figure out where your loyalties lie."

Rumi strode into the tent.

Lexi's brain took a second to communicate with her feet to move. Was she the weak one? Should she volunteer for the experiment and get on board with whatever they learned in their sleep? But what about Kempton's glassy-eyed stare when she'd tried to talk to him? She didn't want to turn into a robot, but once the doctor figured it out, she should consider it.

Inside the tent, she stepped up beside Rumi. Ms. Becky and Fletcher spoke in hushed undertones on the far side. The rebel leader had dressed in the same black clothing all the recruits wore, her hair in a slick ponytail still wet from a shower. When they'd met, Lexi thought Ms. Becky was old enough to be a grandparent, but her hair had to be prematurely gray, as her lithe gait was that of a woman Mom's age.

Rumi elbowed Lexi and leaned in to whisper. "Our first

assignment. What do you think it'll be? I hope we'll need weapons. That rifle *belonged* in my hands."

Lexi returned the jab to the ribs. "And here I was hoping it would involve a basket and long hours in the greenhouse. I heard there was another crop of green beans ready to pick."

"Pfff." Rumi gave Lexi a shove. "Right. Old people work. They need us to do the hard stuff, not greenhouse chores. What do you really think it's about?"

"Hey, a girl can dream, can't she?" If only it would be something simple. Perhaps she shouldn't have been so rash in rejecting her mother's offer to work with the plants.

Ms. Becky waved them over. "Let's focus, shall we?"

The musty scent of canvas mingled with body odor washed over Lexi as she approached Fletcher. He hunched over a map on the table. He acknowledged her and Rumi with a dip of his head. "Ladies."

"I'm afraid my tent isn't as fancy as the main house, but we'll make do." Ms. Becky shuffled in behind them and pointed to her cot. "Sit if you'd like." When neither of them moved, she continued. "Fletcher and I have a mission to accomplish when your mother's team returns to the Imperium. And your mother has permitted me to include you if you'd like to join us."

Lexi's heartbeat ticked up a notch. Maybe she'd get a chance to rescue her father after all. "When are we leaving?"

"Yes!" Rumi's fist jabbed at the air, and she bounced on her toes like someone had tied springs to her shoes. "Do I get to choose my weapon?"

Ms. Becky huffed out a laugh. "Calm, my friend. You won't need any guns or bombs for this job."

She might as well have stuck a pin in Rumi, who visibly

deflated, shoulders sagging. "Not even a handgun?"

"Humph." Fletcher's grunt drew Lexi's attention, grumbling loud enough for them to hear. "They should arm all of us, at all times—if you ask me."

With a pat on his shoulder, Ms. Becky shrugged. "You know we don't have enough weapons for everyone. I'm grateful we brought what we did, or I'd have already scrubbed this plan. But then again, that's the whole point of this mission."

He muttered his next words, and all Lexi caught were curses her mother would have grounded her for in her school days.

Ms. Becky raised a silencing hand. "Anyway, we've got guards with the ability to protect the rest of us if we plan this correctly." She approached the table. "We think we've found a solution to rescue the next batch of retirees."

Fletcher jabbed a beefy finger at a point on the map. "One of our insider connections has been sneaking uniforms out of the laundry systems. She's picked up those that got tossed into the recycle bin as too damaged to repair. They're supposed to be turned into rags for the maintenance crews, but we've salvaged enough to patch together and dress a troop."

"We've also intercepted orders for the squad responsible for the next train detail." Ms. Becky's tone grew serious. "Our people will be on that train instead of the Freedom Force team."

Though the plan sounded simple enough, the pieces weren't fitting together. "My mother agreed to let us join the squad?"

"Ha!" Fletcher's laugh exploded into the room. "Like Mrs. High-And-Mighty would let her princess wear a Freedom Force uniform."

Lexi's face burned. At least now she knew how people viewed her. She opened her mouth to protest, but Rumi beat her to it.

"What about me? Mrs. Verity would probably love to see me in that detail. Who knows? If she's lucky, I might not make it back."

Fletcher's smirk said more than any words could have. "Can't argue with you on that one."

Lexi bristled. "My mother wouldn't send anyone on a mission they weren't prepared for." She ignored Fletcher's glare. "So, Ms. Becky, what *are* we supposed to do?"

"We"—she indicated herself, Lexi, and Rumi—"are going to the Favela to pick up supplies."

"Supplies? From the bedraggled people in the Favela?" Lexi visited there a few times, saw the filthy clothes, the people burning anything they could find to stay warm, eating whatever food they could get their hands on. "What could they have left that's worth going back for?"

"As much as we were able, we've been a peaceful rebellion. Or at least our original group was." Ms. Becky tucked her hands in the pockets of her tactical pants and rocked back on her heels. "But that doesn't mean we didn't stock up on weapons here and there."

Rumi's eyes lit, and her mouth formed an O. "Like what?"

Fletcher—yes, *Fletcher*—smiled. Who'd have thought that possible for him? "Grenades, an assortment of bullets, and one or two grenade launchers, if I recall."

"Wahoo!" Rumi clapped. "Sounds like a good time. When do we leave?"

Unable to avoid Rumi's contagious grin, Lexi grinned back. Her blood hummed. She'd be involved in the same rebellion her mother had joined at her age. Her grandmother even. Then her thoughts froze. Had anyone told Reeves? A pending argument with her fledgling husband dampened her mood.

No. They needed every able-bodied person. Everyone knew that. Reeves would see the truth of it.

She needed to find him and let him know. "How much time do I have before we leave? Will the recruiting team take off before or after us?"

Across the map, Ms. Becky's finger drew a line between the rebels' camp and the Imperium's towers. "We're all going in at the same time—at sunset tonight. We'll travel through the night and end up in the Favela just before sunrise. At that point, we'll split into three groups. Each team will return on their own after they've met their objectives."

The risk that one or more of them might never return remained unsaid. Lexi wasn't about to give it a voice. "We'll all celebrate tomorrow night. I'm certain of it."

After agreeing to meet at the main house an hour before sunset, Rumi and Lexi walked out of the tent, leaving Fletcher and Ms. Becky deep in a discussion about which weapons would have the most value. They assumed the Freedom Force hadn't found their cache. Lexi blinked in the sunlight, having gotten used to the dim tent, and caught Rumi doing the same.

Before she'd walked five paces toward her and Reeves's tent, Lexi noticed Rumi following along beside her. Lexi didn't want to hurt the girl's feelings, but she'd hoped to find Reeves and have at least a few hours alone with her husband before their missions. Perhaps a hint would do. "Sweet seedlings, Reeves better not be stuck in planning all day. We've barely had a waking moment together since we arrived."

Rumi nodded but stayed by Lexi's side. "I just need a minute."

Her voice had taken on a conspiratorial murmur, causing

Lexi to look about for eavesdroppers. Lexi indicated the now-empty mess hall. Once they were both seated across from each other at a far-end table, Lexi raised her eyebrows. "What gives?"

Rumi's gaze darted around the room like she expected a Freedom Force guard to pop out from a hiding spot. "I have an older brother. He works in administration."

And...? Lexi nodded.

Rumi lowered her head and leaned in, the heat of her breath closing the gap between them. "We're going to find him when we return to the Imperium. I'm going to ask him to help us get your father out. Gunner has paid for your mother's crimes long enough."

Conflicting emotions welled into a fury that burned in Lexi's chest. She wanted to defend her mother, but Rumi hadn't lied. Her father betrayed the Imperium to help his daughter. She'd only asked him to because she'd joined the same rebellion her mother left him for. Rumi had been gracious not to place the blame on Lexi's shoulders, but it belonged there.

Their whispered words while hidden away in a corner meant they planned to disobey orders at some point. She'd have to choose between her father and her mother once again. It always felt like disloyalty, no matter which side she chose.

Could she trust this new version of Rumi not to lead them both to an early grave? Would Reeves ever forgive her for putting her life at risk? He'd be furious once he found out, but this might be her only chance to free her father. The tension building in her body was a vise squeezing the air from her lungs. She had to choose. Closing her eyes, she pictured her father standing in front of a firing squad. "What do you need me to do?"

Chapter 6

Lying isn't always wrong, especially to keep a loved one safe. Lexi repeated the thought and paced around her cot as if the reiteration somehow made it true. If Reeves knew she'd be on the team going to the Imperium, he'd freak out—distracted on his mission. A formula for disaster. Besides, it wasn't exactly lying, just a lack of full disclosure.

The tent flap opened, and he strode in, his eyes lighting up the moment they met hers. "I was hoping I'd find you here." He closed the gap between them and pulled her into an embrace. "We're moving out within the hour, but I needed a moment to remind myself why I'm doing this. To keep you safe."

Why'd he have to be so loyal? Guilt writhed through Lexi's veins, a serpent intent on strangling her heart. The air grew thick, clogging her lungs. Maybe it would be easier to confess. To let him know she'd be safe with Ms. Becky's team. But he might push for her to stay behind. Or worse—worry about her the entire time. No, she had to protect him. She forced a light tone. "That's me. Your wife. Safe here in our tent."

"Are you okay?" He eased back enough to look into her eyes. "You're tense like you're bracing for a storm."

Somehow, she managed a warm smile and shrugged. "I'm

fine. Just worried about you." Unable to maintain the façade, she'd better go for a distraction. She hugged him close and pressed her lips against his. Her hands slid into his silky hair. *Finally*. Their chance to indulge in the luxury of married life.

"Scheffer." A shout from outside their tent tossed a cold bucket on their passion. "Thrym's lookin' for ya."

"Grrr." The rumble of his primal growl vibrated through her chest. He stepped away. "We have to stop meeting like this."

In the dim light, his dilated pupils were a mesmerizing pool she wanted to dive into. Her ragged breath matched his, and her words rasped. "No. We need to get some privacy. Lots of it."

"Scheffer!" the voice hollered again. "You in there?"

Reeves rolled his eyes. "Unbelievable." He cupped her face and brushed her lips with his. Then he stormed out of the tent. "I'm coming. Hold your horses."

As he retreated, the cocoon of warmth they'd shared dissipated. Lexi wrapped her arms tight around herself to retain the lingering traces of his presence. Her heart slowed until it returned to its normal rhythm. The excitement exited her body, leaving behind serpentine guilt. "He's better off not knowing. Not this time."

Though her words had no audience, her conscience echoed a response. *Are you sure?*

She met up with Rumi and Ms. Becky as the sun kissed the horizon, sending pinks, oranges, and reds dancing through the clouds. Ms. Becky handed them both black hoodies, leather gloves, and backpacks stuffed to capacity. Lexi patted her pack before hefting it onto her shoulders.

Ms. Becky picked up a third bag. "We'll bring as much food

as we can for those still in the Favela. Once we've unloaded, we'll refill with ammunition and whatever else we can fit. We're going in heavy and, if all goes well, coming out even heavier."

Rumi lifted her bag and stumbled backward when the weight shifted to her shoulders. She growled and muscled both straps into place, then cinched the waist belt tight and planted her feet, widening them until she balanced. "If it gets much heavier than this, we may need to steal another UTV."

The cool evening breeze blew a stray swatch of hair into Lexi's face. She tucked it behind her ear, and they headed toward a line of vehicles, engines humming, ready to carry the teams on their missions.

Armed rebels swathed in black huddled in two circles, murmuring strategies in the tense stillness. One head towered over the others in each group. Thrym and Fletcher.

Weapons, a promise of violence to come, adorned shoulders, clung to hips, and settled into the grip of steady hands in each of the two clusters. The excessive firepower tightened the knot in her stomach. With a food-filled backpack, she might as well be naked if they ran into Freedom Force guards. Now she understood Fletcher's concern. Three unarmed women would be easy pickings.

That is, until they got to the arms storage. That cemented their mission in her mind. She'd haul every bullet, grenade, or knife she could fit, even if she had to drag it to the UTV.

A war whoop rang out as the first group disbursed to their vehicles. One man's gait looked too familiar—Reeves. The knot in her stomach doubled. How could the sight of him create such war of emotions? Half of her wanted to run to him and stick to his side like she'd been glued there, while the other half hoped he wouldn't notice her. She stopped behind Ms. Becky and pulled her hood up, obscuring her face.

Rumi tugged at Lexi's arm. "Over here."

Grateful for some direction, Lexi followed Rumi and Ms. Becky to the smallest transport at the end of the line. Its dinged exterior and torn upholstery were a far cry from the Imperium's well-maintained machines. Would this rattletrap make it the entire trip? Even more important, could it make it all the way back loaded down with heavy ammunition? Surely, they wouldn't break down somewhere in the dead world between the camp and the city. Best not to think of it too much. The motor pool workers wouldn't have put them into a vehicle they couldn't trust. Right?

The first UTVs in the line started off. Ms. Becky took the driver's seat, Rumi in the front passenger spot and Lexi behind. Backpacks loaded their laps, and Ms. Becky's bag joined Lexi on the narrow backseat. The tiny rear bed held tarped containers strapped down tight.

Fletcher loomed over the vehicle. His voice low, he addressed Ms. Becky. "Keep up with the line. Unless some miracle happens, you'll be alone on your ride back. I'll do my best to find you once we've freed the retirees."

"We'll be fine." Ms. Becky patted the giant's arm. "You're the one on the risky mission. Be safe. I've been praying for your success."

Fletcher trotted back to his ride, claimed the driver's seat, and took off with his team.

They might not all return. Lexi winced from a sledgehammer blow of reality. What if Reeves didn't make it back? She should have hugged him one last time.

No. They'd all make it back just fine. Then she'd cling to

him and never let him go.

Until then, they all had jobs to do.

* * *

Bone jarring. It was the only definition for the all-night ride through the barren lands. Had the trip been so bumpy the last time? Now, her back ached, and her limbs shook with her effort to keep her backpack in place and avoid losing it with each rock and dip. Holding on for dear life left little room for conversation.

With headlights too dim to see over ten feet in front of them, they must've lost the rest of the team, who'd barreled away. Better that way. Less risk Reeves would discover her.

After one particularly jarring bump, Ms. Becky braked to a halt. "Look. The city's just ahead."

Lexi peered into the darkness. A glow outlined the horizon in the wrong direction to be the rising sun. The Imperium—their mission—lay in sight. She repositioned her load for the millionth time. "Do you think we'll make it before sunrise?"

In the rearview reflection, Rumi's moonlit eyes gleamed. "If not, we're better off leaving the vehicle hidden. We'd be too conspicuous driving in."

Ms. Becky hit the accelerator, jolting them forward and snapping Lexi's head backward against the hard headrest. "We'll make it. I know where to hide to make loading easier."

The rising sun stained the eastern horizon crimson and threatened to expose them before Ms. Becky angled their UTV down a steep embankment. Broken cinder blocks crunched under the tires, taxing Lexi's sore muscles while she gripped her bag. With a last burst of acceleration, all four tires returned to the same plane, settling everything into place, upright once more.

In the distance, the outline of a tunnel emerged. She looked out and down, a lump rising in her throat. "We're on the train tracks."

Rumi's reflected eyes widened. "If we don't get off before the next train, we're going to get crushed."

Ms. Becky shook her head. "I know what I'm doing. Hold on."

A vibration shook their vehicle, and a distant whistle shrilled. Not good. Reeves would never forgive her if she died because of stupid navigation. "That's a train. We need to get off. *Now.*"

Lexi and Rumi made eye contact in an unspoken conversation. Could they take control and get them off the tracks before Ms. Becky turned them all into train fodder? Like a choreographed dance, both pushed their burdens to the side to free their arms. Rumi reached for the wheel as Lexi stretched out to pull back Ms. Becky's arms. They risked losing control of the vehicle, but the odds seemed better than whatever their leader had planned.

Ms. Becky twisted out of Lexi's grasp and yanked the wheel away from Rumi. The transport swerved left at a sharp angle, tossing them away from the driver. The world went dark, and the transport shuddered to a halt.

Uncertain what to do next, Lexi listened to the approaching train, then held her breath as the ground shook underneath them. Swirls of air danced around her, bringing bits of debris along for the ride. She covered her face, ready to meet her end. Soon the thunder of the passing train subsided, and the winds abated.

"Ha!" Ms. Becky hooted. "That just goes to show you should always listen to your elders." She swatted the steering wheel, then switched the headlights on, revealing a maintenance tunnel. "They don't use this section any longer, so we can hide the vehicle here until we're ready to go."

Every bit of her shaking, Lexi followed the others out and indulged in stretching sore muscles before strapping on her pack. Thrips and aphids, everything creaked. In the UTV bed, the straps held throughout the bumpy ride, but… "How are we going to get all of this to the Favela?"

Rumi shrugged. "It'll take several trips, so we'll need to hurry if we want to unload it and then reload before sundown." She cinched her pack's strap around her waist. "How far are we from the storage hold?"

Ms. Becky's wide grin belied any problems. "It's not far, but we needn't worry about carrying all this. Once we find some friends, they'll help us lug supplies out in exchange for what we've got here." She slid a glow stick from a pocket, activated it, then reached into the UTV, and switched off the headlights. The glow gave just enough light to see her turn in the direction they'd come. "This way, ladies."

They'd traveled further down the tunnel than Lexi thought. Back outside, the rising sun's rays dispelled the need for the glow stick. Ms. Becky motioned for them to stay quiet and follow her. Their path twisted around and about through a maze of crumbling buildings, abandoned vehicles, and trash-strewn streets to a cavernous opening. A ramp led them underground. Ms. Becky, still holding the glow stick, led them in and down, the light from the entrance fading away, their paths more uncertain with each step. Water dripped somewhere in the distance.

Lexi's skin tingled, not from the cool dampness, but from the sensation of eyes watching. She sidled up to suggest they find another route. But Ms. Becky put up a hand.

They froze. A shuffle echoed nearby.

Lexi swallowed the lump rising in her throat. If only she had a weapon. Even a small one like brass knuckles. Anything to give her an edge. Instead, a backpack weighed her down. She couldn't even run. She slipped one strap off her shoulder, prepared to lose the heavy load.

Ms. Becky cleared her throat and shouted, her voice echoing in the cavernous void. "I know a man and his story. Is what I've heard true?"

What in the world? Was that some sort of code?

Rumi moved to Ms. Becky's side, dropped her pack, and planted her feet in a fighting stance. Lexi followed suit so the three women stood in a tight configuration, eyes scanning for movement.

Ms. Becky grabbed Lexi's shoulder. "It's okay. Just give it a second."

"It's true." A male voice boomed from further down the ramp. "Let me tell you how it ends."

Ms. Becky exhaled and squeezed Lexi's shoulder before releasing her. "John, that you?"

The white of his teeth flashed, his grin wide. Then his long dreadlocks and threadbare clothing emerged. The thin man strode up the ramp and hugged Ms. Becky.

When they parted, Ms. Becky waved Lexi and Rumi over. "This is John. We can trust him to get the help we need." She swatted him on the back. "It's good to see you're still alive. I wasn't sure what would happen once we left."

He shook his head. "Patrols are tighter. They take out anyone they catch unless they need a reminder for the nightly news. Then it's the firing squad, live for the masses."

Ms. Becky tsked. "We brought supplies. Food. Figured you'd need some by now."

His grin lit his face like someone had inserted a fresh battery. "That we do, my friend."

More shuffles sounded in the dark behind him.

"It's okay, folks." His voice echoed through the gloom. "You all know Ms. Becky, and I'm sure we can trust her friends."

Rumi stepped forward, fists still balled, and eyes narrowed.

He murmured under his breath. "Well, mostly friendly."

To offset Rumi's defensive stance, Lexi stuck a hand out. "Nice to meet you. I'm Lexi." She jabbed a thumb toward her companion. "And this is Rumi. She's just… cautious."

A harrumph was Rumi's only verbal response, but she stood down and crossed her arms.

Ms. Becky handed John her pack, and he tore into it like a long-awaited gift. The shuffling turned into quick steps. Soon, a group surrounded them, pulling food and supplies out of all three packs. A woman who couldn't have been much older than Lexi ripped open a protein bar, took a bite, and closed her eyes as she chewed. She let out a whistle, and a child of five or so dashed out of the darkness and joined her. The woman leaned down and gave the kid the rest of the bar. He devoured it in three bites.

Lexi's chest ached as he stared at the packs, hope shining in his eyes. Then it hit her. A child. Outside the Imperium towers. Why? The Imperium rewarded anyone who could produce a child. "Why isn't he in school?"

The woman lurched in front of the boy as if to shield him.

Her eyes flashed. "He failed the test. Defective, they said. I wouldn't let them take him, though. He's mine. So we snuck out together." She ruffled the kid's grimy hair. "Rather live hand-to-mouth than be without him."

School tests flashed through Lexi's mind. The Imperium constantly tested its youth, categorizing them like goods on a store shelf. So, this was what happened if the Imperium decided the goods were flawed. The boy lucked out with a parent who wouldn't give him up. She'd heard of special schools where they sent kids who needed help. They probably ended up on the same trains that carried off retirees.

Bile swept into her throat, as bitter as the reality of their world. The Imperium's rule had to end. These people shared what little they could scrounge up. Sticking together for protection and support. This was the way humans were supposed to act. Helping each other.

Ms. Becky clapped to garner everyone's attention. "We must work quickly. Our group isn't the only one, and if something goes wrong with any of our teams, the Imperium will be out in force. There's plenty more for you back in our vehicle, but we need to replace it with some items we left behind. Who's willing to help?"

Every hand went up, even the boy's, a grin splitting his face. John closed the pack he'd rummaged through and swung it over his shoulders. "Point the way, and we'll sort everything in no time."

A quick discussion verified Ms. Becky's team's cache was intact. Then they chose the healthiest-looking adults to join the crew.

Darting through and between buildings, while monitoring the sky for Imperium drones, the group arrived at a two-story structure wedged between burned-out skeletons that used to be high-rises.

How had this building survived when the war decimated its companions? A wooden sign dangled from a single chain, its matching restraint having failed its mission. Faint purple letters still demarked the words *Ole Time Treats*.

The glass front door shattered long ago, and fractured bits glinted in the sunlight from the street's gutter. Following along single file, they entered the building, its floors creaking under the weight of new occupants. Ms. Becky trotted to the back, passing empty shelves picked clean so long ago the dust had grown thick on them. She opened a door labeled Manager. By the time Lexi entered the doorway, people filed through a gaping hole in the floor into an underground room.

When she reached the bottom, Ms. Becky's eyes shone bright. She cracked open a crate in the dim light of John's glow stick and surveyed the contents. "It's all still here." Waving a hand over the room, she pointed out the crates. "We can't take it all in one run, but we'll get as much as we can. I know it's tempting to keep some of this for yourselves, but if we promise to return with backup, will you guarantee me you'll leave the rest until then?"

John looked around at his companions in a circle surrounding the cache. There was no debate—no long discussion. It was as if they communicated everything that needed to be said with their eyes. One at a time, each closed their eyes and tipped their head—until only one member hadn't. A small fellow. Shorter than Rumi, even. Fire blazed in his eyes. He opened his mouth, then closed it without uttering a word. It had to be the most silent protest ever. His gaze darted around the room as if trying to find even one other member who'd agree with him.

No one would make eye contact, though. No one except John—and his eyes pleaded, almost begging for a unanimous decision. The small fellow squeezed his eyes shut, gave a terse nod, then grabbed the nearest crate, and stormed up the stairs. Probably acting before he could change his mind.

John sighed before a crooked smile crinkled his lips. "Sorry about that. We're with you, though. Just point out which ones we're taking."

In two trips, the group loaded the maximum crates the UTV could handle in exchange for supplies and food. As they tightened down the straps, Ms. Becky shook John's hand. "I can't thank you enough. Please know I'm doing all I can to get you help. It's going to take time, though. I have to convince others that all-out war isn't the only—or even best—option."

John hugged her, then backed away, shaking his head. "After what I've seen, you may have to convince me of the same thing. The Imperium embodies pure hatred and a lifestyle dedicated to self-interest. Reminds me of the story of Sodom. I fear the city is too far gone."

Tears welled in Ms. Becky's eyes. "Pray it isn't so."

With a nod, John led his group back to the Favela. The boost to their stores wouldn't last long. The child swung his mother's arm with his own, happy to have a second protein bar in his little hand. He deserved more.

Once they were alone, Ms. Becky gripped their hands. "Before we leave, I have one errand to run. I need to see if a friend is still with us. She was rather ill before I left, so probably not, but I'd like to visit her grave if nothing else."

Rumi's eyes lit. She elbowed Lexi. This was their chance, but Rumi was giving it away. Lexi schooled her face into a neutral expression. Knowing what the answer would be, she asked Ms. Becky, "Would you like us to come with you?"

Ms. Becky's eyes narrowed. "You both need to stay here. With the UTV. If I'm not back in two hours, then leave without me."

"Yes, ma'am." Rumi's response was too enthusiastic. "We'll be here."

Their leader hesitated as if weighing Rumi's words. "Okay. I'll be back."

The moment Ms. Becky turned a corner, Rumi clapped and rubbed her hands together. "We'll need to be quick. You ready to run?"

Lexi had thought the words metaphorical until Rumi took off like a soldier late for a critical mission. Within a few blocks, Lexi's breaths came in jagged gulps. How this could be the same girl she and Reeves had to drag away during their flight not so long ago?

The Administration tower's lights grew brighter as the last bit of the sun dipped behind the horizon.

A hum overhead sent a shiver down Lexi's spine. They dashed into the closest building through a hole that had once been a plate glass window. They stood flat against the far wall as the hum passed by. Lexi counted in her head... fifteen... fourteen... The drones cleared the way for troops. When the footsteps marched by, her breath caught, and her heart pounded.

A high-powered light beam flashed through the glassless window, and they both dropped to the floor, flat and motionless. The light scanned the room, the wall they'd stood against reflecting the beam. It moved on without scanning the floor.

As the crunch of soldiers' boots on the crumbled cement

faded from earshot, Rumi sprang to her feet. "Come on. We need to hurry. That must've been the only patrol in this section for the next hour."

Once again, Rumi took off like a shot, Lexi sprinting to keep up. Then Rumi pulled up short at the first tower's base, and Lexi sucked in air as fast as her lungs could exchange it.

Rumi glared. "You sound like you've never run a day in your life. Don't you do morning calisthenics?"

Lexi frowned in return. "You mean those exercises you're doing when sensible people are catching a few more z's?"

Rumi rolled her eyes before turning her attention back to the building. "I need mud."

Her mind spinning, Lexi sucked in more oxygen. "Mud?"

With a huff, Rumi craned around. A plastic bag wedged itself over a rainspout on a nearby building. She trotted over to it, Lexi on her heels. After inspecting the bag, Rumi nodded. "Yes." The word hissed out like a snake. A few paces away, she picked up an old metal cup and scraped the road where it met the sidewalk.

The cup half full of dirt, Rumi returned to the rainspout and placed the cup under it. She tore a hole in the bag and filled the cup with the water caught during the last rainfall.

Rumi mixed the water into the dirt, then plopped a blob of mud into her palm. "Now we get to see how accurate we are." She frowned at Lexi. "Make that how accurate *I* am."

"Funny. What are you planning?"

"Watch and be amazed." Rumi scuttled back toward the building's entrance and stared at a pole. "This should be fun."

Lexi followed Rumi's gaze to a camera mounted about ten feet up, aimed toward the door. Her voice hoarse from trying to whisper, Lexi eked out her next words. "No way. Absolutely no way you can make that shot."

Rumi waggled her eyebrows. Then, smirking, she flung a glob toward the camera. Her aim was excellent, and the mud stuck to the side like a growth, but not over the lens. She scooped up another blob and aimed once more. This time, she hit a bull's-eye. "Ha." Her gloating grin promised it would be a long time before Lexi heard the end of this tale.

Rumi dashed to the door and slid a knife from her belt. Using the blade like a screwdriver, she extracted the four screws holding the scanner in place. Once she'd pried it out, she cut two of the wires and twisted them together. The door clicked, and Rumi swung it open with ease.

Was there any limit to this girl's new skills? Lexi walked through the open door. "Where'd you learn how to do that?"

Rumi followed her inside and closed the door with an almost inaudible click. "I told you. I've got a brother who works in security."

They hustled through the administrative building hallways as fast as reasonable but slowed their gait at the sight of any citizens. There weren't many in the halls at this late hour. People would be at dinner or helping children with homework. They stopped in front of a door, and Rumi tapped out a rhythm on it.

What if her brother had moved? Or worse—had gotten into trouble after she'd left?

A rap on the door's other side made Lexi's heart jump. Rumi grinned and knocked three times in rapid succession. The door opened, and a hand yanked her inside. She tugged Lexi along before the door closed behind them.

Joyful squeals erupted, and Rumi wrapped her arms around a man five inches taller than her. When they parted, he rubbed her hair, and she jabbed a punch to his biceps.

The man pushed Rumi to arm's length. "Where have you been? I've been so worried about you. Does anyone know you're here?"

She raised a hand to his lips, silencing him. "I'll explain everything as soon as I can. First, I need a favor."

His face grew somber. "Name it and it's yours."

"We need to get my husband out of prison."

Chapter 7

"Lexi, this is my brother, Zane. If anyone can help us, it's him." Rumi hadn't stopped grinning since they'd entered the apartment.

Zane nodded at Lexi, squinting as if in thought. Then his eyes widened. "Lexi—as in the daughter of Gunner Verity?" He goggled, mouth agape. "Are you kidding me, Rumi? You've brought one of the most wanted people in the whole Imperium into my home?"

Rumi smacked him upside his head. "Who do you think I'm married to?"

He glowered at her. "That's not your fault. You couldn't help who they assigned you to. I could still get you out of that. But bringing *her* here? That digs your hole deeper."

Hands on hips, she glared back. "I don't want *out* of my marriage. I want you to help me rescue my husband so he can join me where it's safe. You, of all people, should understand what family means."

A baby's cries drew their attention to the back of the apartment. Behind a closed door, a woman's coos shushed the child before the bedroom door opened. A tall, thin woman around Lexi's age with curly red hair entered the room. A tiny bundle squirmed in her arms. "Rumi? Is that you?"

Rumi rushed over and hugged the woman. "Lexi, this is Zane's wife, Sienna, and this beauty"—she folded back the blanket covering the child—"is Brynn, my niece."

Something twisted in Lexi's stomach seeing the child snuggled in her mother's arms. This family was complete. They'd had their first child, the most important one. So few ever managed more than one. With the baby's arrival, Zane and Sienna attained the status of parents—an honored role within the Imperium's system. Yearning misted Rumi's eyes as she rocked back and forth with the child. No doubt Rumi wanted what her brother had.

They didn't have time to visit. Lexi stepped up. "Nice to meet you. Sorry for the sudden intrusion. We won't be here long as we have people waiting for us."

Rumi took the hint, sighed, and returned the baby to its mother's arms. "Sorry. I got a little off track. Lexi's right. I need your help. There must be a way to get Gunner out. If anyone could figure out how, it's you."

Zane rubbed the back of his neck. "Look, I know you think you're doing something good, rescuing your husband and all, but I've been tracking the rebels for a while now. You need to see the evidence we have against them."

A laugh bubbled out. "Evidence against the rebels? You've got to be kidding me. What about the people the Imperium tossed out into the Favela to fend for themselves? Or the innocents they lined up and executed on the vis screens? You know, the mandatory viewing for all citizens?"

Zane picked his tablet off the counter and swiped through the menus for something. "There are reasons the government deals with rebels swiftly. If we don't, we'll all be dead or under the control of unbalanced people. Watch this."

Lexi accepted the tablet and tapped the icon to play the video he'd queued. The train station came on screen. A group of seniors stood in line for their ride to Solitude. Or, at least, that would be where they thought they were going.

Her mother walked into view, her grandparents behind her—Nana pushing Gramps in his wheelchair while Mom carried a suitcase in each hand. "This was the day of the explosion," Lexi whispered. The day she thought the rebels killed them. Mom paused alongside other travelers and nodded to Nana, who pushed Gramps farther into the room. After setting one suitcase down at the base of a support pillar, Mom followed Nana and Gramps. The second suitcase ended up at the base of another column, about twenty yards away.

Once Mom's hands were empty, she took Nana's place behind Gramps's chair. The three of them strode toward the platform's far end in front of the emergency exit. A glitch in the video turned the image to static, and when the view cleared, Lexi's family had vanished. The emergency door, though still closed, hinted at no other escape route, leaving little doubt about how they slipped away unnoticed. A heartbeat later, the screen erupted in an orange ball of flames and then went black.

Lexi's blood ran cold. No denying it—her mother set the bombs that killed hundreds of retirees. Somehow, they'd timed the camera glitch with their exit, so they had help in the security department. Bile burned in her throat, and her legs gave out beneath her. She slid into a nearby chair. Mom killed all those people. That made Lexi the daughter of a murderer. How was this any different from what the Imperium was doing? Mom had saved Nana and Gramps, but to what end?

The walls closed in as she struggled to catch her breath.

Arms encircled her, and she seemed to float outside of her body, aware someone shook her and spoke, though she couldn't comprehend the words. The rebels were supposed to be the good guys. What she'd just seen was anything but good.

Rumi's face swam into Lexi's vision, her lips forming nonsensical whispers. Lexi concentrated until she could understand Rumi.

"Snap out of it, kiddo. We've got to get going."

"Mom killed those people." Despite sounding like some sort of Captain Obvious, she repeated the thought as if to convince herself. "Mom killed *innocent* people."

"Yes. She did." Rumi helped Lexi back to her feet. "And we need to find out why. For now, we need to figure out our next move."

Lexi stood once more, Rumi's arm supporting her waist. The fire in her eyes both comforted and terrified Lexi.

Rumi spun them back to Zane. "Gunner had nothing to do with his former wife's crimes. The Imperium *must* understand that."

Zane nodded. "I believe they do, but he's the only bargaining chip they have."

Lexi's thoughts were fuzzy like a vis screen with a bad feed. "How is he going to help them? It's not as if he controls the rebels."

A growl rumbled from Rumi's throat. "They think he'll bring *you* to them, and you'd be the key to capturing your mother."

If what she'd just witnessed was true, her mother needed to be brought to justice. Lexi couldn't argue against the logic.

There had to be more to it than what she'd seen. How could she trust anyone to tell the truth? Her father was in prison because he'd tried to help Lexi. Mom might have started the gears in motion, but Lexi had cranked the engine that put him behind bars. It was up to her to make it right.

Adrenaline kicked in. She slipped Rumi's arm off her waist. "Then I'll turn myself in. An even exchange. Me for him."

Zane's eyes went wide. "Is that what you brought her here for, Rumi? To trade her for him?"

Rumi growled. The spark that had been in her eyes burst into raging flames. She grabbed Lexi's biceps and twisted her so they faced each other. "That's *not* the plan. Zane is going to dig into the security systems, find a weakness, and give me the information. Then we'll *all* be free of this place."

Zane let out a breath and scrubbed the back of his neck with his hand. "It won't be easy. I can get in and poke around, but security is no joke around here."

The baby whimpered. Zane strode across the room, wrapped an arm around Sienna's shoulders, and brushed a finger across Brynn's face, wiping a tear away. "I'll do it if you promise you'll protect my family. Take them with you in the end, even if I get caught."

"No." Sienna shook her head, then glared at Lexi. "You can't risk our lives. It isn't fair that we should pay for *her* crimes."

He cupped his wife's chin and brought his lips to hers, placing the sweetest kiss Lexi had ever seen. "You know we can't continue to ignore what the Imperium is doing. We're the fortunate ones. Not everyone can have a family, and we both know what happens to those who fail."

A tear slipped down Sienna's cheek. She hugged the whimpering child to her chest and nodded.

Zane stroked her hair, then strode to a shelf, pulled a thick book off it, and handed it to Rumi. "I need some time to root around and figure out a plan. A friend of mine works in production for Tempest Malachy's newscasts. He says she's as moody and demanding as they come, and he's tired of the drama. I can get him to do me a favor. Keep an eye out for her telecasts. When you see this book on the shelf behind Tempest, that's your signal I've got the information you need."

Lexi grinned at the title, *Love in the Time of Algorithms* written by Mabel Martin. "Perfect."

Rumi hugged her family and kissed Brynn's forehead. "We need to get back. We'll watch for your signal."

Winded from their sprint back to the UTV, Lexi panted between sips of water. How was it Rumi wasn't even thirsty, much less breathing heavily? Perhaps it was time for a doctor's visit to discuss those pills and earbuds. "I'm glad we made it back before Ms. Becky did, but where do you think she went?"

Rumi shrugged. "She's such a bleeding heart. Probably wanted to empty her pockets of anything of value she had left. I just hope someone doesn't turn her in for a reward."

A weight dropped into the pit of Lexi's stomach. The idea hadn't even occurred to her. "No one would do that. She's done nothing but help everyone she could."

Footfalls crunched on the crumbled concrete. Then Ms. Becky stormed from behind the closest building, her pace clipped and deliberate. The flint in her eyes matched the granite set of her jaw. "There you two are. I thought for sure the Freedom Force found you. I told you to *stay put.*"

Rumi smiled, feigning relief at seeing the older woman. "What do you mean? We went looking for *you* because *we* were worried."

Ms. Becky's eyebrows furrowed, then relaxed. "Well, we're all together again, and we got what we came for. Let's head back and see how the rest of the team fared."

The return ride seemed longer, though the distance hadn't changed and they took the same route. Lexi spent every minute looking for signs of Reeves, Fletcher, Thrym, or any other rebel. There wasn't so much as a dust cloud on the horizon. With each passing hour, her stomach tightened into more knots. What if something horrible had happened? Their team might be the only survivors. A shiver tracked through her body, chilling her to the bone.

Night fell before they reached Solitude, and the illuminated compound's glow brought a strange combination of hope and terror. When they passed through the front gate, part of her wanted to sprint to their tent to find Reeves. Another part feared he wouldn't be there. A pain radiated through her chest. She needed to see him, to twine her fingers with his, to feel his lips against hers once more.

A guard decided for her when he pointed toward the main house, implying they needed to park there. Mom stood on the front porch as if she'd been waiting for them, her eyes like hardened steel. She strode down the steps to greet them the moment Ms. Becky shut off the UTV. "I see you have a full load. Everything go okay?"

"Like clockwork." Ms. Becky alighted from the vehicle and joined Mom.

Lexi's heart hitched. Something was off. Her mother's face seemed armored for battle. Had something happened to Reeves? No. Her stare held no sympathy. Could Mom have discovered her knowledge about the explosion—the tragedy that claimed so many innocent retirees? "How did the other teams do?" Lexi tried to sound casual. "Is Reeves back yet? And what about Fletcher's group—were they able to rescue everyone?"

Her mother tipped her chin toward the front door. "Come inside. We're gathering for the debrief now."

Rumi trailed Ms. Becky toward the main house, but Mom caught Lexi's arm and held her back. Once they were alone, Mom cleared her throat. "Reeves is pretty unhappy right now. You should've told him you were going."

Reeves was safe! Lexi's knees wobbled, and she braced herself against the porch railing before the rest of that statement sank in. She'd be walking into an argument. "I wanted to, but he was so bent on being my protector, I just couldn't."

Mom twisted her lips into a wry grin. "Welcome to married life. You're about to enjoy your first fight—if you two haven't already had the pleasure."

The short flight of steps might as well have been a mountain, and Lexi had no desire to reach the top. She'd gone halfway up before a familiar figure walked into the dim porch light. Reeves. Her mother passed by, whispered something to him, then shut the door behind her.

Lexi smiled as she took the last steps to meet him on the porch. "What a relief to see you."

He glowered and yanked her into the house. Instead of heading to join the others, he directed her into a walk-in closet. The door thumped shut, darkness enveloping them.

The intensity with which he pulled her into his arms and held her close took Lexi's breath away. She'd expected a stern talking-to, but his embrace spoke louder than words. The relief of seeing him again after the terrifying ride back flooded through her, and she clung to him, grateful.

Then he pushed her to arm's length. His growl told her she should be glad he'd started with the hug. "Don't you *ever* leave the compound again without telling me," he snapped, his voice shaking with anger and something deeper—fear. "When I found out you'd gone to the Favela, I thought I was going to lose my mind. Do you have any idea how worried I was? If I'd known you were there, I wouldn't have left—not until I knew you were safe and on your way back."

He pressed her into his chest, his hand gripping the back of her head. His heart raced, a frantic drumbeat against her cheek.

He loves me. And yet, she'd betrayed him. A lie of omission. Guilt overflowed through her tears. "I'm sorry. I didn't mean to frighten you."

His viselike grip tightened further, and his warm breath tickled her ear. "I'm *still* glad they assigned me someone so strong-willed and bent on changing the course of history, but you'll be the death of me yet."

He was glad she was his. She snuggled in closer, just as glad to be his. If only she could stay in his arms and share what she'd learned. This wasn't the place, though. "Let's go back to our tent."

He huffed out a breath, then released her. "We can't. Not yet. We need to be in the debriefing."

When he opened the door, a swirl of air sent a shiver down her arms. He stalked out and waited for her, and her heart sank. When would they have time for themselves?

In the light, a red splotch stood out on his neck. Blood. She shivered. He had injuries, and she hadn't even noticed. She touched the swath of crimson. At least it wasn't actively bleeding. "What happened?"

He brushed her aside, revealing matching stains on his hands. "We ran into some trouble. The blood isn't mine." The door to the command room opened, interrupting him. "I'll tell you about it later."

He took her hand and led her along. Good. They'd go into the room as a couple. Such thoughts ended the moment they reached the door. He released her and strode in, taking a stand beside Thrym and crossing his arms over his chest.

Lexi joined Ms. Becky and Rumi across the room.

Mom clapped to get the room's attention. "Each of our teams completed their missions. Thrym's team alone brought back over a dozen recruits, with the potential to add twice that number on the next run."

Thrym, his jaw set like a chiseled stone, nodded.

Mom continued. "Fletcher's squad also accomplished their task. Unfortunately, their success has given us more mouths to feed and more healthcare needs."

Fletcher glared at the veiled snipe.

Lexi couldn't blame him. He'd risked his life and that of every person with him. Why couldn't Mom congratulate him instead?

Ms. Becky's eyes were just as dark as Fletcher's.

Mom went on. "Our third small squad brought back more ammo, which we desperately needed, and for that, we're grateful. The most exciting news, though, is information Thrym's team gleaned from the recruits. Sixty miles west of our location, an old army base, Anniston Army Depot, may still have the supplies for a bomb."

A low hum of whispered conversations intruded.

Mom's raised hand silenced them. "Not just any bomb. One

that can end this battle in one decisive attack. Rumor is the base has chemical weapons and other supplies we can use to create what is called a dirty bomb. If we get this technology, we can deploy it during a high council meeting and put an end to the system that has controlled our lives since the Great War ended. This is our chance for freedom."

Lexi's hands trembled. Her mother wanted to set off another bomb. As if killing an entire train full of retirees hadn't been enough for her, now she wanted to take revenge on the high council. Who was to say the explosion wouldn't decimate the entire building? Rumi's family was there. The cost outweighed the benefits.

Thrym and everyone who reported to Mom wore triumphant grins. They wouldn't argue against the plan. But Ms. Becky and those who reported to her glanced around the room as if looking for a way out.

This wasn't the right way to win their freedom.

Chapter 8

Lexi's stomach churned, sending acid into her throat. The meeting ended, and she followed Reeves out the front door and down the steps. Her thoughts swirled around the mental image of Zane's family lying dead in their apartment. She had to talk sense into someone. If not her mother, then perhaps Reeves would listen.

Her mind settled. The moment they had time alone, she'd convince him to help her find another way to end the fight with the Imperium and persuade the others to join them.

"Reeves, over here." A guy with curly chestnut hair waved and walked toward them. His Imperium uniform marked him as one of the newest recruits.

Reeves took Lexi's hand. "You'll like Ethan. His enthusiasm is contagious."

Something about the way Ethan walked looked familiar. When he joined them, he grinned at Lexi as if they were old friends. "Lexi, I can't believe it's you. I thought I'd never see you again. What are the odds you'd be with this crazy dude?" Ethan jabbed Reeves's arm and winked at Lexi. "Remember me from Reclamation?"

It's him. The guy she'd met on her first day at the Reclamation Center. Ethan had received his assignment at the same time as her. "Of course." She gave a half wave. "I thought I'd die of boredom if I had to work that conveyor belt of junk one more day. Glad to have you onboard Team Rebel."

"Not me." Reeves released Lexi's hand and threw a fake punch at Ethan. "You bring the mental IQ of this organization down a notch or two just by being here."

Laughing, Ethan traded blows with Reeves. Lexi hadn't seen her husband's playful side before. His grin sparked warmth in her chest and eased her tension. "You two have bonded."

Ethan's smile widened, and he thumped Reeves's back. "Who wouldn't appreciate the guy who saved his life?"

A shadow flickered across Reeves's face. His lips twitched, and he rubbed at the blood still present on his neck. "I did what I had to."

The urge to comfort him sent Lexi's hand to Reeves's biceps like it had a mind of its own. They needed time alone. Time to process today. "It's great to see you again, Ethan. Reeves and I were just headed back to our tent for the evening. See you at training in the morning?"

Ethan's smile widened, and he waggled his eyebrows at her, hint taken. "Sure. Can't wait to see you again, Lexi. At training. It's a date."

He walked away, but not before a final wink made her skin crawl. Ethan's friendly attitude cozied up to a boundary he better not cross. She shrugged off the soft warning bell. Probably just the weirdness of seeing him outside of the Imperium.

Reeves cleared his throat and wrapped an arm around her shoulder. "Ready to head home, Mrs. Scheffer?"

Hearing her married name combined with the warmth of

his body sent a delicious shiver down her spine. "Let's go."

The trip to their tent gave her stomach time to birth a swarm of butterflies. Reeves radiated heat, and he snugged her arm around his. Their time together at the camp had been scarce, and the thought of an uninterrupted stretch alone left her breathless. Never had she experienced such a profound connection with another person. Did he feel the same?

Reeves handed her the solar lantern he'd set outside their entryway to charge in the daylight. He lifted the tent flap, ushered her inside, zipped the closure, and tied it shut.

The tent morphed into their cocoon from the world. Her hands trembled, and she fumbled with the light before she found the switch to flip. Somehow, the dim glow set the perfect mood for what she needed—time alone with her husband.

Her chest ached from her heartbeat's rapid tempo. She placed the lamp on a table, drew in a calming breath. Then her heart sank. His eyes drooped. The red stain on his neck reminded her of his ordeal. How could she have been so thoughtless? Though he'd said the blood wasn't his, there'd still been a cost. Perhaps he'd taken a life. He needed her, but not as a husband needed a wife.

A metal water bottle and washcloth rested on a folding chair from her last trip to the showers. She poured water to dampen the cloth and used a gentle hand to erase the bloodstains. "Want to talk about it?"

He grasped her hand and stared at the tinged cloth before his blue eyes focused on her. "No. *Yes.* I don't know." He stepped back and scrubbed at his knuckles as if trying to erase his memory of the stains. "It was life or death. Ethan's or this random Freedom Force guard who'd caught us sneaking out.

He raised his pistol, had Ethan in his sights....."

A shudder ran through Reeves and he clamped his lips shut either unable or unwilling to finish the sentence.

What could she say? Her tongue stuck to the roof of her dry mouth. "I'm sure you did what you had to."

"The guy's hands were shaking. He didn't want to shoot any more than I did." His eyes dimmed. His body shuddered. "But I swear, I saw his finger flinch, like he was pulling the trigger. I reacted. Like they train us, you know?"

She did, and her heart ached. "You saved Ethan's life. It was the right thing to do."

His eyes pleaded with her. "Was it? I'm not so sure anymore."

The pain in her chest grew until her heart might burst. She gathered him in her arms. "I'm so sorry you had to go through that. What can I do to help?"

"Just hold me." The words croaked out of him. "Don't leave me."

* * *

Morning arrived too soon, sunrise granting a reprieve from the arduous night. What might've been their first night together as husband and wife instead turned into whispered assurances she'd never abandon him. Ever.

And maybe that's what their marriage needed more than anything. The love she'd only hoped she was feeling had grown, solidified from a wispy concept into a stable reality. Lexi's body ached from hours spent cuddled next to him in a single cot until he fell into a troubled sleep. He woke twice from his nightmares, and she soothed him back to sleep each time.

She pulled on fresh clothes, then gathered the scattered remnants of the night before. Reeves's shirt, with its earthy aroma, brought a lump to her throat as she tucked it into the laundry duffel. The scent of him lingered in the fabric.

The creak of movement from the cot snapped her attention back, and she found Reeves watching her, his eyes red, his sad grin not reaching them. "Morning." His casual tone sent a desire to protect him shuddering through her, followed by a silent vow she'd never be the one to hurt him. "Sleep okay?"

The deep connection in his eyes drew her. She crossed the room to his side.

"Not much sleep." She reached for his hand, intertwining their fingers. "But I'm here for you."

In this quiet moment, with the morning light wrapped around them, his nod said everything. It was a look of mutual understanding, of love deepened not by physical union but by shared vulnerability and trust.

They were more than husband and wife. They were partners, connected by an unspoken bond the new day only strengthened. If only they could stay hidden away from what awaited them.

A palm thudded against their tent flap, shattering the mood, and Ethan's voice followed. "Reeves, you in there? Training starts in ten."

Reeves rolled his eyes, and he bellowed. "Hold your horses. I'm coming." He threw off a blanket and dressed.

Lexi averted her eyes from his bare chest and fidgeted with the laundry duffel. Married life felt fresh and new—and awkward. She finished buttoning her shirt. "I guess I'll see you tonight?"

His hands grasped her shoulders from behind, and he turned her to face him. "I'll be the king of accomplishment today. I'll finish every assignment in record time and be back in this tent as early as humanly possible." He brushed her lips with his own. "I can't wait to see you again. I'd say next time will be different." He arched his eyebrows in a suggestive dance before he stole her breath away with a deeper kiss. Then he drew back and framed her face between his hands. "But you deserve better, Lex. Our first night… I want to… I don't know. I guess, I want to know I can give you everything, not just a few nights during wartime, but a whole life. And I want to know you're ready to give me your whole life too."

His intensity weakened her knees and stole the breath from her lungs, leaving her unable to do more than dip a vague nod.

The tent rattled again. "Reeves."

He pushed her to arm's length, a gleam in his eyes though the sad smile remained. "Someday."

Heat flamed on her cheeks, and she couldn't put together a single word in response. She stepped out behind him and waved goodbye as if he were a five-year-old leaving for the first day of school.

Ethan smacked Reeves on the back, and they strode off. She hoped for a last acknowledgment from Reeves, but none came. When Ethan instead gave her an exaggerated wink along with an eyebrow waggle, her heart shriveled.

Let it pass. He's a harmless flirt.

She returned to the tent. If only she could race to catch up and shadow Reeves until he was done for the day. Before she could act on her desire, the tent flap opened. Her heart rate ticked up in anticipation—until she recognized who'd entered.

Rumi rushed inside, her eyes gleaming. "There you are. I figured you'd be out earlier. Did you forget they're teaching knife throwing?"

I'd rather spend the day with Reeves.

It wasn't as if he could ditch training for the day. Lexi couldn't either. But she allowed disappointment to taint her response. "I know we don't have a door, but you still need to knock or something and not just barge in whenever you want."

Rumi frowned. The space between her eyebrows wrinkled. She shook her head as if tossing off a pest. "Sorry. But really—*knife throwing*. How cool is that? We don't want to be late."

Her emphasis reminded Lexi of the thrill she'd felt the first time she toured the greenhouses as a child. She sighed. "Lead on."

Though Rumi chattered the entire way, Lexi heard little of it. She wanted the day to end so she could be with Reeves again. Thoughts of him tempted her to daydream.

An elbow jabbed into her side. Rumi's whisper said Lexi missed something. "Pay attention. You're missing the important bits."

They stood in line where they'd practiced shooting, only this time, throwing knives lined the bench. The instructor sent a blade flying toward a target less than a dozen feet away, and it *thunked* into the bull's-eye. "Remember, stand straight, dominant foot forward, sideways to the target, with your throwing arm aligned toward it."

As usual, Rumi picked the skill up like she'd only had to remember how, but it took Lexi a few tries before she got the feel for the motion. Ms. D. paused beside Lexi. "Rotation is important. Less contact on the knife means faster rotation."

Following her instructions, Lexi gripped the knife like a hammer, inhaled with her backswing, then exhaled, and transferred her weight to her front foot as she threw. *Thunk.* Her knife struck and stuck, just as she'd practiced, and she couldn't resist a fist pump. "Yes."

"Well done. You're either a natural, or you've done this before. I've never seen anyone pick it up so quickly." Before Lexi could respond, the instructor moved to the next trainee in line to provide pointers.

Throw after throw, Lexi's aim improved until the butt never hit, the blade seldom missed, and the strike often came close to the center. She *was* good at this.

A hand squeezed her shoulder, and she frowned at Ethan behind her, his grin wide. "Looking good there. I think you've found your weapon."

She brushed his hand away and craned past him to see if her husband had come along. "I thought you were with Reeves?"

He traced a finger down her cheek. "Nah. He's focused on training, but I've got my eyes on something more important."

How dare... She swatted his hand away. "Don't touch me."

His grin twisted into a smirk. He opened his arms to her. "Come on. Don't be shy."

Lead settled in her gut. *He's crazy.*

She backed away until the bench stopped her. "I'm married."

"Don't you get it?" He ran a hand through his hair. Leaning in closer, he slid his tongue over his top lip like a starving wolf expecting a meal. "We're free here. Any marriages the Imperium forced us into are void. You can have anyone you choose—and I'm choosing you."

A whistle sounded—the signal to pause practice.

Ethan winked, and bile rose in her throat.

Two quick whistle blasts followed—the signal to retrieve the weapons from the target area.

He gave her a knowing smile before he sauntered away.

She rushed to her riddled board to reclaim her blades. The task near impossible with shaking hands. She tugged on a deeply imbedded blade when shouts arose. She whirled to find Rumi standing toe to toe with Ethan, her eyes ablaze.

"You can't tell me what to do. No one can anymore." He shoved Rumi backward, and she stumbled.

Rumi recovered, bent low, and charged, a growl rumbling deep in her chest.

A crack pierced the air, followed by a stifled yelp, barely audible above the surrounding commotion. Rumi's body became a blur of unchecked aggression that didn't break even as the man underneath her gasped, blood blossoming across his face from a nose bent out of shape. His arm lay at an unnatural angle.

Ms. D. rushed over and dragged Rumi off the incapacitated man. The instructor's face strained with the urgency of controlling the chaos. Another teacher joined and gripped Rumi's other arm, viselike, and pulled in the opposite direction. Their movements desperate and disjointed.

"Stand down, soldier!" the instructor shouted, her voice sharp as a whip. "Control yourself!"

Rumi jerked against their hold like a beast fighting restraints. Her eyes burned with a dangerous intensity as she strained, her entire being resisting the command to calm.

Ms. D. growled at the other instructor. "Medical tent."

Lexi struggled to control her breathing while they dragged Rumi away. Rumi continued to kick and scream like a madwoman. Part of Lexi wanted to follow, to help calm her father's wife, but the screams didn't sound like the Rumi she knew. Perhaps the doctor could calm her. A third instructor arrived to tend to Rumi's victim, and Lexi gave Ethan's unconscious body a last glance. Served him right for picking a fight with Rumi.

The trainees dispersed into clusters, some repeating their drills while others lost themselves in animated debates over the event. Amid the buzz, Lexi gave in to a pull for solitude. Her feet moved of their own accord, carrying her past familiar pathways lined with budding flowers. It wasn't until the humid greenhouse air brushed against her skin that she realized her subconscious need for peace had led her there.

Inside, moist heat blanketed her. Ms. Becky worked near the rear, picking green beans for the next meal. Lexi joined her, plucked a pod from Ms. Becky's basket, and popped it into her mouth. The fresh crunch reminded Lexi what she'd been training for. What they all fought for. Freedom to pursue their dreams. But were they going to lose themselves, their humanity, in the process of gaining their freedom?

Ms. Becky eyed Lexi. "Did you come to help or to snitch my beans?"

She swallowed. "Sorry. It's been a rough morning. I'm worried about the experiments Dr. Ichtacka is performing on the people here. Rumi lost it this morning on a guy. That's the *second* time I've seen one of his patients go nuts."

Ms. Becky plucked more beans from the vines. "It pains me to see how we treat each other nowadays. We weren't designed to act this way toward one another."

"Designed?" Lexi picked up the pace, helping to fill the basket. "I read about people holding onto such notions in the dark days."

Ms. Becky chuckled, the sound mingling with the rustle of leaves. "Dark days, they say? Funny how they label the era of faith that way, yet they herd us into lives that don't fit. To me, these times are much bleaker."

"But didn't people commit atrocities in the name of their faiths back then? It would be foolish to revert to that chaos."

"I'm not advocating for a return to religion per se—it often became a tool for oppression. But there were always those who made personal sacrifices, choosing others' needs over their own desires."

Lexi's thoughts drifted to Ethan's casual flirtations and her husband's steadfast presence. "Like someone who remains faithful to their spouse, despite temptation?"

"Exactly." Ms. Becky shifted to the next row of plants, her basket brimming. "At our core, humans are inherently selfish. We need a higher power to remind us to care for others."

Higher power? Ms. Becky had weird ideas, but she'd devoted her life to caring for others. She might be crazy, but she demonstrated love more than anyone Lexi knew.

What would Ms. Becky think of Ethan? "Someone wants me to betray my marriage vows."

Ms. Becky's eyebrows lifted. "And how does that make you feel?"

"It would be wrong. I pledged myself to Reeves. Even if the Imperium mandated it, I want to honor that promise. Besides, the guy's a jerk."

With a nod, Ms. Becky patted down the mound of beans. "It sounds like you're learning to prioritize others above your desires. Continue to heed that inner call to sacrifice, and you'll find the right path. I'm always here if you want to learn more." With that, she headed toward the kitchen, leaving Lexi to ponder the true essence of light in their dark times.

She made her way to the tent, anticipating a quiet reunion with Reeves. Instead, she found her mother standing outside.

"Walk with me?" Mom gestured toward the bustling headquarters.

Lexi paused. She couldn't miss time with Reeves, who might return any moment. "I promised to meet Reeves after training."

Her mother's eyes twinkled. "I'm sure I know where he is." She nodded toward the headquarters. "They've been locked in planning sessions since dawn."

Her certainty sparked a smile. Sweet seedlings, the possibility of joining Reeves there decided it. Lexi gestured. "After you."

As they entered the observation room, the vis monitors flickered to life, revealing Tempest Malachy's stern visage. Today's setting departed from the usual. Instead of a news desk, they'd arranged two plush armchairs at an angle before the camera. Tempest sat across from a dark-skinned man with thinning hair clad in the cream uniform of the council. A gold vesica piscis symbol pinned over his heart marked his high status.

The camera tightened on Tempest, her customary smile dissolving into a grave line. "Today, I'm interviewing Councilman Corvinus Vale regarding a pivotal piece of legislation." Her voice carried an undercurrent of severity. "Mr. Vale, could you shed some light on this document?"

Corvinus managed a strained smile, revealing a flash of white teeth. His foot tapped an anxious rhythm beneath the coffee table. "The principle is straightforward. Our military has traditionally harnessed potential violence through rigorous training of both body and mind, crafting a disciplined force unlike any other." His words tumbled out a tad too brisk.

Tempest nodded. Her finger traced her tablet's beveled rim before swiping through screens. "Indeed, our society assigns roles based on inherent strengths."

"As violence wanes and our youth evolve, fewer qualify for intense military training, leading to diminished ranks as we face a rebellion," Corvinus's voice faltered. "This poses a significant threat to our societal structure."

Tempest's eyes narrowed. Her gaze intensifying, she leaned forward. "That sounds problematic, Mr. Vale."

"It is, but we have a potential solution—if we can secure enough support." He shifted in his chair, crossing one leg over the other. Though the stance caged the restless movement in his foot, one finger tapped the armrest. "By lowering the testing age to fourteen, we can utilize a younger, more malleable demographic, expediting their readiness for service."

Nausea swept through Lexi. Her hands clenched. Would they now be forced into adult life even earlier—possibly including marriage?

Tempest settled back, her demeanor one of calculated satisfaction. "An intriguing strategy. When do you expect the council will vote?"

"Soon, I hope. We can't afford delay." Sweat trailed down Corvinus's temple.

The camera pulled back, bringing the background into focus—a shelf hosted a plant, a water pitcher, and, notably, a book. Lexi stifled a gasp, her heart pounding. It wasn't just any book—it was *Love in the Time of Algorithms,* Zane's signal. He had the information to aid in her father's rescue. She needed to move—to find Rumi and hope her friend was ready to help.

Chapter 9

A sour note clinked out amongst a string of others, grating on Lexi's nerves. She'd waited well over an hour for Reeves to be dismissed from the closed-door session. The guards hadn't made her wait on the porch, a minor concession after Thrym kicked her out of the room along with every other person he deemed nonessential. As if she'd turn into a spy at any moment. *Ridiculous.*

The piano tune continued, and she wandered up the stairs, one eye toward the guards. When they ignored her ascent, she took the final four steps two at a time. The music drew her to the one person who ruffled her emotions at the slightest provocation—her mother. Like a stage spotlight, a beam of sunlight illuminated Mom, turning her blond hair into a golden crown. Her fingers stroked the keyboard the way a mother comforted her child.

Envy rolled over Lexi. Her mother had become a rock wall to her only daughter—impenetrable. Why did they have to be at odds? When she thought her mother was dead, she'd wished only to have her back. Now she was losing her again.

No. They needed to mend their differences. Return to their relationship before the explosion separated them. She slid onto the bench, her hip bumping her mother's. "It's a lovely tune. I wish we had more beauty like this, instead of knives and guns. Maybe if we could make peace with the Imperium, more fourteen-year-olds could learn to play piano instead of war."

Finished, Mom placed her hands in her lap and stared forward as if watching the final notes float away. "I couldn't believe my luck when I found this old Steinway. It's brought back so many memories of your aunt." Her lips curved into a smile. "We used to have a secret signal. Did I ever tell you that? We'd tug on our earlobes."

Lexi couldn't help but return the grin. "You mean like in case there was danger?"

"Kind of." Mom chuckled. "It started as a warning in the Favela when soldiers were spotted. But soon it became a sign I'd give her whenever my mother and I argued. She'd make up some excuse to whisk me away—rescue me from the fray, so to speak. We'd giggle about it like five-year-olds."

Lexi's heart warmed at this glimpse of her mother's softer side, the part she needed to reach. "I wish I'd known her. She sounds like a special person. I wonder what she'd think of you being so focused on the war. Would she rather you spent your efforts to help the retirees instead? Like Ms. Becky?"

Mom stiffened, the warmth in her eyes faded. She slammed the cover over the keyboard and rose. "I used to think that. For years, we followed in Ms. Becky's footsteps—sneaking food and whatever clothing I could scrounge from the recycle bins. But I couldn't save them. Not really. Your aunt died in the Favela during a raid. She was protecting a woman who eventually perished from an illness Imperium technology could have cured. Only a select few—those with power and influence—ever get lifesaving treatments past the age of fifty. Everyone else gets tossed out like three-day-old garbage." She stalked to the door, not looking back. "I used to believe in peace. Now I know there can't be reconciliation until every Imperium council member is gone. I'm *going* to be the one who ends this war, once and forever."

Lexi stared at the empty doorway—the silence of the room pressed in on her. If she couldn't convince her mother to focus on anything besides taking down the Imperium, she'd take matters into her own hands to rescue her father. Who knew how much time he had left?

Reeves appeared in the doorway, his features relaxed when he saw her, though worry lines etched deeper with each passing day. His time with the planning committee seemed to be sucking the life from him. "There you are. Your mom said you were up here, but I couldn't imagine why."

With a final glance at the Steinway, she stood. No need to add to his burdens. "We were having a mother-daughter chat. You know. Girl stuff."

He reached for her hand, and she melted into him for a slow, reassuring kiss. A moment of solace in a tumultuous world.

She broke away. A renewed determination settled over her. They all had their tasks, and she needed to get going on hers. Her father's life depended on it.

* * *

Reeves had one final meeting to attend, so Lexi waited in their tent, unable to staunch the thoughts of her parents swirling

105

in her brain. What if her marriage turned out like theirs? Full of lies and secrets. She wanted so much more out of life, out of marriage.

A thud on the tent flap jolted her.

"Can I come in?" Rumi peeked in from the partially open flap. "Just need to deliver a message."

"Come on, then."

"Reeves said to meet him over at the greenhouse." She shrugged. "Said something about one last drill before shut-eye."

A drill? "It's late. Why would they do training now when they've had all day?"

Rumi frowned. "I'm just a messenger. Not sure why they'd invite you and not me, but whatever."

And since when did they do anything on that end of the compound? Maybe they were practicing night maneuvers? "Thanks for letting me know."

Lexi pulled on her boots and headed out. Some solar lamps hung outside of tents, waiting for their occupants to return for the evening while others set tents aglow from the inside. Quiet murmurs of evening conversations wafted in the gentle breeze.

She passed one large tent, and the greenhouse came into view. No teams had lined up discussing tactics, no people anywhere she could see. But its double doors twinkled with lights, and the glow inside said it hadn't been shut down for the night. Small LED flashlights dangled there with their strobe feature activated. She quickened her pace. What in the world?

The door opened, and a grinning Reeves stepped out. "Welcome to an evening under the stars."

"Where is everyone?"

He ushered her inside a transformed room. Someone had cleared the center aisle and positioned a table with two chairs there. Covered dishes rested on it with plate and silverware settings for two. Glass jars holding glow sticks in their centers and greenery entwined throughout provided enough light to show he'd been busy.

"I figured we could use an evening away from the politics and plans for war." He pulled out one chair and waved her into it. "A night for you and me—alone."

A warm medley of spices and roasted vegetables wrapped around her as she settled into her seat.

Reeves lingered beside her. His fingertips grazing her arms in a slow, deliberate touch sent shivers through her. His breath fanned against her skin before his lips brushed the curve of her neck. He traced a trail of soft kisses down to her shoulder and tugged her shirt aside to steal another inch of bare skin.

A hum of contentment escaped her, but before she could react, he stepped away. Smiling, he rounded the table and sat across from her, his eyes agleam in the dim light.

Her heart performed a flip like a gymnast in celebration. "Oh, Reeves. It's beautiful."

"Tonight is about celebrating us. I want to show you how much you mean to me." He lifted a cover to reveal a small pie. "It's all your favorite veggies with whipped potatoes as the crust."

He cut into it and steam drifted up, carrying scents of herbs and spices.

Once he'd plated their servings, she tested a bite, and the flavors exploded on her tongue. She couldn't identify everything, but her taste buds did a jig in her mouth. "I had no idea you knew how to cook."

He snorted. "I had to call in a few favors. One of the chefs helped me—a lot. I hope you like it."

"It's amazing."

Next, he twisted the lid off a thermos and poured a clear, yellow-tinted drink into their glasses. He winked. "Don't tell anyone about this stuff. I got the first one."

She had no clue what he was talking about, but citrus invigorated her tongue when she sipped it. "Lemonade? But, how?"

His eyes glowed. "Ms. Becky's been harboring a lemon tree. It only had one ripe fruit, but when I explained the special occasion, she let me have it."

"Special occasion?"

"I'm wooing my wife." He reached across the table for her hand. "I think that makes tonight pretty special, don't you?"

They ate, savoring every bite until not a crumb remained. How had he managed to put the meal together? He must owe dozens of people favors now. Her heart ached. How had she ever been assigned to such a loving person? "Thank you. It was wonderful."

He rose, came to her side once more, and held a hand out. "Come with me."

A shiver—half dread, half hope—trekked down her spine. Would this be *the* night? The moment they'd danced around? He walked down the aisle to a corner where a blanket lay in the center of a hydroponics section, the trickle of water through the pipes sounding like a babbling brook. Pillows towered on one side, and another covered dish awaited them.

What else could he have cobbled up?

After easing her down to sit on the blanket, he lifted the lid off a plate. Four large dark-red strawberries lay atop a bed of leaves and tiny berry flowers. He picked one up and held it to her lips. "A sweet for my sweetheart."

His mouth opened along with her own, and they both took a bite off opposite sides of the berry, the sweet nectar tingled on her tongue as they touched noses. Then his lips were on hers, and they indulged in a kiss even sweeter than the berry.

He laid her back against the pillows, snuggled in beside her, and pointed toward the ceiling. Stars twinkled through the clear roof. "I didn't put this together tonight to rush you into anything. I just want to be with you. To know your hopes, your dreams. To know who you want to be when all this insanity is over." He ran his fingers through her hair. "Talk to me. Tell me what your ideal future looks like. Tell me I'm in it with you."

Her heart swelled until it might explode with all the love she held for him.

Then she talked about her dream of working in the greenhouses, how even as a child she'd known what she wanted. And how he'd been the one gift she'd never expected but saw at the center of her future.

They talked late into the night until their throats were raw and they fell into silence. And with each breath, she fell more in love with this man, this husband she'd been assigned, this soulmate now lying beside her, gazing at the stars. She'd cherish this memory forever.

* * *

Morning lessons ended with Ms. D. presenting Lexi and a

select few who passed the knife-throwing test with a set of blades and sheaths. The weight on the belt felt like a medal of honor. She'd achieved something not everyone could. If only she could show Reeves her prize.

Unfortunately, he'd gone back into an all-night planning session, and she might not even see him today. He'd said they'd be leaving soon for their next mission. That meant she and Rumi needed to hitch a ride when they went. They had to get back to Zane.

Rumi bumped Lexi's shoulder with her own. "If your head swells any bigger, you won't fit through the tent flap for lunch."

She punched Rumi's arm. "Can't I savor my reward for the one skill I'm better at than you?"

One eyebrow rose. Rumi laughed. "I didn't realize we were competing, but now that I know, expect me to have my set of knives after the next test."

"Fair enough." Lexi tugged at the sheath, rearranging it for the umpteenth time. "We've got a few minutes before the next class. Want to run to see my gramps? I'd love to show him my new knives."

In response, Rumi sprinted toward the medical tent. "Beat you there!"

Hustling to keep up, Lexi dashed after her, amazed by Rumi's speed. Nothing mattered except catching her before they reached their destination. Within yards, Lexi knew she'd lost. Her lungs burned, and a stitch attacked her side. She slowed, gasped for air, and gripped her ribs.

Rumi must have sensed her victory. She turned to see how far behind her competitor lagged, then circled back— her triumphant grin uncontained.

Before she could crow her success, a scream chilled Lexi's

blood. Medical staff and mobile patients streamed out of the nearby tent.

"Come on!" Rumi raced against the flow of people toward the opening.

Pain forgotten, Lexi rushed to catch up. What could have scared the staff out of their own space? Fear fueled her pace, and she entered only a yard behind Rumi, anxious to reach her grandfather on the shelter's far end.

Shrieks echoed from that direction as they sped past abandoned medical equipment. A nurse crouched on a stretcher, tightening a tourniquet to staunch the tidal wave of blood flowing from the occupant's shredded leg. White-faced and not attempting to stem the flow himself, the man appeared to be in shock. Rumi stopped to help while Lexi continued further in.

The closer she got to the end, the quieter the cries grew. A gust of wind slapped the tent's end flaps against the poles, and a low hiss drew her gaze to her grandfather's bed. An unfamiliar animal, somewhat like the archive images of raccoons, stood with its back legs on her grandfather's chest while its front legs rested on the bedside table.

The beast measured twice the size of a bean plant. Blood-red hues stained one eye, and a grotesque growth protruded where the other should be. Foam and blood dripped from its jaws as it gnawed through a protein bar.

Terrified eyes met hers. Gramps was awake but doing his best to look dead and unappealing. He mouthed one word, "Rabid."

The hairs on the back of her neck rose. Her mind raced back to her school lessons. After the Great War, radioactive and chemical pollution ravaged animals with a variation of rabies.

Nothing. They'd taught her nothing about how to deal with these beasts. They were all supposed to be gone.

The creature hissed as she advanced, their gazes locking. She paused and drew her blades. Her heart hammered her ribs. If she missed, Gramps would pay the price. "Lie still."

Movement to her left caught her eye. Nana stood frozen against a tent pole.

A second animal, twice the size of the one on Gramps, squared off in front of her. A growth on its head left its mouth in a permanent sneer. Its growls spewed foam.

Nana wielded a heavy wooden cane. "Take care of your grandfather. I've got this one."

Another hiss drew Lexi's focus back to Gramps's bed. The animal's ears lay flat against its head, its growl growing angrier.

No time to waste. She planted her foot and sent two blades flying, one after the other. The first lodged in the animal's good eye. The second struck its neck.

She pivoted and hurled the next two blades at the creature cornering Nana, each hitting its mark. The animals screeched and thrashed, and Lexi rushed to finish off the one on her grandfather. With a final strike, she drove the blade into its chest, the follow-through pushing it off the bed and onto the floor.

Nana kicked the dying animal away and ran to Gramps's side. She flung her arms around him, sobbing as she kissed his cheeks.

* * *

Lexi tossed the last shovel of dirt onto the mound and tamped it flat. "I'm going to have nightmares about this."

With a swipe of her brow, Rumi nodded. "Better nightmares since you won than if you'd lost. We're lucky your grandparents weren't torn up like some others."

What could have happened brought Lexi's breakfast into her throat. They'd been fortunate.

While they'd dug the graves, she and Rumi had discussed getting back to Zane as soon as the opportunity arose. It would be soon. If they weren't left behind.

A UTV sped past, on a beeline toward the headquarters. Rumi squinted against the sun. "Looks like they're gearing up for the next mission. Let's see how we can get in on it."

They reached the house to find the convoys lined up with Ms. Becky and Fletcher in the rearmost vehicle. Fletcher looked their way and glared before saying something to Ms. Becky. She left the vehicle and met them halfway. "Morning, ladies. We weren't planning on taking passengers today. We've got a full load with no room for extras."

The UTV's back seat overflowed with blankets, dried vegetables, and a smattering of protein bars. Fletcher tugged on the rope holding it all down, indicating he'd finished packing and had no plans to rearrange anything.

Before Rumi could argue, Lexi stepped in. "We won't take up much room and can hold plenty on our laps. Plus, you'll have extra hands for unloading and reloading."

Ms. Becky's eyes narrowed. "Why would you want to come with us? It's a long, dirty, and bumpy ride—both ways. What's in it for you two?"

It was time to be honest—sort of. "When we were there last time, we found Rumi's brother, Zane. He's married now and has a baby. We want to see the little one again. She's adorable."

A knowing smile spread across Ms. Becky's face. "Oh, you've got it bad, don't ya? I remember when I was first married. I wanted a baby so much it hurt. Any time I saw a wee one, I'd beg to hold it." She sighed, closing her eyes as if to savor the memory. "But it wasn't meant to be for me. No matter what the Imperium said about me being fertile, and no matter how hard my sweet husband and I tried… Nothing."

Lexi could work with that story, no matter how far off the mark it fell. After all, she and Reeves would have to be intimate to make a baby. And, despite parts of her wanting more, she wasn't quite ready for that. "I'm glad you understand. Please, can you take us?"

Fletcher harrumphed. "We don't have time for this. I just finished tying it all down."

Ms. Becky ignored him. "We'll squeeze you in."

Expletives flew as Fletcher's giant paws tore the bindings off the supplies. In one huge armful, he swiped a pile off the left side and glared at Lexi. Once she scuttled into the open spot, he dumped the load in her lap before clomping to the opposite side. He repeated the process and buried Rumi under a similar pile.

Thankfully, the blankets weren't heavy, just hot, though something within the bundle kept poking at Lexi's arm. By the time they reached the Favela, every inch of her sweat-drenched body ached from holding onto the load. Rumi's movements appeared just as stiff when they crawled out from under the blanket piles.

Ms. Becky spoke first. "I know you ladies want to get plenty of time with that little one. Don't you worry about helping us out with this stuff. Just be back within an hour and, for heaven's sake, don't get caught."

Heart pounding, Lexi kept one eye on the hallway while Rumi knocked on Zane's door. The camera above it moved left and right, scanning. A click preceded the groan of the opening door. Zane waved them in and shut the entryway behind them.

Inside, Lexi's shock mirrored Rumi's face. Zane had dark circles under his eyes and looked dehydrated. His cheekbones sharp as if carved from marble, his face pale. Even his eyes seemed to have faded. His gaze followed Lexi's to his shaking hands before he stuffed them into his pockets.

Rumi embraced him and held on for a long moment. Though he failed to return the hug, Rumi kept one hand on his arm. "You don't look so good. What's going on?"

With a headshake, he dismissed her question. "I'm fine. It's good to see you." His words came out flat, like an automaton.

Rumi's brow furrowed. She looked around the apartment. "Where's Sienna? And Brynn?" Her eyes narrowed. "Zane, where are your wife and baby?"

He barked a single word. "Out." He ran a hand through his hair and wandered back to the door. "Look, what you need to know is that your husband's trial starts soon. That's your best chance to rescue him. They figure they've gotten all they can out of him, so it'll be a quick trial and an even faster execution." He pivoted to Lexi. "Evidence is building against your mother for the train bombing. Your father will be assumed guilty by association. Awareness without action is enough to earn a death sentence."

Her legs wobbly, Lexi eased toward the couch and braced against its arm. Her father would pay the ultimate penalty for her mother's scheme. "How is the trial our best opportunity?

Security will be tighter than a starving person's fist on a protein bar."

"They have to transport him to the courthouse. That's your in—when security is weakest. He'll only have a couple of guards on him. A driver and a gunman. They hold prisoners close to the work buildings for free labor. They'll need to move him the day of the trial."

"A checkpoint." Rumi slammed her fist into her other palm. "We capture a checkpoint, and we've got him."

Zane nodded. "Exactly."

Were they insane? Lexi leveled a glare at Rumi. "You act as if taking over a checkpoint is as simple as handing out food in the Favela. In case you haven't noticed, there are only two of us, and neither of us knows how to take down professional Freedom Force guards."

"What do you think we've been training for every day?" Rumi rolled her eyes. "You haven't learned knife throwing to protect us from animals." She jabbed a finger into Lexi's sternum. "Remember, you owe your father. He's in there because of you." Another jab. "Recruit that husband of yours so I can get mine back."

The pressure on her sternum had nothing to do with Rumi's finger. The girl was right. Lexi's father sat in prison because of her. Now Rumi wanted her to pull Reeves into this mess too. Convincing him would have been challenging at best, but how could she explain their little expedition today? He'd be furious.

She swallowed back the acid burning in her throat. All her fault.

* * *

A crowd had gathered around the UTV when they returned to Ms. Becky and Fletcher. The usual ragtag group of Favela dwellers mumbled amongst themselves. Lexi elbowed into the center, then gasped. The councilman that Tempest Malachy recently interviewed faced off against Fletcher. Ms. Becky gripped the giant's biceps as if restraining him.

Fletcher growled, looming over the shorter man. "Why should we believe you? For all we know, you've got that witch on a com right now, listening to every word we say." He shook Ms. Becky's hand from his arm. "I'm telling you, we need to get out of here *now*."

"No, please." The man ripped his shirt open. A button flew off and hit Fletcher's chest. His terror-filled gaze darted between Fletcher and Ms. Becky. Sunken cheeks and worry lines etched deeper since his vis interview. "Look, no wires. Search me. I'm telling the truth."

Rumi passed Lexi, joining Fletcher as if forming a human shield. "What's *he* doing here?"

Ms. Becky tutted at the pair of warriors. "If you'd just listen, he's been trying to explain. *Please*."

Fletcher's harrumph settled the issue, and the man wrapped his shirt around himself again as if it would protect him from their scrutiny. He focused on Ms. Becky, the one person who seemed willing to listen. "You must understand—I had no choice. They're holding my parents. They say it's for their protection, but it's to force me to back their agenda. After election day, they'll vote me off the council. If that happens, my parents are dead, and I'll be next."

Cold sluiced over Lexi and settled in her heart. How unfair that the privilege of status allowed this man's parents a longer life, but it was her father's situation all over again—another puppet of the Imperium forced to choose between horrible options. This was her chance to help make things right. She edged closer to Ms. Becky, who faced off against Fletcher and Rumi. "We have to help him."

Chapter 10

Lexi's eyes burned from staring at the crude map in the tent's dim light. "Are you sure you can trust Ethan's information? You'd think the Freedom Force would change their routes or patterns with all the recruits we've been bringing back."

Her right eye twitching, Rumi prowled the inside perimeter. "It's not like they're going to move the courthouse, right? And we know where he's been working, thanks to what Zane told us. There's one logical path." She jammed a finger on the map. "This is the only checkpoint remote enough to target."

They'd been over the plan a few times, with Lexi throwing what-ifs at every opportunity to thwart potential obstacles they might face. "I agree they're running short on manpower, but I still count a minimum of four guards—two at the checkpoint and two with the transport vehicle. Even if we manage to overtake the guardhouse by ourselves, I'm afraid either my father or one of us will end up dead when we try to take out the van. We just don't have that much experience."

"Exactly why you've got to convince Reeves to join us."

"You don't understand what it's like to be married." Lexi rubbed her neck, working at the knot that had formed. "He's going to argue against this entire plan. Then we're back to sneaking behind his back. Which I'm tired of doing."

Rumi's eyes flashed, and she stalked into Lexi's personal space as if she planned to eat Lexi for an after-breakfast snack. "You think I don't know what it's like to be married? Are you really going to say that to *me*? You're the reason my *husband* isn't with me right now."

Forced to step away, she cringed. If only she could take back her words. How could she have forgotten Rumi had known married life? Probably more of it than Lexi had.

Rumi advanced another step.

Lexi pushed her hand into Rumi's chest, hoping the physical contact would calm the firestorm reddening her face. Fearing the same snap in control that landed Ethan in the medical tent, Lexi added soothing promise to her tone. "You're sorry. I'm sorry. I'll talk to Reeves."

After a moment's hesitation, Rumi relented. She blew out a breath and stretched her neck side to side. "We need his combat skills and tactical knowledge on our team. He's been on enough missions to be an asset. Be persuasive. I'm sure you know how to convince your man."

Lexi could almost feel the temperature of the room going down as anger seeped out of Rumi. Then Lexi realized what Rumi suggested, and her cheeks heated. "Got it."

Rumi's knowing smirk added to Lexi's embarrassment. "And after you've got Reeves on the team, get him to recruit Ethan."

What? She must have misheard. "Ethan? I thought you hated him."

"He's learned his lesson where I'm concerned." Rumi walked to the tent flap and raised it, but turned back to Lexi, the sun spotlighting her. "He's become Reeves's best friend. We need another body, and he'll fight hard to protect someone he cares about. Maybe he'll kick in an extra punch or two to keep you safe."

Lexi swallowed rising bile. It was already difficult to imagine Rumi working with him without another incident, but his flirtatious behavior made Lexi feel like she needed a shower.

* * *

The sun dipped behind the mountains, setting the horizon ablaze with crimson tones as Lexi waited in their tent for Reeves. When he stepped through the flap, she searched his eyes for any tell that tonight might not be the time to discuss her father's rescue. The moment their gazes met, his shoulders lowered, and he grinned.

His long legs ate the distance between them in two strides. He pulled her into an embrace, capturing her lips and her breath with his kiss. He released her mouth but continued to hold her close, his breath low and warm in her hair. "When this is all over, we're going to spend a month locked away in some secluded spot. Just the two of us." He murmured in her ear, sending tingles down her arms.

Her hands slid into his hair, and she dragged his lips back to her own. Plans to convince her husband of anything melted away. His spicy scent filled her lungs while his kisses stole her determination to tell him of her plans.

Then the image of Rumi crying while Dad wasted away in prison invaded. Lexi couldn't indulge in the luxury of her husband while Rumi slept alone. She forced herself to push Reeves to arm's length.

It wasn't fair. Time to hold up her end of their agreement.

The passion in Reeves's eyes changed to confusion.

How to begin?

Better just spit it out. "I need your help."

He dragged her back into his embrace, squeezing the breath out of her before running his stubbled chin over the top of her head. Contentment rumbled in his chest with his relaxed grumble. "Anything you need, love."

Maybe this would be easier than she'd thought. He loved her. He'd want her to be happy. "Rumi and I have a plan to rescue my father. We could use a few extra hands."

The luscious movement of his fingers over her skin froze midstroke. Their gazes met. "You *what?*"

Aphids. Perhaps easy was too hopeful a term. "It's a good plan. Her brother, Zane, figured out the dates they're moving my father for the trial." The words tumbled out, rapid fire, as if she could convince him if he heard it all at once. "Ethan's intel on the checkpoint locations shows us where we need to intercept—"

He laid a finger on her lips. "What does your mother think of the idea? We'll need her approval to assemble a team."

Pushing herself away from him, she looked him in the eye, willing him to listen with his heart. "My mother's focus is on other things. We need to move on this ourselves. There isn't time to convince her."

He shook his head and snugged her back into his chest. "It's dangerous enough with a team of trained soldiers. No way will I let you go on a mission like this without the proper support."

With her hand splayed on his muscled chest, she swirled soft strokes. "*You're* my best protection. No one would fight to keep me safe more than you would. And you could find someone to help us. The smaller our team, the more agile we'll be. Besides, have you seen Rumi when she's determined? I swear she could tunnel through a mountain to get what she wants. And she *wants* her husband back."

Part of her hated herself for manipulating him, but she needed his help. She kissed his chin, his cheek, then focused on running tiny pecks down his neck. "Please. For me."

A low growl rumbled through his chest. "Ugh. You don't play fair, but… you win."

His lips captured hers, but she struggled to respond. She couldn't let their first time together as husband and wife be part manipulation. He meant too much to her for that to be the way.

How could she explain?

She pulled back, her world cold without his touch. "I promised Nana I'd sit with Gramps tonight. He's been restless, and she needs a full night's sleep. I'm sorry." The lie tasted bitter on her tongue.

Brow furrowed, he gave her a slow nod. "I'll come with you."

"No." She kissed his cheek before heading to the exit. "You get some sleep. I'll be fine."

She wanted to kick herself on the walk to the medical tent. Reeves deserved better. She owed him more.

* * *

Morning came too early, and Lexi's body ached from sleeping

in the uncomfortable chair beside Gramps's bed. There was no sign of Reeves when she returned to their tent, but a note lay on the tiny bedside table with a heart-shaped locket on top of it. She picked up the note.

I'll love you forever.

Unable to imagine what he could have put inside it, she pulled the heart open. On one side, the tiniest scrap of paper had a hand-drawn heart with minuscule letters around it: *For my love.* On the other side, he'd pressed a bitty purple flower.

Her eyes filled. Would he feel the same if he knew everything? They had to trust each other completely if they ever wanted to be as close as Nana and Gramps were. She wanted that, not the lies her parents shared.

She removed the piece her mother had given her, the weight of it and all it represented lifting like a broken curse. Her heart swelled as she slipped Reeves's gift on in its place, the cool metal warming her neck. She'd do better from now on. Be honest with Reeves.

Rumi paced outside the training tent. The moment she saw Lexi coming, she jogged to meet her. "Did you talk to Reeves?"

Ever since Rumi started seeing the doctor, she'd changed from a simpering girl into a hardened soldier. But today her eyes were wide, pupils more dilated than normal, and her body seemed to vibrate as if ants had invaded her clothing. Her normally pale skin looked almost translucent.

"Yes, he'll help, but are you okay? You don't look so hot."

Rumi brushed the concern aside, avoiding eye contact. "I'm fine. Dr. Ichtacka changed my dose last night. I feel like I could take on this mission on my own, honestly. It's a rush. Maybe we should get you on the program."

Lexi rested a hand on Rumi's arm to focus her friend. "Or

perhaps we should get you off instead? You might feel great, but I'm worried about you."

Rumi spun toward the tent. "Come on. We're going to be late."

"What about breakfast?" Lexi rushed to catch up, her question ignored.

They reached the training tent in record time. She trailed Rumi inside and joined a group pairing off to spar.

Ms. D. pointed to them. "You two, get going. No weapons this morning, strictly hand-to-hand."

They found an empty mat and faced off. Lexi lifted her fists in front of her, ready to protect herself. Rumi's amped-up jitters and unfocused eyes made her an easy target. Though Rumi's fighting stance should have had her balance rock solid, she wobbled side to side as if caught in some undetectable breeze.

This wouldn't be a fair fight.

"Are you sure you're all right? You don't seem steady."

Rumi shook her head, perhaps trying to clear mental cobwebs. "I'm fine. Let me show you."

She swung and missed without Lexi having to dodge.

Lexi stepped back. "I'm serious. Something's not right. We need to take you back to the medical tent."

In response, Rumi growled low in her throat. She attempted a round kick but lost her balance and fell with a scream. Her body went rigid, then shook like someone hit her with a thousand volts of electricity. Then it spasmed out of control.

"Ms. Draven!" Lexi screamed and dropped to Rumi's side. White froth formed on Rumi's lips, then bubbled out. "Help me!"

* * *

Rumi's fluids seeped through Lexi's pant leg. The itch unbearable. She'd waited too long for Dr. Ichtacka to return from the curtained-off area. They'd refused to let her stay at Rumi's side, even when Lexi insisted they were family. One nurse assumed they were sisters, and she hadn't corrected him. They felt more like sisters than their actual connection.

When the doctor emerged, he stalked past without a word.

She hustled to catch up. "Dr. Ichtacka, how is she? What happened?"

He didn't slow, much less look at her. "I thought the larger dose would…" He paused, flicked his etablet to life, and scrolled through pages as if looking for something. "Maybe the formula…"

Lexi's heart stopped, and she lost her breath. He hadn't even realized she'd asked a question. All he cared about was the experiment.

She blinked at the cordoned-off area where Rumi lay. Fire burned in her chest. She ran back and shoved the curtain aside, despite the nurse's protests. Her friend, her father's wife, her stepmother—it all jumbled together in a confusing swirl—lay unmoving. Her face was so white it made the sheet under her look gray. Lexi pressed her palm over Rumi's icy hand.

A huff reminded Lexi the nurse stood nearby, injecting some concoction into an IV bag. "Hasn't she had enough of your poison by now?"

He glared. "Just a hiccup in the experiment. The doctor will get it straightened out soon enough."

The ground dropped beneath her. She fought back tears, but her trembling lips gave away her emotions. They'd kill Rumi with their experiments and have no more remorse than if she'd been a rat in a cage. "You need to stop. Can't you see how sick she is?"

The nurse paused. "It's too late for that. We need to figure out the right dosage to correct the issue."

He injected tan liquid into the IV bag from a syringe, turning the IV into a dirty-looking concoction. "I've got to update the data. She's doing so well. One of our best yet." He hurried out, leaving the curtain wide and exposing Rumi's inert body.

Lexi reached over, shut it, and swiped the tears out of her eyes. She needed to be strong now.

She clasped her friend's hand again and rubbed warmth into Rumi's too-cold unconscious body. "I'm here for you. You're going to be fine."

Rumi lay still for a long time. At the snail's pace the IV bag drained, her color returned to normal. Heat seeped back into her extremities until Lexi feared fever and infection.

The nurse returned with another syringe. This one tinted lilac. He jammed the needle into the port and infused the contents into the half-empty bag. "This will finish the healing cycle. She'll wake up shortly. After the doctor runs her through a few tests, he'll discharge her."

Though Lexi couldn't argue that Rumi looked better, it seemed too soon for her to return to a normal life. To return to training. "I think she's got a fever, maybe an infection. Shouldn't you take her vitals or something?"

The nurse shook his head. "Mild fever's normal during the healing process. She's fine."

Giving the unfeeling jerk a piece of her mind was a temptation Lexi would have to pass on for now. The moment the nurse tossed the syringe into the bin, Rumi moaned. Not as if she were in pain, but like she struggled to pull herself out of a deep dream. Lexi laid her hand on Rumi's shoulder. "Hey, there. How do you feel?"

Rumi's eyelids sprang open like she'd been waiting to surprise Lexi this whole time. She pushed up on her elbows and frowned at the tube that tugged on her arm. Her gaze roamed the room, but she didn't look surprised to find herself in the medical tent. "I felt a little off, but figured I needed to adjust to the extra dose." Her words came out thick as if her throat had dried out while she'd been in bed. "What are you doing here? Are you joining the experiment?"

Shaking her head, Lexi poured a glass of water on the side table, then handed it to Rumi. "You collapsed in training. I thought you were going to die."

Rumi scrunched her eyebrows together. "Why would you think that? I've never been stronger."

Lexi's gut twisted. "You had a seizure. Foaming at the mouth and everything. I thought I'd lost you."

Rumi's shoulders stiffened, and she sucked in a breath. "Whoa. He said there might be side effects, but... whoa." She gazed at the IV and traced the tube to where it entered her body. "I'm feeling pretty good right now. The doctor seems to have figured it out."

Unbelievable. Rumi'd almost died, and she still trusted that quack. "You need to stop. Get out of the experiment. It's going to kill you."

Rumi raised her face, her eyes wide. "No. It's a little setback. I'm fine." She swung her legs over the side of the bed and set her jaw. "I'd do it again if I had to. I'll do anything to get him back." She stood, wobbled, then flopped back onto the bed. "Maybe give me a few more minutes."

A chill squeezed like a vice around Lexi's heart. This once terrified mouse willingly risked her life to turn into a warrior. Her friend, her father's wife, had sacrificed so much. Too much.

I should have done more.

* * *

Lexi headed toward the greenhouse. Ms. Becky should be there about now, picking green beans if Nana's information was correct. The doctor had kicked Lexi out of the medical tent so he could run Rumi through more tests. Before Lexi left, she'd agreed to find Ms. Becky to get transportation on the next trip to the Imperium.

She still struggled to process what Rumi agreed to. She'd risked her life to turn into a super soldier to save her husband. Who knew what lasting effects the doctor's experiment would have. If it had been Reeves behind bars, Lexi might be tempted as well.

From behind, strong arms slipped around her middle. Reeves's solid form flattened her back against him. His head lowered, and his warm breath wisped across her neck.

She melted, closing her eyes and tipping her head to give him better access to nibble her neck, but no kiss followed.

Instead, a low growl issued from his throat, and his arms gentled, cradling her as if he'd never let her go, as if she were something exquisitely precious. "Has your husband told you yet today how beautiful you are?"

The words mumbled against her ear, more breath than sound, birthing delicious shivers. "No, you haven't."

His chin skidded across her neck, but still, he didn't kiss her. "He's a fool, then. Unworthy of you. I'd never make that mistake."

Wait. What? She opened her eyes. Was that dark hair in her peripheral? That wasn't Reeves!

Her elbow rammed backward, and she jerked away. Breathless.

Ethan's eyes glazed, the emotion in them almost undoing her. Then a mask came over his face. He winked as if she'd be happy to see him. "You're something else, Lex." His breath, like hers, came far too fast. His smirk quirked one side of his mouth. "I missed ya after you ran away from Reclamation, you know."

Ms. D. walked past, one brow raised. "Morning, *Mrs. Scheffer.*"

Heat climbed Lexi neck. Had the trainer seen them in each other's arms? How to explain? But she'd already walked away anyway. Lexi pivoted back to Ethan, her hands fisting. "How. Dare. You."

"Oh, I dare a lot of things. In case you hadn't noticed, I'm a rebel, not a conformer." He blocked the swing, caught her wrist, and snugged her against him. His breath warm on her neck, his head lowering to whisper against her ear. "No need to get all upset. I'm just appreciating you as you deserve to be appreciated, is all. If you know what I mean."

She stomped his instep, relishing the sight of him hopping on one foot while he cursed. "Touch me again, and I'll make sure your manhood ends up as broken as I hope your foot is." She quickened her pace.

Shuffling followed her.

He caught up, his gait pleasingly not as sure as it had been. "Give me a break. I promised Reeves I'd help you out. You know, with your dad."

Her hands balled into fists at her sides, and she stopped midstride. Every bit of her was shaky, the violation assailing things she held sacred, but they needed all the help they could get. She blew out a calming breath and centered her thoughts. "Never approach me again. This is the last time I accept an apology from you. I'm happily married to *your new best friend* and have no intention of messing that up for anything or anyone." She met his eyes dead-on. "Do you understand?"

"I hear your words, but I also read your body language. I don't believe you mean it—not after the way you responded." He lifted a finger to touch her neck, tracing the line his chin had traveled. "You and I, Lex, we're rebels through and through. You won't conform with your marriage. Ha, you're already keeping secrets from your so-called husband, even avoiding him. Don't think I haven't seen you sneaking from your tent at night. And you've been drawn to me since our first day in Reclamation. Don't forget the way you looked at me—like you wished they'd assign us to mate, like I'd be at the top of your list of guys to get to know if you had the choice."

She shivered, almost leaning into his touch before she knocked his hand away. Today, she'd responded because she thought he was Reeves, but she couldn't deny his words echoed her thoughts from that day. Best he understood now though. "That was another reality. *I'm married now.*"

"Means nothing. Not really. Not your choice. You'd have chosen me like I'd have chosen you, Rebel Heart. Don't forget—*you* dragged Reeves along for the ride, but *I* sought the rebels out myself." He leaned in closer, his breath and intensity warming the space between them. "Because I wanted to find *you*."

He couldn't mean that. Could he?

He reached as if to touch her again, then jammed his hands into his pockets. "So *I will* help you free your father, *I will* help you free our people, and *I will help you free yourself from your marriage*. But I'll let you make our next move, lover."

* * *

By the time she'd reached the greenhouses and located Ms. Becky, Lexi's heart rate had returned to normal, Ethan's assault and claims leaving her drained. Still, her encounter must have shown.

Ms. Becky's face first registered surprise, then compassion as she stopped her work and hugged her. "You look like you've had a rough day. Want to talk about it?"

Ethan could've seen her on the vis and known she'd joined the rebels. He could have followed her here.

Why did that even matter? She'd committed to her husband, so why let such thoughts create an unwelcome thrill? Was it pride? Or something more?

"Thanks, but I wouldn't know where to start." Lexi bent to the plants and breathed in the heavy, damp air. She plucked beans off the closest one and deposited them into Ms. Becky's basket. "I need your help, though."

Seeming to understand Lexi's need to get down to business, Ms. Becky returned to harvesting. "That's a coincidence. I'd like some help of my own. Perhaps we can trade."

"I like the idea of a negotiation." When all was said and done, no one would owe anyone else. Would she owe Ethan if she let him help free her father? What would he think he had the right to ask in return?

And what if someone told Reeves about her letting Ethan nuzzle her today? Ms. D. couldn't have been the only one to see them. Should she tell Reeves first?

But he needed a friend. If he knew what Ethan was up to, claiming…

Aphids! Why'd life have to be so complicated?

"Talk to your mom for me. Convince her to rescue the councilman's parents. We need him to be our witness to the rest of the Imperium. He'll reveal the truth only if he knows his parents are safe."

A laugh escaped before Lexi could pull it back. "I can't convince her to rescue my father—her *husband*. Or ex-husband. It's so confusing." She scrubbed the back of her neck. "Regardless, how could I convince her to rescue strangers? Unless they're a resource for her plans, she won't give it even a moment's thought."

Ms. Becky tapped down the heaping pile of vegetables so the basket could hold more and moved on to the next plant. "Give it your best effort. Use the most persuasive arguments you can come up with, and I'll accept the outcome, win or lose."

That much Lexi could do. "Deal." She unloaded a handful of beans onto the growing pile. "I need a ride to the Imperium. Myself and three others. No questions asked. We'll have a fifth passenger on our return."

Ms. Becky raised an eyebrow. "You'd need a larger vehicle to make that happen. I suppose I could lend you mine. But why?"

Would Ms. Becky try to talk Lexi out of it? Or worse, tell Mom? "Can't say. No questions asked, remember?"

Awkward seconds ticked by. "You're going to rescue someone. I could guess at your short list, but won't. Anyone we save from the Imperium's grasp is a win to me." Ms. Becky's shoulders drooped. "Fine. You can take mine. It's not as if Fletcher and I could fit along with that many passengers."

"Thank you. I'm certain Reeves can drive. He's traveled the distance enough times."

"Then it's a deal." She held out a hand for Lexi to shake. "There's no time like the present. Your mother is in meetings right now, planning their next mission. It would be an ideal time to add the rescue to her list of extractions."

After dropping off their produce, they approached the headquarters where Ms. Becky gained them access. It irked Lexi that her name didn't grant her the ability to see her mother. Even more frustrating, the leadership circles had readily accepted Reeves.

The meeting was in full swing, her mother at the center of the discussion. A familiar look hardened her face—one that meant someone wouldn't like what she had to say. "Look. I know he's young, but this guy knows his stuff. He's studied the weapons of the Great Wars and would know how to put a dirty bomb together. Even more important, he'd know how to activate it for the most impact without contaminating everything."

A shudder ran through Lexi. She'd looked into a *dirty* bomb. Weren't explosives bad enough without poison added in?

Not everyone looked convinced.

Fletcher gave his usual harrumph. "He's a kid. How could

he know enough to build something from scratch no one has built since the Great War? Even if he could, would he? He's too young to know what it looks like to face retirement."

Reeves caught Lexi's eye from across the room, and she made her way to him. They touched fingers, and he leaned over to whisper in her ear. "Didn't think I'd see you today. Did you get my gift?"

His gift? She'd forgotten it after the morning she'd had.

How could he think of gifts at a time like this, anyway? She wanted to crawl out of her skin with the conversation going on. He must have known Mom's plan.

Still, she rewarded him with a smile and lifted it out of her shirt. "I'm wearing it now. Thank you."

Shoulder to shoulder, they faced the argument.

Mom smacked the table. "You don't seem to grasp my point. This weapon is our best shot at ending this once and for all. I won't let anything stand in the way of getting the only expert in existence, regardless of his age."

The heated temperature didn't bode well for Lexi's chances of convincing her mother to add a side mission of any sort. Trying would just waste time.

A technician at one monitor called out. "We've got an incoming announcement. It's mandatory for all Imperium residents, so you'll want to pay attention."

Mom motioned for the room to quiet as the vis screens came to life. Tempest Malachy sat center stage across from two students dressed in school uniforms. Their huge smiles showed gleaming teeth, their eyes aglow. Tempest grinned at the camera as if her best friend sat on the other side of it. "I've got two very special guests with me today. Let me introduce you to William and Stephanie, the first two recruits who are graduating early to enjoy wedded bliss and serve in the Freedom Force."

Their smiles grew wider while canned applause filled the surrounding room. Confetti rained down on their heads. The girl caught pieces of it, and the boy sat up taller in his chair. He pushed his chest out, announcing to the world his manhood was solid.

When he noticed what the girl was doing, he reached over and touched her shoulder. At his slight headshake, she let the colored paper she'd collected settle into her lap along with her hands. Her faltering grin returned when a patriotic tune started up in the background.

Tempest continued. "So, Stephanie, tell me what it feels like to be the first one chosen at such a young age. Do you think you're ready for what comes next?"

The girl joined hands with the boy like they'd rehearsed the move and had been waiting for their cue. "I couldn't be more grateful to the Imperium for recognizing the fact that I'm ready"—she nodded to the boy—"*we're* ready to take on our responsibilities."

The camera focused on the young man. Acne dotted his chin where a beard might grow—if he lived long enough. Off camera, Tempest continued the questioning. "William, what would you say to those who might think fourteen is too young to start a family or to serve your country?"

He released the girl's hand, stood straight as a board, and placed a hand over his heart. "I've been ready for as long as I can remember." He pulled the girl up beside him and wrapped an arm around her waist. The camera zoomed in on them, and they recited their lines.

Unity above all else.

Hard work lifts us all.

A young Imperium is a thriving Imperium.

One marriage—many children.

Focused on Tempest, the cameras zoomed in. "We'll leave this excited new couple to their honeymoon. Others are eager to accept early adoption of marriage and military service. Hopefully, council will soon see fit to mandate it so all those who are ready to serve their country will have their chance."

The camera panned back to look at the beaming kids. An image of the Imperium flag waving in the breeze accompanied the crescendo of the city's anthem. Then the screen went dark.

Lexi's chest tightened to the point breathing became a task. They were *children*. How could anyone expect them to understand what marriage or babies or war entailed?

Around the room, the leaders' faces became stony.

Her mother's eyes flashed, and she pointed at the closest screen. "That is why we must use the bomb. Next, they'll be after the twelve-year-olds. We must stop them. *Now*."

With few exceptions, the room nodded.

Lexi's stomach twisted. The Imperium had to be stopped, but...

This wasn't the way.

Chapter 11

Another day of body-punishing drills left Lexi exhausted and ready for bed. True to what the doctor predicted, Rumi arrived with dark circles under her eyes, the only evidence of the previous day's trauma.

During their lunch break, Lexi tried to talk about the experiment, but Rumi changed the subject and left early to work out before the next lesson. If Rumi didn't want to talk about it, Lexi would let it go. Or try to. Her brain refused at the moment.

The sun had begun its descent in earnest, and she'd returned to her tent to wait. Reeves's team should be back from their recruitment mission any time, and spending time with him sounded better than anything. If only she could stay awake until he finished the debriefing.

She brushed her hair with long strokes, willing it to gleam with the same warmth pumping in anticipation of their evening. This night would be special. She'd make sure of it.

A shout from outside caught her attention, and she shoved the brush back into her duffel.

Feet rushed by her tent, and cries of alarm sounded. "Invasion!"

She tore outside. People rushed to the front gates, and she joined their surge.

Just inside the fence, UTVs lined up like sentinels—but the scene beyond them left her stunned—immobile. New recruits shouted, shoved, and clashed against the team who'd brought them back. And the numbers—there were so many of them, far too many for a single mission.

Newcomers in their Imperium uniforms—white, green, and brown—fought against the black-clad rebels.

It should have been over as soon as it started with the rebels outnumbering the Imperium team, but the Imperium fighters had some sort of stun weapon on their wrists. Each time they touched or struck their opponent, the victim fell to the ground in convulsions.

The invaders were trained and armed.

She needed her weapons.

Lexi ran to the tent and gathered her knives. On her way into the fray, she found Rumi, her eyes wild, squared off against a recruit.

Before Lexi could make it to her friend's side, Rumi dodged a swing and let the guy's momentum turn him around. She jumped on his back and twisted his neck the way their instructors taught.

He dropped like a sack of sand—dead by the time he hit the ground.

She dashed to the next one.

This battle would test who could kill—and who would die.

Lexi froze, fingered the knife hilt, and searched for Reeves. Heart pounding, she couldn't get enough air. She didn't see him but refused to search through the fallen. He was *not* dead.

"Lexi!" Reeves's voice came from behind. "Here."

He's okay! She spun and rushed toward him when something hit her from behind, knocking her off her feet.

She flipped to her back, knife out and ready to strike.

A pimple-faced boy hovered over her. He reached to touch her with his wrist device.

Knowing what she had to do, she steeled herself to strike. "Please don't make me do this. Back off."

Fear flickered in the boy's eyes as her blade glinted in the setting sun's last glimmer, but he gritted his teeth and kicked her wrist.

Her hand exploded with pain, and her knife went flying.

He backhanded her, and spots dotted her vision. Then he brought his wrist weapon to her cheek.

She tried to jerk away from his stunner, but too late. Every muscle in her body contracted, and her skin burned, on fire from within.

He raised a boot-clad foot above her face.

How could she be so helpless? So stupid? She should have struck first.

A furious roar distracted the kid.

Reeves plowed into him, knocking him to the ground.

Then her world went dark.

* * *

"You're going to be fine." A warm hand smoothed Lexi's hair while the words coaxed her to consciousness. "There you go. Come back to me."

She dragged one eyelid open, then the other. Canvas and

tent poles blurred into view. Then Reeves's gorgeous eyes looked into hers. "That's right. I'm here."

Memories of the boy who'd bettered her swam through her mind. "Is he—dead?"

Reeves shook his head. "Don't worry about him. We got them all… eventually."

The effort to lift herself onto her elbows took all she had. Every muscle ached like when she'd come down with the flu last year. She gazed around the dark tent, their renewable lamp's glow close to death. "The recruits. What happened?"

"They planned it perfectly." He scrubbed his neck with one hand. "We thought we'd scored, big time, with this latest recruiting mission. Thought the kids were fleeing the Imperium rather than being married off and pressed into the Freedom Force."

Reeves lifted a cloth off their bedside table, dipped it in a basin, and pressed it against her swollen cheek. "Turns out they were plants—sent to find and destroy our weapons cache. Seems they'd been training for a while now. Almost got to the armory too."

Lexi struggled to sit the rest of the way up, and he helped her ease her legs over the side of the cot. She fought through nausea until the surrounding room settled into place.

The pimple-faced kid's image returned, along with Reeves's attack. She didn't want to know if he'd killed for her. "How would they have known where the armory was?"

"That's just it." He took the cloth, doused it in the water, wrung it out, and handed it to her. "The only way they would have known is if someone told them. We've got a mole."

A mole. Someone they trusted worked for the Imperium… and almost cost them everything. But who?

A thud slapped against the tent flap. Rumi asked, "Can I come in?"

Reeves locked gazes with Lexi. She nodded, and he hollered, "Come on."

Once inside, Rumi shuffled toward Lexi, each step deliberate and heavy. She lowered herself to her knees beside the cot, her movements stiff. Her dilated pupils stood out on her pale face, and her right eye twitched. "You had me worried there. I thought that kid knocked the stuffing out of you."

Rumi killing with such ease flashed through Lexi's mind as if she were watching a vis recording. Bile burned a path up her throat and lay bitter on her tongue. "I'm fine."

Rumi turned to Reeves, who'd sat beside Lexi. "I saw you save her. I couldn't get to her in time, but I'm so grateful you did."

He squeezed Lexi's hand. "This is why trying to rescue your dad is a bad idea. What if I'm not there next time?"

Before Lexi could return Reeves's gesture, Rumi popped up from her knees and paced. Left two steps, one-eighty turn, then right two steps. Repeat.

Her hands shook.

Lexi snagged one of them when she strode close enough. "Stop. We'll figure this out."

The turbulence on Rumi's face dulled. Then her eyes rolled back as she collapsed.

"Rumi!" Reeves bent over their fallen friend. Her body vibrated and shook with her eyes rolled up in their sockets. "She's convulsing again."

* * *

When Dr. Ichtacka came from behind the curtain, he glanced between Lexi and Reeves as if trying to decide who he should talk to. She stood—her body stiff but functional. "How is she?"

"Stable, but she isn't recovering as quickly this time. I can't figure out why the recurring episodes." The doctor stuffed his hands into his lab coat pockets. "She keeps asking for someone. Do you know who Zane is?"

"Yes." Lexi pressed a fist against the ache in her chest. "Her brother. He's not here, though. He's still with the Imperium."

"That's too bad." Shaking his head, the doctor nodded at a nurse entering Rumi's curtained room. "She's hallucinating and switches between thinking she's talking to him and asking for him. If we could bring him to her, she might calm enough to heal. I don't know why our protocols aren't working anymore. They're still experimental, but she's done so well on them so far. Well, except for…"

Easy to fill in the blank space the good doctor left. *Except for the life-threatening seizures.* "I know where to find him."

Lexi pivoted and left the tent. She couldn't move fast enough.

"Lex, slow down. Let's talk about this." Reeves pulled at her arm as she strode toward headquarters.

"No. We need to get Zane now, and my mother is going to help us."

The guards stopped her at the door until one of them recognized Reeves and let them in. She ground her teeth. As the daughter of the rebels' leader, she should have some perks, shouldn't she? Even if it's only access to her mother's office. But no. Not her. Instead, Reeves got them in.

Her mother stood in a semicircle with Thrym on her left and

Fletcher on her right. Other leaders flanked them, Ms. Becky notably absent. In their center, a table held a hand-drawn map.

Fletcher shook his head. "There's no guarantee the stuff is still there. Even if it is, can we trust it's stable?" He gestured around the group. "Besides, shouldn't our focus be on figuring out who the mole is?"

Mom's jaw tightened, and she pinched the bridge of her nose. "Never mind the mole. We need to keep moving. We need an expert. Why do I have to keep repeating myself?"

The timing better be right for an interruption. "Mom." Lexi marched across the room. "We need to talk."

"Not now." Her mother dismissed her with a wave. "I'll be free in about an hour."

"No." Lexi ground her teeth. She grabbed Mom's arm and twisted her to face her. "Right now."

In a flash, Thrym wrenched Lexi's arm behind her back.

She yipped.

Reeves shoved Thrym, knocking him backward and freeing her.

"Stop!" Mom wedged herself between the two men, then thrust a finger at Lexi. "You. Upstairs."

Lexi rubbed her sore shoulder. Being ordered aside as if she were a disobedient five-year-old rankled, but she'd gotten her way. She'd take the meeting, no matter how it came.

On her way to the door, she made eye contact with Reeves and gestured for him to stay. He glared at Thrym as if ready to block any further attack. She headed for her mother's favorite room and the piano.

Mom entered, steps behind her, and slammed the door shut. "What is so important that you needed to barge in on my meeting?"

Dark circles shadowed her bloodshot eyes, and her shoulders slumped the minute they were alone. She'd taken on a lot of responsibility.

Lexi breathed deep to calm herself so her words would come out right. "It's Rumi. She's had a seizure again, and I'm worried she won't make it. She's asking for her brother, and I need your help in getting him."

A look flashed in her mother's eyes—regret? Lexi couldn't tell.

"I'm sorry." Mom's jaw hardened. "I wish I could help, but I have to consider the entire camp over a single person. We don't want the perception of favoritism."

This conversation wasn't going the way Lexi imagined. "Who'd ever think your husband's new wife would be *your* favorite?"

"Can't you see we're under attack? Any minute, the Imperium's entire Freedom Force could be at that front gate." Mom jabbed a finger at Lexi's chest. "We need to end this fight or risk losing everything—everyone."

She swatted her mother's hand away. "So, you want to abandon Rumi like you abandoned me." She couldn't believe she'd said it, but the words emboldened her. "Like you abandoned Dad."

Mom winced and jerked backward. She turned her back on Lexi, opened the door, and stepped through it, then straightened her spine. Tall and proud. "I'm sorry you can't understand the responsibility I have to this cause and to these people. The needs of the many outweigh the needs of the one."

She slammed the door behind her.

After calming herself, Lexi headed out. Reeves waited at the bottom of the stairs, and his expression reflected her anguish. His arms opened, and she stumbled on the last step in her rush to their strength.

Confusing emotions—betrayal, loss, sorrow—threatened to bring on tears. But she wouldn't let anyone in this building see her mother best her. She braved a smile. "We're on our own."

He brushed a kiss across her lips. "I figured it hadn't gone well when your mom stormed past."

Beyond Reeves's shoulder, the man guarding the door smirked. This world belonged to her mother. "Let's get out of here."

If strength could flow from one person to another, she would draw it from Reeves. They walked, hand in hand, to their tent. With each step, she stood taller, prouder to be with him and to be his. Conquering the world was within reach with him by her side.

Together, they were strong enough to bring Zane back and rescue her father. They'd let her mother deal with the Imperium.

* * *

After a quiet meal—aka planning session—alone in their tent, Lexi left Reeves to check on her grandfather. She paused after zipping the flap. Was that a tall silhouette outside Ethan's tent? Surely, he wasn't watching their tent. Hadn't seen her leave Reeves there. Wouldn't be there waiting for her.

Maybe she should have asked Reeves to walk with her.

She snorted. Since when was she a wuss?

Shivering, she quickened her pace. Her heart rose in her throat when she found Nana and Ms. Becky by Gramp's bedside, heads bowed. Ms. Becky mumbled. Gramps lay unmoving, eyes shut, his face pale and translucent.

Her breath whooshed out. He couldn't be dead. She laid her hand atop his, and a chill ran up her spine at the lack of warmth. "Gramps?"

Ms. Becky's mumbled words ended with amen. Then she faced Lexi.

Nana's tear-filled eyes, red and swollen, looked at Gramps. "Don't wake him, dear. He's had a rough day. It took a while for him to get to sleep."

Lexi fought air into her lungs. What if he never woke? When had she last told him she loved him?

Ms. Becky leaned down to Gramps's ear, whispered something, then stroked his hand as if soothing a newborn to sleep. To Nana, Ms. Becky said, "I'll come back to check on you both."

A tear trickled down Nana's cheek, and she swiped it away. "Thank you. It's been too long." She yawned, her eyelids drooping.

Ms. Becky gestured Lexi onward. "Walk with me. Let's let your grandparents rest."

She allowed Ms. Becky to lead her out of the tent, casting one last glance over her shoulder. Nana was mumbling with her head bowed, her hand resting on Gramps's arm. "What were you and Nana talking about when I walked in?"

Ms. Becky slipped her hands into her uniform pockets. "We were praying. For your grandfather."

"Praying?"

An uninterpretable look flittered across Ms. Becky's face.

"Your parents… your grandparents… no one taught you anything about God?"

The confusion deepened. Everyone knew this stuff. "I learned all about the gods in my first year of school. Myths that brought on the Great War that polluted the land. Everyone learns about them. So what?"

As if she'd hit an invisible wall, Ms. Becky stopped. "No. Not myths. Beliefs. That's what started the rebellion in the beginning. Our right to believe. Our right to worship."

Thrips and aphids! No wonder the Imperium exiled Ms. Becky to the Favela. "You're a believer?"

"Just like your grandparents and your mother. Your father, not so much." She continued her stroll. "I thought for sure one of them would have taught you."

Her mother and grandparents were believers? How was that possible? They'd never said anything that might suggest…

Brainwashing—that must have happened before she'd been born.

Good thing her mother had seen reason. But why would Ms. Becky think they still believed?

As much as Lexi wanted an answer to that question, she needed to change the subject. In school, she'd learned how convincing believers could be. She wouldn't fall for it, but she also needed Ms. Becky on her side. "Why weren't you at the meeting today? Fletcher came, but not you."

Ms. Becky's eyes flashed. "Your mother and I have parted ways. It's for the best. Fletcher represents our group on your mother's planning committee."

"I don't agree with her plan to build that bomb, either."

"Your mother won't listen. Just because the Imperium got one over on us doesn't mean we need to rush into some half-baked plan." Ms. Becky's jaw tightened. Her frustration rushed her pace so Lexi had to hustle to keep up. "Kidnapping the scientist to poison the Administration sector is insanity. We don't need more war, more killing. We need less." She gripped Lexi's arm. "You must see that."

The truth rooted in the pit of Lexi's stomach. She did see it. Everywhere she looked outside their patch of green, the lifeless dirt that once produced vegetation screamed for them to listen.

Ms. Becky's idealistic belief that some all-knowing and all-powerful being existed drove every decision she made. Ridiculous.

And yet, Ms. Becky fed the poor, rescued those slated for death, and fought for what she knew to be right.

Hadn't the Imperium brainwashed its citizens in the exact opposite? Look down on the outcasts, ignore the aged or infirm, and follow the rules... no matter the outcome.

Opposite sides of the same coin.

* * *

Lexi lay on her cot, cold but not covering herself—penance for the suffering everyone else was undergoing. Rumi lay near death. Dad faced a rigged trial. Gramps might breathe his last at any moment. Reeves prepared to help rescue her father—at risk to his own life. And Ethan lurked around, insisting he'd joined the rebellion just for her. Could the world couldn't get any messier?

Perhaps it would have been easier if she'd done what the Imperium expected her to do. Take the test. Become an engineer. Make babies and live her life until the Imperium decided she'd passed her prime. Years would've come and gone before they retired her. Would a life with Reeves have made the end bearable?

But if she'd aced the test, they wouldn't have assigned her to Reeves, and that thought she couldn't bear. She'd figure this out. Keep her husband safe. Save Rumi and Dad. She had to. She'd never be able to live with herself any other way.

Chapter 12

"Lexi… Lexi, wake up."

She kept her eyes shut. The desire to stay asleep, to make up for the long night alone, pushed aside the voice and the hand resting on her back. "Go away."

"Lex, it's me. I'm sorry, but you've got to get up."

She knew that voice. Reeves. Her blurry husband came into focus.

His face projected sorrow. "It's your grandfather."

The blanket landed on the floor seconds after her feet, and she wriggled into her shoes without bothering to locate socks. "What happened?"

He grabbed her arm and drew her to him before she could reach the tent flap. "He's gone, Lex. I'm so sorry."

Her legs wobbled like gel, and she slipped toward the floor until he wrapped her into an embrace. He whispered into her ear. Though she understood nothing he said, his words comforted her—kept her mind from fracturing into a million pieces.

Gramps was gone forever, but Reeves was still safe. She wasn't alone.

She wasn't… "Nana. I need to go to her. She shouldn't be

by herself." She fisted her sleeve and scrubbed the tears from her face. After rooting around, she found a cloth and blew her nose. She needed to be strong for Nana.

"Your mom and Ms. Becky are with her." He brushed a stray tear from her cheek. "Come on. I'll take you to them."

They'd cordoned off Gramps's bed at the back of the medical tent. Nana sat in the chair beside him, as if waiting for him to wake from slumber. Mom stood behind, one hand resting on Nana's shoulder. Ms. Becky acted the sentry, guarding the entrance to the private area and turning back anyone who ventured in.

Lexi eased to the bedside. If Gramps's body weren't so still, she might think he was asleep. She touched his arm, then jerked back as if he'd burned her. Unfortunately, the opposite truth—that his body lacked any heat—became her new reality. Reeves's arm slipped around her waist, warding off the chill.

While she appreciated his support, her pain paled compared to what Nana must feel. Lexi squeezed his arm before releasing it to walk around the bed and kneel in front of Nana.

With Gramps gone, this woman was one of the few remaining people in the world who loved her unconditionally. When their eyes met, it wasn't pain or sorrow she saw. Nana looked lost, as if she couldn't remember her own granddaughter's face. "He's gone. Just his body's left."

Nodding, Lexi covered Nana's icy hands with her own. "I'm so sorry."

The connection seemed to break something in the older woman. Nana pulled Lexi into a crushing hug, and together, they sobbed and allowed sorrow to seal their bond.

* * *

Without the proper funeral facilities, they laid Gramps to rest that afternoon. For as often as Ms. Becky had visited her grandfather, her absence at the funeral seemed conspicuous.

While Lexi and Nana continued to leak tears, Mom remained stoic. She somehow held in all emotions to the point Lexi wondered if her mother had a jar where she secretly hid her heart.

Reeves said little, comforting Lexi with a gentle squeeze before joining the men in charge of digging the grave.

While the men filled the grave, Lexi and her mother took Nana to the main house. In her room, Nana stared at the second cot. She dropped onto her makeshift bed as if too exhausted to stand a moment longer. "I need some time with my thoughts." Without another word, she lay down and flopped the covers up and over her head, cocooning herself away from the world.

Mom tucked the blanket down over Nana's feet. "I'll come back later to check on you, Mom."

Though they waited, Nana didn't respond, and Mom gestured for Lexi to follow. "She's been up all hours the last few days. The sleep will do her good."

Mom went up the stairs to the piano room. "We need to talk."

"Yes." The word faltered on Lexi's tongue. Gramps's death brought new understanding to her world. Today could be the last day for any of them. There were no guarantees.

Rumi might not make it out of the infirmary, and Lexi hadn't lifted a finger to bring Zane or Dad back for her. This changed everything, and though she missed Gramps, at least it had shown Mom the need for expediency. "We can't waste any more time. We need to move now."

Mom's eyes widened as she dropped onto the piano bench. "I couldn't agree more. I'm glad you're ready to listen to reason. We've got everything set for the trip to pick up the materials once we've secured our scientist."

"Scientist?" Lexi must have heard wrong. "Are you planning to get the scientist on the same trip as we get the councilman's family, Zane, and Dad? That's a lot to do at the same time."

"No–o." The word came out as if it had two syllables. "We're only going for the scientist. That's our priority."

Heat flared, the flames in Lexi's chest sparking until she saw red. "You mean that's *your* priority. Not mine."

"Young lady, it's time you saw reality." Mom stood, hands clenched at her sides. "As my daughter, I expect you to contribute to this community. Since your husband's proven his loyalty, others have turned a blind eye to your haughty attitude. That changes today. You're going to take part in the rescue of the one resource we still lack."

"Kidnap, you mean." Lexi jabbed a finger at her mother. "You're going to kidnap some poor guy and force him to build a bomb that might kill everyone he loves. Let's at least be honest about this."

"We're putting an end to the killing." They drew closer, her mother's breath warmed the air between them. "Permanently."

Lexi closed the remaining gap, fists clenched at her sides to mirror her mother. The explosion she'd thought left her motherless flashed in her mind. "You're nothing but a murderer."

The slap came without warning, and she stumbled back before regaining her balance.

Her mother loomed closer. "Don't you ever call me that again. I've been fighting for your freedom, for your life, since before you were born. When are you going to grow up and stop letting others fight your battles?"

The freshly ignited heat churned through Lexi's body, the desire to strike out—to wound her mother with as deep a cut as her mother's faked death once scarred Lexi's soul—left her hands itching. "I'm ready now, but not to follow you in killing innocents. So good luck with that." She spun on her heel and stalked toward the door.

"You get back here." Her mother's shrill tone tore at Lexi's resolve. "I'm not finished."

Lexi paused halfway through the door and blew out a breath. "I'm not a child anymore, Mom. You told me to grow up. This is me doing that."

She shut the door, muffling her mother's commands.

* * *

Reeves gestured for Lexi to stay close as he pressed the door's crash bar. Yesterday, she'd poured out her argument with her mother, her voice raw. Hours of pleading had followed, her tears unstoppable until he'd given in.

The hours-long drive from Solitude got them there under the cover of darkness. They hurried through dank storm culverts into the Favela. The food and medications they'd brought as gifts earned them a place to hide until the wee hours when distracted guards allowed them to slip into Zane's building and up to his floor.

Easing through the open door, Reeves slipped behind the hall camera and disconnected the feed from the wall. The green light went black, giving them precious minutes to get to Zane's door before someone arrived to check on the dead video feed.

Reeves kept watch while Lexi ran to the apartment she'd followed Rumi to not so long ago.

A combination of pressing the doorbell while tapping resulted in the lock's click disengaging. The door eased open an inch. "Yes?" Zane's voice?

"Zane?" She kept her voice low, almost a whisper. "It's Lexi. Rumi's friend. We need to talk."

The door eased open to reveal Zane, face haggard, eyes wide. "Lexi? Where's my sister?" He looked behind her and scowled at Reeves waiting down the hallway. "Who's that?"

"My husband. Can I come in?" Not waiting for his response, she pushed past him. He relented, letting her shut the door behind them. "You need to come with us. Rumi's sick. She's asking for you."

She expected an argument. Instead, his eyes widened. "I'll get dressed."

He disappeared into another room and soon returned, shoes on and ready to go.

Lexi had heard no conversation behind the bedroom door. She'd never take off in the middle of the night without letting Reeves know. Something seemed off. It was too quiet. "Where's your wife and daughter?"

"Visiting her mother." He rushed to the door. "Let's go."

A tingle tickled up her spine. "Shouldn't you leave a note or something?"

"No." Opening the door, he shook his head. "Not worth the risk. She's visiting all week to help with her sister's new baby."

Lexi hesitated. It seemed reasonable, but—

Reeves poked his head in. "We need to get going."

Not wanting to argue, she followed them out.

* * *

Grime from the two trips through the dead lands covered Lexi head to foot, including grit she couldn't seem to spit out, no matter how many times she tried. Reeves looked no better than she felt with his face two shades darker than normal where dirt caked in his two-day stubble. Still, they didn't stop to clean up before escorting Zane to Rumi's bedside.

Lexi swept the curtain aside to find Rumi asleep, her freckles standing out in contrast with her lily-white skin. Not wanting to lay her filthy hands on the girl, Lexi rubbed Rumi's leg where a thin blanket provided a barrier. "Wake up, sleepy. You've got a guest."

Rumi's eyelids fluttered as if she wanted to comply but didn't have the energy.

Zane moved to his sister's side, crowding out Lexi. He leaned close. "I heard you slacked off in bed just to get my attention. Well, you got it. Now let's get you moving. How about it?"

Her eyes moved to half-mast, and her cracked lips twitched toward a failed smile. "Za–Zane?"

His face split into a grin. "Present and accounted for. Now let's talk about you getting better."

A hand gripped Lexi's shoulder. Reeves gestured for them to leave the siblings alone. She clasped his hand and followed him out of the medical tent.

The sunrise bathed the compound in orange, making the tents look like flickering flames as the flaps danced in the breeze. Though elated they'd reunited Rumi and Zane, Lexi couldn't shake the sense that something evil lay in wait.

Reeves squeezed her hand. "After we get cleaned up, I promised Ms. Becky we'd finalize the plans to rescue the councilman's parents, along with your father."

Sweet seedlings, he'd been there for her and still planned to help with the rest of her agenda. His touch, warm and strong, made her long to snuggle up in his arms. They were so good together. They could conquer anything as long as they stood united. Couldn't they?

* * *

Cleaned and changed, they arrived at the tent where Fletcher and Ms. Becky talked strategy. Fletcher waved them in. "Heard you were back. Everything good?"

Reeves nodded. "Like clockwork. If the trip to save her father goes half as smooth, we'll be fortunate."

Ms. Becky hugged Lexi. "Any change with Rumi?"

The unexpected embrace hinted at what Lexi needed now more than anything. Unconditional love like she'd received as a child. How could her seventeenth birthday have been only weeks in the past? It sure felt like a lifetime ago.

Back then, her mother sat on a pedestal, one of Lexi's heroes. Now she doubted they could agree on anything as minor as a breakfast selection. "She's awake—mostly. But Zane is with her now. I'm hopeful it'll give her the mental fortitude to get better."

With a jab toward the map, Fletcher waved them over. "It's a simple plan and shouldn't take more than a few men to make it happen—you said you had a guy in mind to help?" He rubbed his clean-shaven chin. "Which is a good thing since your mother's plans to get that scientist will stir the pot, big time."

"Yeah, Ethan will come along. I'll brief him on the way to the mission." Reeves blew out a breath. "When's that scientist escapade happening? No way I'll be able to back out of that one."

Ms. Becky shook her head. "Actually, it's already taken care of. Fletcher worked out a deal."

Huh? Lexi's head snapped up. "A deal? With whom?"

The fierce eye contact between Ms. Becky and Fletcher hinted at a long-standing argument. Fletcher rumbled a low growl, like one dog warning another off a bone. His chin jerked up. "She's excused Reeves from his next assignment. It's with the understanding that your mission happens the same night we're retrieving the scientist and the councilman's family."

Ms. Becky crossed her arms.

Fletcher continued. "Figures we'll cause enough of an uproar with the primary aim that we'll distract the Freedom Force."

Sweet seedlings. Her mother knew about the plan and would let Reeves help? Lexi blinked at her husband, and his grim determination bolstered her. "Let's get this done, then."

Within a half hour, Fletcher outlined the plan. One main road connected the jail to the courthouse with a single checkpoint midway. Their sources revealed two guards would be at that post. The vehicle carrying her father would have a driver and guard in the back.

Two people to take out at the guard post and two at the

vehicle. They could do this.

Finished with the map, Fletcher rolled it up for storage. "We've got a few of those stun bracelets we took off the recruits who attacked us. Since you'll have the advantage of surprise, you may get away with stunning them. No shots fired."

A no-kill mission sounded good. So far, she'd gotten away without ending another human's life. If possible, she'd keep it that way. "I can't wait to bring my father back. But I'm not sure what that'll mean for my family. What a shocker it will be when he finds out Mom's alive."

As they prepared to leave, something heavy thudded into the tent.

Fletcher rushed out the entrance, Reeves on his heels.

By the time Lexi made it outside, Fletcher had hoisted Zane off the ground, his glare menacing. "What are you up to, sneaking around?"

Zane's wide-eyed terror made him look like a child caught in the act. "I was just…" He sought Lexi's eye. "I was looking for Lexi. Rumi's asking for her."

A signature growl emanated low in Fletcher's throat. Then he released the smaller man. "Then why didn't you knock or something?"

Rubbing his arm, Zane glared. "I didn't have a chance. I tripped over the tent spike before you snatched my arm."

Ms. Becky intervened. "Lexi, why don't you check on Rumi? She'll be happy to hear of our plans."

With a nod, Lexi jogged off to the medical tent.

An IV bag fed strange blue liquid through tubes connected to Rumi's arm. She sat up, wide awake.

"Wow. You look a lot better than the last time I saw you."

A smile, weak but true, bunched up Rumi's now rosy cheeks.

She pointed at the concoction flowing into her veins. "I feel a lot better. Dr. Ichtacka's new formula seems to be the trick."

Aphids! Another one? Somehow, Lexi kept her tone in check. "I'm glad you're feeling better. Perhaps it's time to get out of the trial once you're released. I don't like what he's doing to you."

Her shoulders slumping, Rumi ducked her head. "He's helping me." She lifted her arm as if the abnormally colored liquid were proof. "I'll be stronger than ever. More focused."

How could Lexi convince Rumi to step away from the doctor's promises before he killed her? "We're heading out soon, and we'll bring my father back with us. Once he's here, you won't need to be a warrior any longer. Right?"

Rumi's eyes went wide. She shoved her blanket aside and swung her legs over the bed. "You're not going without me."

Before she could yank out the IV, Lexi pushed her back down. "Hold up. You're not going anywhere." She snugged the blanket back over Rumi. "Not until you are back to one hundred percent."

A struggle ensued with Rumi fighting Lexi to get up, but Lexi had the advantage of full health. By the time Rumi gave in, her face lost some of the color it had gained. "Fine. When are you leaving?"

Triumphant, Lexi stepped back and gave Rumi space to rearrange herself in bed. "Around midnight, so we'll be ready first thing in the morning when they move my father."

Rumi nodded. "I wish I could come, but I trust you and Reeves. Bring him back safe, will you? I don't want to be here anymore without him."

"That's the plan."

* * *

Back in their tent, Reeves held Lexi close in his cot to calm her jitters. They needed at least a few hours of sleep before they took off, but she couldn't get her mind to let go. Though she'd almost hoped it would lead to more intimate relations, he'd drifted off within minutes while her mind continued to swirl.

The plan should work. Her mother's team, much larger and better armed, would cause several diversions to take the Freedom Forces away from the true targets of the day. If all went well, they'd all sleep sound tomorrow night, back at the compound. Her father included.

Well, all except for the scientist the rebels planned to kidnap. Thoughts of him and those who loved him wouldn't leave her.

Why did people need to plot against each other? The scheme to poison the Administration building couldn't be allowed to move forward. But how could she stop it?

For now, she needed to focus on her father.

Reeves snuffled in his sleep and pulled her tighter against him. She reveled in his warmth. At least, she had him near.

Tomorrow would be a big day for them. For the whole rebel camp.

If only she didn't have this sense of foreboding. Premission jitters. Had to be.

She burrowed into his chest, breathed in his scent, and let the thought go.

Chapter 13

"I can't believe Mom wouldn't give us even one more person—especially when Ethan vanished this morning." Sure, they hadn't told him they were embarking today, but he hadn't been in his tent. Where could he have gone in their encampment? Could he be their mole? Was it all a lie, him saying he'd joined up for her? Had he been using her to worm into Mom's trust?

But no, the way he'd looked at her… That couldn't have been faked, could it have?

Better refocus before her thoughts spilled into words. Just imagining Reeves learning about Ethan's attempts to woo her sent Lexi's heart crawling into her throat. Shuddering, she joined Reeves and pulled the shock cuffs on in the beam of their UTV's headlights. "I guess I should be grateful she let us have a couple of these."

Around them, the various teams finished last-minute preparations as the day's first glimmer of light warmed the horizon. Five squads, the smallest being Lexi and Reeves. One group, composed of the most experienced fighters, would target the scientist Mom wanted. Anyone observing could tell their mission held the highest priority as they carried the best weapons.

Two larger squads looked almost gleeful. Their only aim for the day would be distraction and destruction. The backpacks in the middle of their circle bulged with every ounce of explosive firepower they could afford to expend.

Fletcher gathered his men around him. Under Ms. Becky's orders, he'd locate and rescue the councilman's family. Lexi wished for their success as much as her own. If they could free his loved ones, they'd also loosen his tongue. He'd promised to have his say at the next meeting and encourage others to vote against the increasing violence. But only if his family were safe.

Reeves checked his sidearm. "We should be thankful for every bit of assistance." He gestured toward the other teams. "What they're doing today will distract the Freedom Force. That's huge."

She knew the truth—she should appreciate all the missions today. But she struggled to let the bitterness go. Was she partly saving her father to get even with her mother? Ridiculous.

This wasn't the time to sort through the mental morass of her family dynamics. She needed to focus if she were to have any hope of success.

Family. Only months ago, it seemed so simple. Her parents, grandparents, and her—uncomplicated. She could barely recognize the person her mother had become, and she had a stepmother just a year older than herself.

To top it off, Lexi was married and in love. Something she never expected.

Reeves. Her husband. The man preparing to put his life on the line to save someone he barely knew—for her. Today needed to be quick and painless, with Reeves out of harm's way before the sun set. Once they were all together again, she didn't care if they lived in the tent city for the rest of their lives if her loved ones surrounded her. Of course, Reeves had a family too. He never mentioned them since they left the Imperium, though she'd carried on about her own. They'd need to discuss that when they returned. They should all be together.

Her heart ached to tell Reeves how much she loved him. Words didn't seem to suffice anymore. "Ready to head out?"

He nodded, then waved both arms overhead to catch Fletcher's attention. Reeves flashed a thumbs-up signal, and Fletcher returned it. Then Reeves pointed north. "Let's go."

They hadn't gotten past the first broken deserted buildings when someone hollered from behind. "Wait up." Zane jogged toward them, only a club for protection.

Reeves's eyes narrowed. They paused for Zane to catch up. When he reached them, he bent over, hands on knees and out of breath. He raised one finger for them to wait while he sucked in air.

Within seconds, Reeves's impatience came out via his toe, tapping on the crumbled cement under their feet. "We don't have time for this."

Zane stood straight and drank in a steadying breath. "I promised Rumi I'd do this, so I'm coming with you."

Sweet seedlings. A third person gave them more of an advantage.

But Reeves's face hardened into a granite façade. "Why now? Why not offer while we were still planning things out?"

"I didn't think I could." He held his palms out to Lexi, eyes pleading. "I know what it means to have those you love in danger. Solitude is better than I could have hoped for. If I get involved and save your father, all I ask in return is that you'll allow my family refuge."

Afraid Reeves might reject the late offer, Lexi jumped into the conversation. "Of course. We appreciate the extra set of hands."

Her husband's glower said he had other thoughts, but he kept them to himself. The harrumph that followed mimicked Fletcher's. Then he started out once again. "We're losing time."

* * *

The low morning sun lit their target, the guardhouse's white siding gleaming. Because all four sides boasted windows, they couldn't walk up to it. Not unless they wanted the battle to end before it even began.

Lexi staggered from between two burned-out businesses, a blood-soaked rag she'd brought from the medical wing tied to her head. She let out a moan, needing to convince the guards an injured Favela dweller staggered toward them—not a rebel.

If the red-stained cloth didn't do the trick, the stench of the ragged and holey clothing she'd traded her uniform for should. Dealing with someone else's body odor from a distance was challenging, but wearing it nauseated her.

One guard took notice and exited his protective hut, but she needed them both by her side.

Time to move to part two of her play.

Doing her best impression of a weak, injured female, she groaned louder. "Help me. Please." Then she stumbled to one knee.

The second guard moved from his shelter as the first

advanced on Lexi, rifle leveled at the ground. "Stay down."

He didn't have to tell her twice. The chest-high weeds kept her lower half hidden, and with her free hand, she eased the stun cuff out of her sleeve.

"Help… me." She had to sell it. "I don't think… I can…" Then she flopped into the grass.

Rustling weeds told her at least one guard rushed toward her. Would the second be close behind?

Mustering every ounce of patience she possessed, she stayed still when a beefy hand touched her neck and felt for her pulse.

She sensed the large man turning away from her before he shouted. "Come give me a hand."

Patience. Wait for it. She counted down. Ten… nine… eight…

A second set of legs joined the first as she peered through barely open slits.

Both laid their weapons down and leaned in to inspect her. Hands touched her side and rolled her.

Now or never. She struck, touching each of them with her stunning cuff.

Their faces pinched in pain, then went slack. Their bodies followed suit, and they crumpled to the ground.

The rustle of quick steps through the weeds caught her attention, and she spun to face her attacker.

She lowered her clenched fists when her two partners came running.

Zane's eyes shone when he reached her side. "I can't believe that worked."

Reeves pulled her up and into his arms, squeezing the breath out of her. "You will *never* do that again. I thought I'd die when they rolled you over."

Nervous laughter bubbled up as she wiggled out of his

embrace. "You thought you'd die? I almost added more body fluids to this already disgusting outfit."

Knowing they were on a schedule, they dragged the guards into their original hiding spot and disrobed them. Within minutes, Reeves and Zane had the uniforms on and stood sentinel at the roadblock as if it were just another day of work.

Lexi huddled in a corner below the windows. "Any sign of the transport? I should have swapped this outfit for yours."

Reeves chuckled. "You *are* ripe, my love."

The tease, out of place, eased some of her tension. She swatted his leg. "Just keep your eyes peeled."

Zane tensed. "I see them. Look."

Body close to the ground, Lexi peeked out the door but couldn't see anything past the weeds. The tension in her shoulders flowed through the rest of her like she'd become a tightly wound spring ready to explode at the slightest touch. For their plan to work, she had to remain hidden, so she crawled to her corner and curled into a leg-hugging ball.

"This is it." Reeves picked up his handgun and moved to the doorway. "Our turn, Zane."

The transport van stopped in front of the guardhouse, and Reeves stepped out of the building, Zane close on his heels. Lexi wanted to see, but to keep her husband safe, she had to stay put.

A hum nearby. The driver's side window lowering.

She held her breath.

A voice she didn't recognize. "Quiet day?"

Reeves should step up to the vehicle…

"Hey…"

The crackle of the stun cuff followed by footsteps said they'd taken out the driver. All that remained was the guard in the back.

She itched to help rather than stay hidden while Reeves risked everything. Now she knew how he must have felt watching her play her role.

Thump. Thump.

"Checkpoint." Reeves and Zane would be at the back of the truck.

Any minute, her father would recognize Reeves. *Please don't give him away.* Her father wouldn't intentionally give her husband up, but the surprise of seeing him might be hard to hide.

Another sizzle verified someone had deployed their cuff. Reeves should now holler out for her to join them.

They'd have her father and be back in Solitude before nightfall.

Any second...

Boots stomped back into the hut, and Zane stood over her, his gun pointed at her face. "Get up."

Ice snaked around her heart, squeezing painfully. She sprang to her feet, ready to attack, but froze when Zane's finger played at the trigger. "What have you done? Where's Reeves?"

"Turn around." He gestured with the gun. "Face the wall."

Gladly. She needed to see where Reeves was. A slow turn to the windows revealed the truth.

Three Freedom Force soldiers stood near the back of the van. One had his weapon aimed in her direction. The glass walls wouldn't offer much protection if he fired.

A second stood by the van driver's window, checking on him.

The third hung out at the back of the van, towering over another uniformed person lying in the dirt. She recognized those shoes—Reeves.

The chill around her heart tightened further, and her breath caught. There'd been no gunfire, only the stun. But what if someone had used a knife or Zane's club? The desire to run out and check for a pulse fought against the need for self-preservation. "Is he…?"

Zane yanked her hands behind her back and zip-tied her wrists. Rough hands searched her before removing her blades from their sheath. "Sleeping like a baby. I'll bet he has a whopper of a headache when he wakes up, though. Hit the dirt pretty hard."

The pressure thawed a bit. He'd be fine. For the moment.

Zane twisted her to face him.

If her hands weren't bound, she'd have taken a swipe at him. Bile rose in her throat. She'd convinced Reeves to bring this viper into their camp, and he'd betrayed them all. Once again, her fault. "Where's my father?"

Ignoring her question, Zane hauled her from the building and shoved her toward the back of the van. They'd already zip-tied Reeves and dropped him on the van's floor.

Her gagged father sat on a bench seat, his hands manacled and bound to the floor with a long chain. His wrinkle-lined eyes glazed when they met hers. His prematurely gray hair shocked her. She'd have sworn he'd aged ten years since she'd last seen him. Now, instead of rescuing him, she'd added herself to the Imperium's trophy shelf.

A push to her back unbalanced her, and she stumbled against the van's step. Zane ordered, "In."

The desire to strike with her feet, her elbows, even her teeth if she could, quickened her blood. She wanted to call Zane every name she could think of starting with *traitor*, but she knew better.

He'd never been one of them, so she couldn't label him a traitor. Not to the rebels, anyway. If anything, she'd been the one at fault in this mess. She'd prioritized Rumi over the entire camp by bringing Zane back. "You're betraying your sister. She trusted you."

His weapon jabbed her lower back. "My sister chose poorly. Get in while you're still able to stand, because my next strike won't be as kind."

Her father's eyes pleaded with her, the message clear, so she stepped up and in. Before she could find her seat, the door slammed, cutting off all light except for a slanted skylight.

Reeves hadn't budged. Her need to check on him got helped along when the van took off without warning, dropping her hard to the floor. Her knees smacked the metal before she toppled over her husband.

The warmth of his body and the steady inhalation and exhalations comforted her. Sweet seedlings, he was alive. If he were conscious, they could plan their next move. On her own, she couldn't even fathom what escape might look like.

Muffled words, incomprehensible through the gag, emanated from her father. She struggled back to her knees and then onto the bench with him. If only she could free her hands.

She tried to bring her arms forward. No good.

Using her teeth, she pulled on the cloth while he tugged in the opposite direction. His captors had tied it tight. It took some back and forth before they inched it down far enough for him to take a full breath. "I can't believe you're here, but you should have left me. Now they've got another pawn to parade around."

Aphids. Those words stung. She'd made things worse.

Tears singed her eyes. "I couldn't leave you." Her husband's prone figure lay before her, emphasizing her error. "*We* couldn't leave you."

"Oh, honey." Her father leaned into her as best he could while connected to the wall. "I'm sorry. I had no idea I had such an amazing daughter. You've grown up too fast. In my mind, you're still a kid, but here you are, all married and turned into a warrior."

The warmth of his head against hers was more connection than she'd ever felt with the man who raised her. She should have appreciated him more. "I love you, Dad."

A tear dampened the top of her head, and her heart twisted. He sniffled. "You've never called me dad before. It sounds good. And… I love you too."

The truth was hard to swallow, but he was right. She'd preferred her mother's and grandparents' coddling to her father's all-business, all-Imperium disconnection. But her mother had a different agenda the whole time, and they'd paid the consequences for it.

Mom. Did he know? "Mom's not dead." She searched his face for his response. "She's a rebel."

A bitter laugh huffed out of him. "I heard. In fact, that's *all* I've heard since they imprisoned me. Somehow, they think I knew about her and could assist them in tracking her down. Weren't they disappointed to find out they knew more than I did about my wife." He cleared his throat like the weight of the world had settled in it. "You can't beat the truth out of someone who doesn't know it."

Words wouldn't come. Her mother had betrayed him in so many ways. What must he be feeling now?

It seemed strange to bring up, but he'd cared for more than

one woman. "Rumi's alive, but she's been sick." Should she explain the experiment? No, that would be Rumi's story to tell. "She wanted to come, but she isn't well enough yet."

The dim light revealed the pain crossing his face. "I'd have never asked for a new wife if I'd known."

Lexi let the words hang in the air. Sometimes the truth sets you free in ways you'd never expected.

The van slowed to a stop, and the rear doors opened. Blinding sunlight streamed in.

A soldier waved a rifle. "Out!"

She inched toward the door until gloved hands reached in and tugged her off the bench. She stumbled forward, lost her balance, and dropped to one knee in front of a six-foot-plus guy. The guard still held her. Otherwise, she might have face-planted.

The muscle-bound jerk yanked her to her feet like she weighed less than a stuffed doll. Pain shot through her shoulder from his rough handling. He ignored her cries and marched her toward the aging courthouse they'd parked in front of.

Though she tried to look back to see what they'd do with Reeves and her father, the pace her captor set left her stumbling over the cracked pavement.

She gave up and took in the aging building they raced toward. Massive pockmarked marble columns held up a roof that sagged on one side. Though it must've once been white, black soot crawled up the siding like flames, a reminder of their society's troubled past.

No one stopped or even slowed their progress inside and then down a side hallway. Their footsteps echoed under ceilings at least twelve feet above the floor. Faded murals had huge sections missing where some past invader gouged out the plaster.

She couldn't fathom its history or how many prisoners previously walked this corridor. The musty air clogged her nose and lungs. She might suffocate if she didn't get a fresh breeze soon.

A door waited at the hall's far end. They entered an open room where a desk separated them from another door beyond. No one sat at the desk, but two Freedom Force guards flanked the second door. The one on the left reached backward and knocked once.

They waited. Seconds ticked by, and each one increased the patter of her pounding heart.

When the door opened, a woman with grim-set lips and the white uniform of the Administration personnel stepped out. Her eyes went wide when she took in Lexi. She gestured for them to go in.

Instead of pulling Lexi into the room, the guard shoved her from behind, knocking her off-balance, but into the room. He shut the door behind her.

Once she righted herself, she scanned what once must have been an opulent office, though it currently featured chipped paint, stained floors, and a weathered desk with one broken leg propped up by a brick.

"I've been looking forward to our conversation." The voice drew her attention to a faded and cracked leather chair and the person who'd spoken.

Tempest Malachy—the voice of the Imperium—gave her a wicked grin.

Chapter 14

Lexi shivered and searched for a camera. One must be in Tempest's vicinity so she could be on a vis screen within minutes. An etablet rested under her hands. One perfectly polished fingernail tapped it, her eyes laser focused on Lexi.

Aphids! She squirmed like a bug under a microscope. "Are you planning to televise my execution?"

That sickening grin widened. "Maybe someday, but I hadn't planned for that possibility today. Don't tell me you crave the spotlight *that* much."

Somehow, the news she wouldn't die immediately set Lexi's teeth on edge instead of bringing relief. The sparkle in Tempest's eyes said Lexi had become the latest toy in her playroom. "What do you want?"

"Please, sit." Tempest waved at a rickety guest chair. "It's time for a talk. Just us girls."

A whiff of cloying perfume turned Lexi's stomach as she sat, hands still bound. "I can't imagine what we'd need to discuss."

"Oh, we can think of something." Tempest picked up a stylus and twirled it between her fingers. "How about your mother and her ragtag group of wannabe rebels?"

The missions planned for today… Had their plan to rescue Dad been the only one thwarted? The itch to know crawled up Lexi's arms. "Considering that Zane works for the Imperium, I'd think the council already knows more than I can tell you."

"Hmm…" Tempest clicked the stylus on the desk, the slow rhythm grating. "Zane is a good boy. Knows what's best for him and his family. His daughter is precious. I'd hate to see anything *bad* happen to her. Zane will get to see the little rug rat for an hour as a reward. I can be generous."

A lump formed in Lexi's throat. The Imperium prized children and rewarded new parents. How could this woman use them as baubles? She'd backed Zane into a corner, the same as Lexi. Understanding sparked, but not forgiveness. Rumi should have been his priority too. He could have told the truth. Lexi would have helped. "Does the council know what you're up to? I would think they'd frown on your mistreatment of babies."

"The council knows what they need to." Tempest's stylus stilled. "But let's talk about you, shall we? You've got star potential, did you know? You're young, freshly married… and you've got a symmetrical face. The camera will love you."

Lexi drew her shoulders back. "I thought you coveted the spotlight for yourself."

Eyebrows quirked, Tempest relaxed back in her chair. "Before the Great War, an animal called a sheep wandered the north pastures. Back then, it was too hot to raise sheep here, but further up, the animals thrived. People used their wool to make clothing, if you can believe it." She flipped the stylus between her fingers. "They also had sheepdogs back then. Animals to herd other animals. Imagine."

"Stop ruminating and get on with it. We learned about them

in school."

"Sheep were vulnerable, tasty creatures. The dogs protected them from predators. You'd think sheep would love dogs because of that, right?" She paused but shrugged when Lexi didn't respond. "Nope. They hated the dogs and ran away from them. People are like that. Weak. In need of direction and protection, and yet they hate those of us who provide it."

"You're wrong. We're strong. The rebels prove it every day."

Tempest's frown warned Lexi'd scored a hit. "All the rebels prove is that they're reckless fools. We had a system. An arrangement. They get the Favela, and we turn a blind eye when they fritter away resources on people they should've allowed to die when their time came up."

Wait. "We?"

"The council, of course. Mind you, they're smart enough to listen to my suggestions." Tempest's eyes narrowed. "Most of them, anyway."

Not only was Tempest the face of the Imperium on the vis but she treated the council like her puppets. That explained the councilman's family. How had one woman gained so much control? "We've disproved your sheep theory. We're not all willing to accept your system."

"Right you are, my dear. Your mother isn't some fuzzy stupid lamb. She leads a wolf pack." She leaned forward. "And I'm the exterminator."

A chill skittered down Lexi's spine. If ever a person embodied evil, this woman was it. "You'll never get rid of us all. Even if you take out Solitude, others will start new rebellions. People crave freedom and will sacrifice to earn it."

"Look, it's like I said. I can be generous." Calm returned to her face. Glee faded. "If you'll do your duty as a loyal

Imperium subject, reject the rebellion on vis, I'll forgive you. You can have the Favela back. No more troops cleaning it out. We'll look the other way while your kind scurries around like rats, stealing away the protein crumbs from under our tables. Just like before."

"Not exactly a bargain. Why would I agree to that?"

"Because I always get what I want." She activated her etablet, typed a few commands, and tipped the screen to show Lexi a video feed of Reeves, bound to a chair, one eye swollen shut. A split lip oozed dark blood. "Of course, I'm assuming here. Since he left with you and, even more brazenly, returned by your side, you must have bonded with your husband, whether or not you chose him."

Acid burned in Lexi's throat. She swallowed it and the desire to climb over the desk and pummel Tempest's gorgeous face. If only her hands were free. She couldn't let Tempest win, but where was the exit for this wild ride? "You're evil."

"Oh, you… flatterer." Red tainted Tempest's cheeks. "Seriously though, your father's trial can go either way. In fact, I could even delay it, perhaps permanently. Your call, but… you need to choose now. Shall we continue your husband's interrogation? Punish your father for his crimes?"

Seconds passed.

Tempest wiggled her eyebrows. "The suspense is killing me."

At Lexi's nod, Tempest signaled the guards and gestured Lexi out the door ahead of them.

What choice did she have? But two friends had betrayed her today. Could she expect better from the enemy?

* * *

Heat emanating from the studio lights sent a trickle of sweat down Lexi's back. The uniform they'd dressed her in itched, and the too-tight collar acted as a vise. Caked-on makeup suffocated. If only she could crawl into some hiding spot instead of sitting exposed for the Imperium to see.

A makeup artist performed final touches on Tempest's hair and face, ensuring every strand lay just so and no shine would be visible on her cheeks under the light's harsh glare. Tempest crooned at the woman, who held a mirror for her. "You're a magician, dear. If I didn't know better, I'd think I was ten years younger."

The assistant beamed with the compliment, then backed out of the camera's path. Tempest and Lexi sat in overstuffed, cream-clothed chairs facing each other. The table between them held glasses of water. Just out of the audience's view, a split screen showed a feed of Reeves on one side and her father on the other, chains stretching both their arms to the ceiling. Freedom Force guards stood at their sides, armed with menacing batons.

The message was simple. One wrong word out of Lexi, and the men she loved would pay the price.

A man with enormous headphones stood between cameras before the stage. He counted down as he lowered fingers one at a time. "Three... two... one..." He gestured for Tempest to begin.

Her face took on the scowl of a reporter bearing critical news. "Today, I'm joined by an important person in the Imperium's war against the rebellion. Mrs. Lexi Scheffer, the daughter of the traitor, Gunner Verity." Tempest turned toward her, and a cameraman panned to Lexi. "Welcome, Mrs. Scheffer. May I call you Lexi?"

As if Lexi had a choice. How many people would believe the act she was on the brink of performing in the Imperium's ongoing play? She forced her hands to lie still in her lap, fingers clenched tight to minimize their trembling. "Of course, Tempest."

Tempest smiled. It sure appeared warm and genuine. "Lexi, you've experienced such a harrowing month. Captured by rebels, tortured for information on the Imperium, and then rescued by your brave new husband. It must be overwhelming, and yet such a relief to be back in the safety of the Imperium."

The response her interviewer expected lingered on Lexi's tongue, glued there by the injustice of it all. She had an idea to thwart the charade of an interview, to take back the power the Imperium stole from her, but the risk unsettled her.

A glance at Reeves's swollen face settled the matter. Even if she played by Tempest's rules, she couldn't guarantee anyone's safety. To win, she needed a countermove—and for that, she needed to draw her opponent in closer. She cleared her throat. "I can't even tell you how it feels to be back where I started."

She'd deviated slightly from the script, but it was close enough.

A flicker of irritation flashed in Tempest's eyes, but she let the slip pass and continued addressing the camera. "As my viewers understand, the rebels, known only as Y, have one goal—to wreak chaos where our citizens have built peace and prosperity."

The director pointed to the second camera.

Tempest faced it. "Our young people are our future, but the rebels target them. Children murdered in their parents' arms. They even kidnap our young women to prevent them from fulfilling their roles as mothers. Only by destroying them can we protect our citizens."

Fire burned in Lexi's chest as propaganda spewed for the vis screens.

Headphone guy pointed at Lexi, and the first camera panned toward her.

As did Tempest's gaze. Her eyes reflected a pretense of concern. "I don't want to make this interview more difficult than it has to be, so we won't go into detail. But our audience wants to know how the rebels tried to brainwash you. Tried to make it seem like you were one of them. That must have been horrific."

The scenarios Lexi rolled around in her head refused to solidify. She knew her lines, per the script, and she'd practiced several variations while she'd waited. Now, the time had come, and words scrambled away from her. "I almost trusted them—the rebels. Their stories were so convincing." Lexi tugged at her ear, hoping her mother would recognize the significance of the move. "After all, as you said, they tortured me."

Once again, not what they'd instructed her to say, but close enough.

Tempest didn't hesitate. "At any point did you sense this Y group had your best interests at heart?"

Lexi's ear warmed when she pulled on her lobe again, desperate for the people she'd left behind at the camp to know she hadn't turned on them. "Never."

Tempest's pink lips parted, prepared for her next diatribe.

But Lexi didn't stop. "And I'd like to thank you, as well as the council, for uncovering the conspiracy to discredit my father as well and for allowing him to join Reeves and me, once again, to experience full citizenship. The three of us look forward to testifying. Live on the vis, just as you wanted, at the next council meeting."

Having made her move, Lexi held her breath. Tempest had a choice to make. If she played along with Lexi, she'd need to leave all three of her new captives alive and relatively unscathed to be at the next council meeting and to show it live.

Tempest soon recovered her composure. With a twitch of her head, she let the camera operators know to move their focus off Lexi and return it to herself. The all-business frown returned. "I'm certain we'll have plenty of opportunities to talk to our returned citizen again, but for tonight, we'll let Lexi get some rest. Until then, a reminder to all that a young Imperium is a healthy Imperium."

* * *

Lexi's clothes—a scratchy ill-fitting uniform—clung to her worse than a straitjacket. She paced in tight circles between the cement slab they called a bed, the hole serving as a toilet, the cinder block walls, and the solid door. Six steps— exactly—to tour her enclosure.

Her head spun with a dizzy nausea from the path, the thick suffocating air, and the invasive thoughts. Her cheek throbbed from Tempest's cobra-strike slap the moment the cameras were off. Had Lexi pushed too far? Tempest's final verbal jab still stung. "Maybe I can't put your father on public trial, but that doesn't mean he'll live."

The fire in Tempest's eyes told Lexi she'd touched a nerve. If the witch wanted to keep up the pretense of loyal Lexi, then both Reeves and Dad must show up on the vis soon. But a

182

reckoning lurked beneath the surface. No way Tempest would let Lexi's move be the final one.

A beep sounded from the door, and a red light above it flashed green. When it slid open, Lexi's pulse jumped into a feverish gallop. Two Freedom Force guards, each towering over her, their biceps strained against their uniformed shirts, glared. "Let's go."

Blood froze midway to her heart, and she backed away. "Where are we going?"

Rough hands grabbed her and hauled her out of the room. "Council meeting."

Tempest's counterplay. Get Lexi in front of the group immediately. Then the game could continue. If only Lexi knew what her own next move should be.

Each footstep echoed down the hallway with finality. Like a slow march to a firing squad.

Chapter 15

A time warp captured Lexi the moment she entered the Administration building. At the formative age of five, she'd come with Mom to see where Dad worked among the white-uniformed elite. She'd been awestruck, walking among the select few who ran the Imperium. Those who wielded the power.

Now the hallways bustled with pallid faces that rarely enjoyed the sun's kiss. The contrast to her tanned skin stood out more than if she'd worn the gardeners' green uniform she'd always coveted. Administration workers' eyes widened at the sight of her, then looked away as if offended. Little did they know her mind had morphed even more than her tanned body had.

The two guards flanking her took up most of the corridor's width. People scuttled around them, taking in the spectacle of a freckle-faced girl in military dress uniform. They couldn't shackle her and keep up the pretense of her rescue, but her escort's breath tickled the back of her neck. The message clear—behave, because the situation could change in a heartbeat.

The woman Lexi met coming out of Tempest's office earlier

joined them and hurried their group through a room animated by vis screens and cameras. A window linked the room to the studio where Lexi made her false confessions.

Men hunched over keyboards, their monitors playing scenes of Tempest interviewing various government officials, young teenagers, and military leaders. As they passed, her interrogation played back in slow motion on one screen. The woman watching it stopped, backed up, and played it again. Lexi could only imagine the propaganda concocted here.

Near the far end, the assistant knocked twice on a door, then entered, waving Lexi and her escorts inside. Tempest sat before a mirror while her makeup artist perfected the arch of one eyebrow. With a wave, Tempest dismissed the assistant and narrowed her eyes at Lexi. "You played me once, but you won't have another chance. The council is waiting for your testimony, and though we'll record it for the world to see, it won't be live. We can snip and cut, even add in, whatever we'd like before it's made public."

Lexi swallowed, her throat drier than the dust kicked up in the dead zone. "Where's Reeves? My father? People expect to see them."

Tempest stood and patted her perfect hair into further submission. "They'll be in the room. Seen and not heard, like obedient children." She inspected her red-glossed nails. "And if you hope to see them again after today, you'll answer my questions appropriately. A prompter will guide you since your brain can't seem to keep up on its own."

Lexi gulped. Would it matter? If she played the puppet, would Tempest keep her promise, or would it all be for nothing? "Let's assume I play along. How can I know you'll let us go? We're not who you want, anyway."

A wicked grin spread Tempest's lips so thin she looked frog-like. "I guess we'll see, won't we? But you're right. Tora's the one I want. I so wish I could see your mother's face when she hears your testimony today. Your mother *does* hate to lose."

She snapped her fingers, and a guard spun Lexi toward the door and shoved her in the back. They marched down a hallway she'd never seen. At the far end, two sentries blocked the entryway. Without a word, the guards ushered them into an overwhelming room.

A wall of windows displayed the shell of a once great city. Dark clouds blocked the sun's warmth. Her footfalls on the cold marble floors echoed off the high ceiling. A gleaming wood podium with a microphone faced a semicircular table on a dais. People in starched cream uniforms, decorated with blue trim and silver buttons, occupied the chairs. Their gazes followed her in, and their chatter quieted.

Once they'd placed her behind the podium, her guards moved out of camera range. As promised, a screen filled the top where she'd have expected solid wood. The words *Testimony of Mrs. Lexi Verity Scheffer* in block letters scrolled across it. Looking up at the people on the dais gave her the sensation of sitting in a pit while others peered down at her. Like being under the magnifying glass of a young child spotting its first spider mite. Some whispered. Others remained silent, their lips twisted into interested puckers. The central chair remained empty.

Cameras and darkened floodlights stood at the ready. Today, she would play the part of a well-trained Imperium drone, ready to take her place back amongst the breeding stock the council had amassed. But only if Tempest delivered her payment—Reeves and her father.

As if the witch heard her thoughts, a door on the left opened. Lexi clutched the podium. Reeves walked in, followed by two guards. Caked makeup disguised the bruises she'd seen earlier. They'd dressed him in a matching uniform as if they'd both graduated from military school and stepped out of the commencement ceremony. The trio stopped at the edge of the semicircle, within eyesight of everyone in the room, including the bank of cameras.

He gave her a small nod. A sign he supported her crazy plan as if he knew it?

Sweet seedlings, her interpretation better be correct. The urge to run to him and apologize for getting him into this mess, to soothe his aches and pains, and to kiss his battered lips brought pain to her chest. Being assigned to him was the best gift the Imperium ever could've given her, and she'd done nothing to earn an ounce of his love. Yet, a spark in his eye brought her a sensation of invincibility. She could conquer anything with him.

Once again, the door opened. Her father, dressed like them, shuffled in on unsteady feet. A guard remained close to his elbow, as if ready to catch him if he lost his balance. He lined up beside Reeves. They must've received specific instructions, which didn't include joining her to testify. At least they wouldn't have to lie. She'd do enough of that for all of them.

The room quieted, preparing for the show.

Lexi stared at the stone columns lining the chamber. What of her mother's plans for a dirty bomb? The device's true destructive power lay in the poison it would spew, but the explosive properties would wreak havoc as well. If her mother got her way, would these columns soon lie in ruin and the pristine pale faces surrounding her become part of the destruction? Or would this panel seal the rebels' fate and restart the cycle of starvation and death in the Favela all over again?

Neither outcome sat well. Both brought destruction and death, but to different segments of their world. If only her words could stop both sides. Ms. Becky's care for the people of the Favela seemed the best example for all of them, but no one paid any attention to her or her methods. Both Tempest and Mom treated the older woman as an annoyance when they should have adopted her standards.

The double doors behind her opened. Each member stood, backs ramrod straight, arms glued to their sides like plastic dolls stuck in a pose. Their faces were clear of all emotion, and the room fell silent except for brisk footsteps on the hard floor.

Tempest strode in, cape billowing behind her. She stalked to the table's center and glared at Lexi while an assistant removed her cape and pulled out the massive, throne-like chair. Once ensconced in the middle, she flicked a finger, and the entire council seated themselves in unison. Tempest lifted her chin to the assistant, who tapped a message into an etablet. Tiny green lights popped on around the room, revealing locations of dozens of built-in camera feeds.

A sickly sweet smile parted Tempest's lips. "Mrs. Scheffer, it's good to see you again. You're looking better by the hour in the freedom of our glorious capital."

The monitor in front of Lexi glowed. The words she needed to parrot appeared, and she read aloud. "Thank you for your generous support, Tempest. I'd like to thank the council for taking the time to hear from me." Her heart flipped in her chest when Tempest scowled.

The viper cleared her throat. "Let's try that once again. I know you're nervous, but if you plan to be a star, you mustn't sound like you're reading your lines. It must come naturally. Woo your audience, dear. The Imperium wants to hear the truth from you." She flickered her fingers toward her assistant. "We'll edit that out."

The guards standing by Reeves and her father inched closer to the men Lexi loved.

Tempest's voice drew her attention back to the room's front. "Again."

Lexi plastered on a smile and tried her best to sound natural as she repeated her lines, drawing an approving nod.

Tempest moved on. "You've revealed to me one of your deepest sorrows—that your mother is the leader of the rebellion. Tell us how you feel about that?"

Nausea welled in Lexi's throat. She forced bile down before it ruined her ruse. "My mother lied for years to both my father and me. It's pathological with her. A person like that isn't capable of love."

Tempest's smirk acted like salt in a wound before she schooled her face. "This council has worked tirelessly to maintain order, peace, and prosperity for our people. Do you believe your mother's tactics—bombings and sabotage— are the actions of a sane person? What does she think she'll gain from all that destruction?"

It couldn't have been clearer. Lexi's testimony had a sole purpose—discrediting her mother and those who followed her. She might not agree with her mother's tactics, but the rebels were right to oppose the control the Imperium held over their lives. People deserved the right to choose whom they married or *if* they wanted to. The right to seek a profession they enjoyed and to switch careers if they changed their minds.

A shuffle behind her drew her attention. Reeves stared at her father, who had grown paler and listed to one side. Her eyes met her husband's, and he nodded, his features set in grim lines.

The play must go on. She licked her parched lips and read her response. "'These are not the acts of a sane woman. I encourage all of those who have fallen for my mother's deceptive lies to lay down their weapons and return to the Imperium. The acceptance I've received from this council proves we've taken a fresh path of reconciliation and are ready to welcome back any who wish for peace.'"

False empathy softened Tempest's eyes. Anyone who didn't know better might think the tear she wiped from her cheek was genuine. "It's so heartbreaking to hear the sorrow in your voice, Lexi. I know this is difficult for you. But isn't it true the council has offered peace terms many times, and yet the rebels refuse repeatedly? What does your mother want for the Imperium?"

The council members sat rigid in their chairs. The councilman she recognized from the Favela meeting shifted, crossing his legs. The heat from the spotlights didn't help, but were those beads of sweat slithering down his neck? Had the rebels rescued his parents? Another woman's feet jiggled, though she clasped her hands in a white-knuckled ball on the tabletop. How many of them had reasons to fear the woman sitting in the center chair?

The prompter displayed a single-word response to Tempest's question. Lexi cleared her throat. "Chaos."

"This council will vote today on whether to lower the age

of adulthood to fourteen. Some have volunteered already, but our citizens have proclaimed the need for unification, for all to have the same privilege of serving our great society at an earlier age." Tempest motioned around the room.

Lexi could imagine the camera panning to each man and woman. How well could the editors clean up the feeds so they all looked confident, not terrified?

"What would your advice to them be before this critical decision?"

Images of children holding weapons and babies paraded through her mind. She didn't want to look at the prompter, much less spit out the words it would reveal. Her heart thumped against her rib cage. How many kids would watch her face and hear her words and believe she'd betrayed them?

Someone cleared their throat.

Tempest raised an eyebrow at Lexi. Once again, this woman had outschemed them and held the winning hand. Lexi may have saved three lives today, but she would ruin so many more.

Her lines blurred. The space below the dais beckoned her to crawl in and disappear. Instead, she read the words aloud. "'My advice to the council would be to vote in favor of a younger age of adulthood. Let those who've reached the age of thirteen join in the fight to preserve the Imperium and all it stands for. Assign them mates immediately.'"

Chapter 16

What have I done?

As Tempest demanded perfection and grilled Lexi again and again, the same questions required the same answers until the result satisfied Tempest. Why make Lexi repeat the words so many times? The vis engineers would cut, paste, and then manipulate the video until it told the story the way her tormentor wanted.

Trembling, Lexi stole another glance at her father. He teetered closer to toppling with each passing hour. From exhaustion, starvation, or illness? Green tinged his pallid skin. It might have been a makeup job gone wrong, or it may have been hiding something worse. Reeves remained stoic, not uttering a word, but he inched closer to her father every so often. Now, nearing the day's end, Dad leaned on him. At least the guards hadn't prevented it.

"All right. We have what we need." Tempest pushed back her chair, ending the charade. "You're free to return to your cells."

Free. The word grated. The ache in Lexi's chest twisted into a sharp pain.

A guard pushed her father, and he toppled to the floor.

"No!" she screamed as he thumped against the marble, and nausea sluiced through her. Woozy, she tried to get to him, but the lout who'd brought her in captured her arms and hauled her in the opposite direction.

Another prevented Reeves from stepping in. Then two brutes grasped her father up by the armpits and dragged him from the room.

Held between two giants in white uniforms, Reeves reached out as she passed by. Their fingers touched. His gaze captured hers longer than his body could, and he mouthed, "I love you."

Her throat constricted, and her vision blurred. Tears threatened the entire walk back to her prison cell, but she'd refused to let them fall.

A guard shoved her into her cell. The door clanged shut. She eased her aching back down onto the cold cement slab of a bed. Who'd have thought she'd miss the sagging cot back at camp?

She fisted her hands. The time for sorrow had passed. She'd gotten them into this mess, and she had to find a way out. Soon, Tempest would have enough propaganda video. Lexi would be worthless then. The witch might not publicly execute her, but that didn't mean her fate would be better than death. Far worse, her father's and Reeves's destinies would mirror her own.

Her gut rumbled a protest. She hadn't eaten since before the mission. Perhaps the plan for her demise revolved around starvation. That could explain why her father had been so weak and thin. Tempest could claim anything she wanted if he died. Blame any sort of illness. No one would be any wiser.

Lexi couldn't sit here and do nothing while they all wasted away. Her feet throbbed when she stood. Thrips and aphids!

Too many hours standing behind that podium, sweating under the scorching lights. She hobbled to the door and pounded on it. "Hey! Is anyone out there?" She slammed her fists some more. The door's hollow interior thumped like a drum. "I need food and water."

Pausing for a beat, she pressed an ear to the door.

Nothing.

Could no one hear her? Or had they chosen to ignore her?

She repeated the process, thumping, hollering, and even kicking at the metal enclosure. Her throat grew drier by the minute. Perhaps shouting had been a poor choice.

About to give up, she lashed out in a frantic final effort.

The green light glowed, and as the door slid open, a scowling face appeared in the opening. He snarled and smacked a baton against the doorframe. "Back up."

She stepped further into her cell.

A second guard moved around the first to set a plastic cup of water and a thin sandwich on the bed. While the food bearer backed out, the grouch glared at her. "Don't think every time you act up, you'll get something. If it were up to me, you'd go hungry. But you'll be out of my hair soon enough." A grin slithered across his face, and he pressed in close enough that his body odor assaulted her nose and left a sour taste on her tongue. "You're going to the place all troublemakers go. Then we'll see how much noise you make."

He backed out, and the door's slam reverberated in her chest.

Where troublemakers go. She shivered. The Imperium slaughtered older adults and called it "retiring to Solitude." Unlikely any better fate awaited her if they were transferring her to a place for agitators. But wouldn't Tempest want to keep her alive in case she needed more video?

Lexi eased back onto the hard bed and gulped down the water, forcing herself to save an inch in the bottom. She'd need something to wash the sandwich down. They wouldn't be bringing more. Peeling apart the two slices of bread revealed a gray wedge of what might be protein. Her stomach lurched. She brought it to her nose and sniffed. An earthy aroma filled her nose, like the scent of digging through a dirt pile. Even a protein bar would have appealed more.

Who knew when she'd get another opportunity to replenish calories? She held her breath and chomped a mouthful, chewing and swallowing before gulping in air. The bread's sweet tang offset the slab of disgust in the middle. Four bites later and she no longer had to worry about the taste, but it balled in her gut like she'd eaten a weight. She gulped down the last of the water. Would it help the sandwich dissolve?

What about Reeves and her father? Had they been served the same garbage? If they hadn't complained, perhaps they'd gotten nothing at all. Tears sprang to her eyes, and she gritted her teeth. Crying wouldn't help anyone. She needed a plan.

* * *

A hand covered Lexi's mouth in the dark, jolting her awake.

"Shh." A guard, much smaller than the others, stood silhouetted in the light from the hallway. "It's me."

The voice, familiar but out of place, whispered, "Stay put." With a swift step backward, the intruder hit the button on the outside wall that activated the cell's interior lights. After a few blinks to adjust to the brightness, Lexi could see her visitor was a woman. Her back to Lexi, the tiny guard looked left, then right down the hallway before easing the door shut and turning.

Lexi's heart leaped. *"Rumi. But how?"*

Rumi shushed her again, rushed to her side, and hugged Lexi. "I've been so worried about you. We all have."

Her body heat ebbed into Lexi, easing the tension and reminding her people still cared about her. Lexi grabbed her friend tighter. "I can't believe you're here." She pushed Rumi to arm's length and swiped at a stray tear. "How'd you get in?"

Her grin widening, Rumi darted to the door and listened. "Zane helped me."

A chill crawled down Lexi's spine. "No. You can't trust him. He works for Tempest."

"Shh…keep your voice down." Rumi returned to the bedside. "I went to his apartment, and he confessed everything. Said he didn't have a choice. They kidnapped his wife and baby. But he realizes he made the wrong decision. You understand that, don't you?"

Lexi shook her head. How could Rumi fall for her brother's treachery again? "Don't you get it? That's why we can't trust him."

"Look, I get it, but my brother isn't lying. I know him too well." She scowled, sat on the bed, and patted for Lexi to join her. "Yes, I fell for his fib too, but I wasn't looking for a lie back then. I was this time, and I believe him." When Lexi crossed her arms over her chest, Rumi put up a hand in protest. "Besides… we know where his family is, and a team is getting them out. By tomorrow morning, his family will be in Solitude, waiting for him."

Lexi still didn't trust the guy. But, if her mother approved the rescue, she'd let the issue pass—for now. "So, what are you doing here? What's the plan?"

Rumi's satisfied nod swished her ebony hair. "They're moving you, Reeves, and Gunner to a camp on the outskirts of town. They don't want word getting out that you're all prisoners, so moving you to a more remote area where you'll be 'safe' is a better bet."

"Better to be moved farther out than in front of a firing squad."

"We couldn't agree more. Your mom is bragging about your move to everyone she sees." A shadow lingered beneath Rumi's eyes, the faint smudge of exhaustion offset by eyes atwinkle. She was back in the game. "Says you're a born strategist."

With a gesture toward her cell door, Lexi smirked. "Yes. It's obvious I've outsmarted the Imperium."

"You're still alive, and that's more than anyone expected when you didn't rendezvous with the rest of the teams." Footsteps in the hallway paced toward them, and Rumi held a finger to her lips until they'd moved past the door and their echo faded down the hall. "We're going to get you all out during transport tomorrow, but this time, Zane is *our* secret weapon, not theirs."

The lump of alleged food Lexi'd eaten threatened to come back up. Their plan was too risky. What if even more people ended up stuck here—because of her? "Won't they expect the rebels to try again? Mom must know that."

"Of course she thought about the possibility. Thrym and Fletcher went toe to toe, arguing over the whole thing. If Ms. Becky hadn't stepped in, your mother would've had to." Rumi shrugged. "Honestly wish she'd let them be. Fletcher would've won."

They were getting off topic. "What do you need me to do?"

"Be prepared for anything, but most of all, help me keep your dad safe. He didn't look good on the vis feed, and I couldn't risk an attempt to get into the men's side of the prison to warn him." Her face fell, worry lines forming around her eyes. "How did he sound when you talked to him?"

In their brief ride to the courthouse, he'd leaned into her and told her he loved her. But then he'd looked so beaten down during her "testimony." His eyes drooped—someone who'd given up on any chance of freedom. Rumi didn't need to hear that. "He'll be fine once we get him out. Get him some decent food, rest, and fresh air. He'll perk up." She cringed. Sweet seedlings, she'd described a plant that needed repotting or fresh water in the aquaponics system instead of a human on the edge of collapse.

Rumi frowned. "I need to get going before the guy we paid off to let me in gets greedy or changes his mind." She embraced Lexi, squeezing the air out of her lungs, then released her. "The next time I see you, we'll all be together again. A real family, just like before."

The words hitched in Lexi's chest, leaving her speechless as Rumi exited the room and the heavy doors locked in place once again. The room went dark, and so did Lexi's thoughts. *A real family?* In retrospect, she realized her parents never agreed on anything because of her mother's secret ambitions to take down the Imperium. Her father's desire to move up in power within the elite had to have rubbed her mother's emotions raw. Oil and water—never capable of blending.

Since her mother's decision to play dead, her father had every right to request another bride to continue his climb in rank. It hadn't been his or Rumi's fault that the Imperium system assigned someone his daughter's age. When Lexi met

Rumi, Lexi hated her father and his new wife. Would she have treated the interloper any differently back then if she'd known what her mother had done?

How could they be a family now? Who would be her father's wife in Solitude? The entire situation was too weird and twisted.

Her thoughts shifted to Reeves, to their time cuddled close on a cot. Warmth shot through her. She closed her eyes, picturing him beside her, embracing her. His lips would be soft at first, drawing her in, soothing her frazzled nerves. After languid minutes of indulgence, his kisses would grow more demanding. Tingles ran up her spine, every nerve aching. She turned in his direction, and her elbow smacked against the unforgiving cinder block, yanking her out of her reverie.

The need for him buzzed through her. Did he feel it too wherever he lay tonight? This plan—it *had* to work. She'd move the earth itself to free them all. When that happened, she'd never put him at risk again. Ever.

Chapter 17

The lock's sharp click gave too little warning before the overhead lights blazed. Lexi's heart drummed a frantic rhythm, and her sleep-deprived brain struggled to keep up. A guard Fletcher's size slid the door open, raising her hopes Rumi had brought more muscle along, but his glower didn't belong to Ms. Becky's sidekick.

"Out of bed and face the wall."

Rough hands yanked her arms against her spine and zip ties cut into her wrists again. *So much for parading me in front of the vis screens.* Not a single camera would memorialize this day, which was just as well. If they were going to get out of this mess, a distinct lack of attention would help.

His fingers clamped around one arm, and he hustled her toward the open door. "Move."

Another Goliath led the way down the hall and into an elevator. Once inside, they flanked Lexi as if itching to tackle her at the slightest resistance.

Where were the rebel rescuers? Who would she see? When?

Nerves left her jumpy like she drank caffeine all night instead of going thirsty.

Water. Her parched tongue stuck to the roof of her pasty

mouth. Still, she croaked out the words, "Where are you taking me?"

Her stomach dropped when the elevator bounced, and the doors opened. Instead of answering her, one of them shoved her forward. "Out."

Their vocabularies weren't nearly as big as their hands. Probably not the time to get snarky, though. Once again, the smaller one moved in front of her and led the way to a loading dock in a Lexi parade. A security van waited, its doors flung open to swallow her.

Six uniformed and heavily armed Freedom Force members spread out and focused on the street ahead.

Too many. They must suspect.

The rising sun's rays tinted the skyline orange. If only she stood on those distant hills, Reeves by her side, his arms cocooning her while they watched the world awaken.

Instead, another hand to her back pushed her into the vehicle's dark interior.

Her heart skittered. Two prisoners sat inside, their hands shackled to the ceiling. They turned to see the newcomer, and she sucked in a breath—her father and Reeves.

Reeves must have washed the makeup off his face, or perhaps it had worn away. Either way, his bruises had mottled into shades of green and purple. The healing had begun, and she hoped no permanent damage would haunt him.

Two long benches hugged either side of the van's interior. She slid onto the bench beside Reeves, capturing his lips with her own in an awkward kiss before anyone could prevent it.

"Give it a rest, you two." The whispered words came across as more of a warning than a threat.

Mom. Adrenaline pumped through Lexi. The game pieces

slid into place, ready for the next roll of the dice.

"Hands." Her mother barked the command like the other guards. She winked at Lexi but shackled her next to Reeves.

Goliath joined them, and the van sank lower as he plopped onto the bench beside her father. His head mere inches from the low ceiling.

His eyes narrowed into slits as he took in Mom. "I don't recall working with you before. Who do you report to?"

Lexi's heart stuttered. Mom was no match for this guy, and with the rest of them chained to the van, they wouldn't be much help.

Her mother tipped her chin. "Been stuck in the Favela for years. Now that they've cleaned most of it out, I've been reassigned… twice already."

"Humph." He pointed at her uniform's breast pocket. "We don't wear that insignia on this duty round. You need to pay attention to the dress requirements."

"Cleaners mixed 'em up."

If the guy could hear Lexi's heart pounding, he'd know his day was about to go sideways. Instead, he glared at the man standing behind the van. "What're you waiting for? Close it up and let's get a move on."

The doors slammed, and the engine rumbled to life. Lexi swayed with the movement, first into Reeves, and then back against her mother. If only she could ask a few of the million questions zooming in her brain.

When would the rebels make their move? What did she need to do? Even if Rumi'd told her more, successful strategies remained flexible. Maybe Rumi hadn't known the full plan herself.

The van bounced, sending them inches into the air and then

back down hard.

Her father moaned, and Lexi saw him with fresh eyes. He'd lost so much weight—his wrists were those of a skin-clad skeleton. Dark smudges underlined his eyes, and his cheekbones stuck out in sharp points. Had they been starving him this entire time? Or had he come down with something? His pale cheeks belied any fever, but his lips had a gray tint.

A half hour into their ride, a jolt rocked them, and the massive guard's head smacked against the low ceiling. He cursed, his face twisting.

Leaning forward, he pounded his fist against the divider separating them from the driver's cabin. "Hey, watch where you're going." His voice echoed in the cramped space, and his proximity made Lexi's skin crawl.

When he thudded back onto the bench, the van swayed and dipped on his side. Her father moaned again. His eyes rolled back in his head, and he slumped backward.

"Dad!" Lexi lunged to help, but the manacles bit into her wrists, holding her back. "Mom, help him!"

Everyone froze at her fatal blunder.

Then chaos exploded.

Her mother reached for her gun, but the big guy beat her by a fraction. "Don't move!" He leveled his pistol on Mom.

Lexi kicked as far as her restraints permitted at the same moment he squeezed the trigger. Her toe connected with the barrel.

Several deafening rounds sent bullets whizzing past her side and punched holes in the compartment's walls.

Reeves jolted into action, his longer legs striking the guard's shin before Mom crashed the butt end of her rifle into the guy's temple.

The van weaved, throwing them against the walls while the big guy crumpled to the floor.

Gravity yanked Lexi sideways as if the van stood on two wheels before smashing down on the road, hard.

The vehicle swerved left, then right, tires squealing. What was the driver trying to do?

Moisture splashed Lexi's cheeks as the maneuvers tossed them around like rag dolls stuck in a washer's spin cycle. Her father dangled, unconscious, flecks of red spattering his clothing.

Her frantic gaze searched him for wounds. Had a bullet hit him?

Then something crashed into the driver's side. The van's outer shell crumpled, and it toppled onto its side.

Metal ground across concrete, and the sound scraped her nerves. Her body collided with Reeves, and her shoulders wrenched with the pull of the manacles.

Silence filled the compartment while Lexi cleared the ringing in her head. She hung suspended by her arms, every muscle in her body ablaze. Everyone else lay crumpled in a heap.

Reeves's manacles had broken with the last hit, and he scrambled to his feet. Blood slithered down his cheek. "Are you okay?"

She shook off the brain fog and rattled on her shackles—still stuck. "I'm fine. Find a key."

A moan drew her attention. Her mother wobbled to a sitting position where she'd landed, splayed across the unconscious guard's chest. She heaved his muscled arm off her leg and yelped. A baseball-sized spot of blood on her pant leg doubled in diameter within seconds.

The growing red puddle sent Lexi's already pounding heart into triple time. "Reeves, help Mom!"

Reeves rushed to kneel at her mother's side. He ripped open the soaked pant leg to a pulsing, bright-red bullet hole. He clamped a hand over the flow, causing a sharp intake of air from her mother, followed by a groan.

Mom's eyes squeezed shut, then opened. She grimaced. "We can't sit here. Need to move."

Reeves nodded. "Can you keep pressure on this?"

Already holding the back of her calf, Mom bent forward and clasped her hand over the front when Reeves pulled away.

Macabre red handprints stained Reeves's shirt after he swiped his palms clean. "I need to find something to tie it off."

He removed the unconscious guard's belt and used it as a tourniquet to slow the bleeding.

Lexi raced her gaze over the compartment interior. Her father hadn't moved since the crash. Tears welled in her eyes. His pale face and unmoving body lay in a skewed heap. Was he…?

She kicked her feet, swinging back and forth. She needed to get loose.

Metal grated at the back of the van. Reeves scrambled for the guard's sidearm and aimed at the face that appeared in the half-open door. Rumi and Reeves faced off—barrel to barrel.

Rumi's eyes widened. She lowered her weapon and rushed into the van. "Gotta go—" A heart-wrenching wail screeched out of her. "Gunner!" She scrambled over the guard, knocking Reeves into Lexi's mother, and hugged her husband's head to her chest. Tears poured down her cheeks. "No."

She placed two fingers on his neck, then whispered, "He's

alive."

Relief shuddered through Lexi. "Find the key to our manacles."

Mom pointed with her chin, both hands still clamped to her leg. "It's here. In my pocket."

Reeves extracted the ring and rushed to Lexi.

Free, she froze, uncertain which parent to focus on first. She couldn't do much for her father, but her mother… "I'll be right back."

She rushed out the back and almost tripped over the door that now served as a ramp.

Outside, Fletcher and Thrym circled the van like hawks guarding their nest, weapons ready. Fletcher acknowledged her. "What's taking? We're going to have visitors soon."

A bruise already bloomed on his face. One of the rebels' two UTVs waited beside the road, its reinforced front end lopsided from the impact.

"I need a medical kit."

Thrym headed toward her, a new limp in his gait. "In the back."

They retrieved the supplies out of the UTV, and Lexi scrambled into the van. Thrym close at her heels, despite his injury.

Reeves and Rumi passed her, carrying her father out. His chalk-white face bobbed with the rhythm of their steps. Too white. *What if we're too late? My fault.*

Lexi nudged the unconscious guard. "Thrym, can you get him out of the way?"

While he muscled the guy out by a foot, she dashed inside. Her mother's complexion had grayed to the shade of their medical tent's sheets.

Lexi kneeled in front of her, ripped open the red bag, and dumped the contents. One container labeled RapidClot stood out. She tore it open, white gauze popping up. She'd seen this in training. Its chemicals slowed bleeding. "I've got what you need, Mom. Let me see the wound."

Mom stared at her, eyes unfocused. "It doesn't hurt much." Blood oozed from under her hands and down her calf, the expanding pool too large to contemplate.

Lexi pushed her mother's hands away and shoved a wad of the cloth down hard, ignoring the agonized scream, then packed the exit wound. She wrapped the long tail around and around until she ran out. The bandage turned red, but the flow ended there. "The bleeding's stopped. We'll get you to the doctor."

Her mother shrugged. "Did you know I wanted you to have a sis… sister? Or a bro…" Mom's eyes rolled back in her head.

"Reeves!" Lexi screamed. "Fletcher!"

Both men lunged to her side.

"I stopped the bleed, but she just keeled over."

Fletcher took in the spilled medical kit. "There should be an IV bag. She needs fluids."

She found what they needed, but Fletcher stole the needle packet from her trembling hands. "I'll do it."

He inserted the lifeline into Mom's arm and connected the bag to it. Once he secured the IV with tape, he positioned himself behind her shoulders. "Time to get out of here."

Thrym nudged Lexi aside and grabbed hold of Mom's thighs in time with Reeves lifting under her arms. They trundled her out and aided her in the undamaged UTV.

Lexi climbed in beside her and then caught Rumi's gaze where the girl sat by Dad in the other vehicle.

Thrym pointed east. "We gotta go."

Distant specks, looked like a flock of birds, headed their way. But birds only lived in zoos.

Lexi's blood ran cold. *Drones.*

Reeves joined Fletcher in the front, and both vehicles took off, racing away from their pursuers.

In the other vehicle, Rumi held Dad's head in her lap, trying to protect him from the jolts as they left the paved road and rumbled back to camp.

Lexi warmed Mom's icy hand in her own. As frustrated as she'd been with her mother, she never wanted to see her like this. Her mother's gray appearance left her nauseous. "Hold on, Mom. We're going home."

But what lay between them and their destination?

Chapter 18

Lexi brushed a damp strand of hair from her mother's pallid face. Her fingers trembled as she fought to steady her breathing. The ache in her chest threatened to crush her. She'd already grieved her mother once—not so long ago—and the thought of losing her again... "Hold on, Mom." Her voice cracked. "We're almost there. The camp's just ahead. I can see it."

She'd endured the brutal, seemingly never-ending ride with her mother drifting in and out of consciousness the entire way. Mom opened her eyes and ran her tongue over her dirt-covered lips. "Drink."

The canteen lay just out of sight, but Lexi knew better than to share its contents. Advanced first aid in school taught her that much. If the doctor had to sedate Mom, they wouldn't want her stomach full of fluids she could aspirate. "Just a little longer." She'd have killed for a sip the night before, and here she sat, denying Mom the relief she craved

Grime crusted every crevice on Lexi's body and, though she'd tried to protect her mother from the billowing crud, the dirt coated her. The two UTVs drove side by side to avoid the vehicle behind eating the dust of the lead, but some areas through wrecked towns didn't permit the luxury. But at least they'd outrun the drones.

The gate swung wide when the guards recognized them. Without slowing, both vehicles drove straight to the medical tent. At the entrance, Fletcher bolted from the driver's seat and sprinted into the tent, Reeves hot on his heels.

She eased herself behind her mother's shoulders to sit her up. Why hadn't one of them stayed to help? "We made it, Mom. The docs will fix that leg before you know it."

Reeves darted back out of the tent. Beside him, a muscled guy in scrubs carried a folded field stretcher. Lexi's heart cramped at the concern in Reeves's eyes as he helped ease Mom onto it.

The medical professionals took over once they'd gotten Lexi's parents in the tent. Doctors shouted orders to nurses, and nurses to aids. Technicians swirled, making her dizzy. Once they'd moved both patients into separate areas, curtains secluded them from each other and their rescuers.

Lexi, Reeves, and Rumi huddled together by the cordoned-off rooms. A shiver snaked down Lexi's spine at the heartrending sounds coming from her mother contrasting with the lack of her father's voice in the opposite room. But which bothered her more—her mother's agonized screams on the left or her father's silence on the right? Both set her teeth on edge.

An arm wound around her middle, and Reeves snugged her in tight. "Let them work. We'll clean up and come back when they can have visitors."

She twisted her shirt hem. "What if they need me?"

Rumi grimaced. "He looked so fragile."

Gentle fingers brushed Lexi's shoulder. Ms. Becky appeared at Lexi's side. "I'll stay and find you if necessary. I'll pray for them as well."

Would it matter if Ms. Becky spoke to her invisible deity? Lexi wished she could believe as easily as her friend. Once this was over, she'd learn more about Ms. Becky's beliefs. Even ask Mom and Nana about it. What had so thoroughly separated them all? It had to be big to accomplish so much.

Reeves tugged Lexi toward the exit while Rumi straggled behind, turning to look back every few yards.

The tent felt foreign when Lexi entered. A musty odor clogged her nostrils. If she didn't know better, she'd think no one had lived in it for years. Reeves closed the flap and gathered her into his arms, his breath warm on the top of her head. His brawny arms, like a cocoon of love, blocked out every bad thought and welcomed her home.

She'd missed this feeling the most, being his. "I'm so sorry and thankful at the same time. Sorry I got you captured, yet thankful you helped me save Dad."

He eased back to look her in the eye. "The worst part was worrying they might hurt you." He winked. "But you're one skilled and crafty negotiator. I'm so proud of you."

Her fingertips brushed his bruised cheek. If only she could take his pain on herself. "I wish I could've protected you better."

A tear tickled her face as it slid toward her chin. Why did she have to leak like a faucet now of all times?

His lips curved into a lopsided grin, and his thumb wiped the drop away. "Don't cry. We won." He led her deeper into the tent. A washbasin waited on the table. He soaked a cloth into it, then wrung it out. "And you, Mrs. Scheffer, are a mess."

Delicate swipes belied the strength of his hands. He ran the cool cloth over her forehead. He took extra care when sliding the fabric over her lips, sending a luscious shiver down her spine. When he dipped his mouth to hers, she put a finger up, then stole the cloth. She rinsed the rag and reveled in the brush of his hands on her hips while she wrung it out.

She returned the favor, careful to avoid too much pressure on his bruises. His hands explored her back, drawing her closer until she tossed the cloth over her shoulder and claimed his lips.

Her desire to sleep in Reeves's arms tugged at her, but rest would never come until she knew her parents would recover. They finished cleaning up as best they could with the washcloth, put on fresh clothes, and got a meal before heading back to the medical tent.

She hadn't seen no-show Ethan around since they'd gotten back, but no way would she ask *Reeves* about *Ethan*. Was he their mole?

She shook the thought away. Unable to concentrate on anything besides her parents, she managed to eat, but even her favorite, fresh-picked green beans, lacked flavor. What would they find when they returned?

Reeves's hand on the small of her back grounded her as they moved past the rooms where the medical team had worked on her parents.

Ahead, Ms. Becky waved them forward, her smile reassuring. "Down here."

The tension building in Lexi's gut eased as she passed a curtained-off area and found her mother lying in bed, a thick bandage covering a good portion of her lower leg.

Arms crossed over her chest, Mom frowned when she saw Lexi. "Go get me a set of crutches."

Ms. Becky walked around Lexi and set a glass of water

on the bedside table. "Now, Tora, we talked about this. The doctor said you should wait until tomorrow."

From the curtain's other side, Rumi's voice sounded. "Let me get that for you, love?"

Her mother jabbed a finger toward the curtain. "If I have to listen to *that* one minute longer, the doctor will deal with more serious injuries than a bullet."

The curtain jiggled, and Rumi growled. "Someone, find her crutches, or *I will.*"

Reeves tugged the curtain open, revealing a clean Rumi holding her husband's hand in one of hers while smoothing his hair back with the other. Dad looked like a changed man. Though still gaunt, he sat up in the bed, his face no longer pallid.

Dr. Ichtacka's blue concoction dripped from an IV hooked into Dad's arm.

A lump formed in Lexi's throat—the doctor's experiments. "Dad. How are you?"

Rumi beamed. "Doesn't he look great?"

Dad patted Rumi's hand. His wary glance found the dividing curtain. "Would you mind seeing if you could snag me a protein bar? I'm getting hungrier by the minute here."

She sprang up and kissed his forehead. "I'll get you something better, even if I have to bribe the cook. Back as soon as I can."

When Rumi passed, Mom murmured something less-than-complimentary under her breath.

Ignoring it, Lexi opened the partitioning curtain the rest of the way. "You two look loads better than the last time I saw you."

A sneer twisted Mom's face. "I told the doctor not to give

him that stuff, but your father's *new* wife wouldn't hear of it. She insisted he needed it."

Dad glared at Mom. "And if you'd been honest with me from the beginning, I might never have required the good doctor's treatments in the first place. For that matter, I wouldn't even have a second wife." When Mom turned away from him, he jerked up his chin. "Rumi was only doing what she thought was best."

Their fight transported Lexi back to her childhood where they disagreed on every topic. Her arms hung limp at her sides, helplessness taking over as if she were ten years old again and powerless to stop their arguments. She'd grown up. Why hadn't they?

Ms. Becky strode between them, patting Lexi on the shoulder as she passed. Ms. Becky reached over and squeezed shut the valve between the blue IV bag and Dad's arm. "You've had enough of this. The nurse'll come disconnect it." She then nodded to Mom. "And I'll find a wheelchair for you. Time for a spin and some fresh air."

The knot in Lexi's stomach eased as Ms. Becky yanked the curtain closed, giving each patient privacy once again. Reeves must have noticed Lexi's indecision as to which side of the curtain to stand on because he placed an arm around her waist. "We should let your parents rest."

She loved her husband. This might have been his best rescue yet. "Yes. We should go." After a kiss on her father's cheek, she popped over to the other side and kissed her mother's as well. "Take it easy, Mom."

When they emerged from the tent, the air smelled like freedom, and she grasped Reeves's hand. "Thank you. Again."

He gave her a gentle squeeze in response. "Anything for you, love."

* * *

Within the hour, Lexi and Reeves joined Fletcher, Thrym, and the rest of the leadership in the planning room. Ms. Becky rolled Mom in with a wheelchair, her bandaged leg elevated. Once she'd applied the brake on the chair, Ms. Becky leaned in. "Can I get you anything else, Tora?"

The words of endearment seemed so foreign, directed from the other woman to Mom. Ms. Becky couldn't help herself, could she? Her caring gene kicked in and overrode any past disagreements.

"No." Mom attempted a smile, but it came across more as a grimace. "Thank you."

Lexi captured her lips between her teeth to keep a straight face. Mom needed to work on her gratitude.

Thrym stepped up to Mom. "Good to see you back in the mix, ma'am. For a minute, I feared I might be stuck leading this ragtag bunch of wannabe soldiers."

Mom cleared her throat, her nod terse. "We've run out of time. Tempest has shown her true colors, and we're in the strongest position we've been in yet. We've recruited and trained enough soldiers to take over any remaining resistance after our initial strike."

She rolled up to the table, the Imperium's layout displayed on its top. She jabbed a finger at the Administration tower. "This is our target." With a swipe of her hand, the image changed to the building's schematics. "Once the bomb is ready, we place it near the heart of the building where the servers control their military resources, administration files, and most importantly, Tempest's studio feeds." Her finger traced a path from the server room and stopped at the sizeable council chamber. "The initial explosion will take the chamber out. Then the air ducts will feed the radioactivity throughout the building. If we time it right, Tempest's entire council goes down with her."

Ms. Becky uttered the only word rattling around in Lexi's mind. "No..."

Mom's raised hand cut her off. "It's the only way. We've embarrassed Tempest and shown her up in front of the council. Word of Lexi's escape, with Reeves and her father, will spread uncontrolled." She looked at Thrym, who nodded before she continued. "Tempest's back is up against the wall, and she has to prove she's still in control. We must strike before she does."

Lexi's heart pounded out of control. "How..." Her voice stalled in her throat. "How does killing everyone in that building make us any better than her?"

Mom's eyes softened as she took in Lexi, but then hardened again. "We're wiping the slate clean. Then we can build it new without the influence of the old."

* * *

Lexi huddled outside their tent, unable to sleep, her gaze on the stars. They twinkled above her, unchanged from the first time she'd seen them as a child. Back then, she'd thought they were fairies. She'd whispered her wishes to them and hoped for the day when she could work in the greenhouses and grow plants to feed the Favela's hungry.

Even on their special picnic, the stars had been magical. Now they looked cold and uncaring. The entire world overflowed with hatred—the same loathing that started the Great War and scorched the earth. So little had survived the last time. It wouldn't turn out any better if it happened again. There had to be another way.

She wanted Tempest defeated as much as Mom did, but not if it meant forfeiting her humanity. What alternative could she push?

Chapter 19

After her fitful night, Lexi's eyes burned from too little sleep. The sun glowed in the east, ready to bring a new day. Reeves's predawn goodbye kiss lingered on her lips. Her brain whirled with her mother's plan to win the war. Lexi couldn't be a part of it. Polluting one of the few habitable buildings with radioactivity—insanity.

Outside, the cool air clung to her skin like she'd walked through a cloud. Dew sparkled from every surface. She needed to find Ms. Becky before the day started. The moment had arrived to embrace Ms. Becky's lifesaving mission.

At least she didn't have to worry about running into Ethan alone in the semidarkness. Discreet questions revealed he'd vanished. Had he managed to make it back to the Imperium on foot, or had someone helped him?

"Don't forget—you dragged Reeves along for the ride, but I sought the rebels out myself... because I wanted to find you."

The liar. Not that she cared. She'd never have chosen Ethan. She had Reeves.

While most of the camp's residents slept later, Reeves would be in the training area getting in his morning exercises with the rest of the planning committee. They'd wrap that up, shower, breakfast, and return to her mother's briefing before others even crawled out of their cots.

One resident would also be wide awake and starting her day—Ms. Becky. Lexi swore that woman could live on five minutes of shut-eye a night when someone needed tending. In order to catch her, Lexi needed to get moving.

At Ms. Becky's tent, Lexi raised her hand to knock but froze at a woman's angry whisper. "What am I supposed to do with you? I should turn you in and let Tora deal with you."

Ms. Becky angry? Who could disturb her? The woman had nerves of steel and a never-ending well of patience. After looking both ways, Lexi leaned closer, curiosity overriding etiquette.

"You'd never do that, and you know it." Fletcher's voice. "I've been telling you for years we must join the fight. I can't continue to wrestle people out of the Imperium's clutches one by one. That's not the solution."

Guilt over spying raised a cold prickle on Lexi's skin. This argument ran deeper than a simple tactical disagreement. She scooted around the side with soft footsteps.

A huff inside. Ms. Becky, for sure. "So you serve as Tempest's mole? What could you hope to gain with that strategy?"

Chills ran through Lexi's body. *Fletcher? A traitor?*

He'd been in so many planning meetings, had so much information on the rebellion. If he'd been informing on them, why hadn't Tempest wiped out the camp?

"I'd hoped you'd see reason." His menacing tone chilled her. "I only told that woman enough to get the little raid started. Figured it would convince you to join forces with Tora. Use your resources to end the Imperium instead of being a part of this crazy system."

"How can I trust you now? How can any of us?" Ms. Becky groaned. "For all I know, you've already got plans to bring the Freedom Force here and tear everything down."

Lexi clamped a hand over her mouth to squeeze back the words that wanted to pour out in Ms. Becky's defense. Would she turn Fletcher in? Or had they been together too long?

Silence inside the tent set Lexi's teeth on edge. Why wasn't he responding?

When he spoke again, his words were so quiet she had to press her ear to the tent canvas to hear.

"I've done everything you've asked of me for five years. *Five. Years.*" He sighed. "And where has that gotten us? Nothing has changed, and neither of us is getting any younger. At least Tora wants to end it. You only want to placate Tempest. I want to stop her."

A sniffle came from Ms. Becky, and Lexi ached to comfort her. "You…" The older woman's voice cracked. "You need to turn yourself in. I can't…"

Her words hung in the air, sending Lexi's heart rate stampeding.

"I never gave Tempest enough to do any *real* harm." Desperation filled Fletcher's voice. "Even though I may disagree with you, I'd never let that woman hurt you."

"No. You didn't let her hurt me. You did that all on your own."

The urge to run in and hug Ms. Becky nudged Lexi on, but she stayed frozen to the spot. What if Ms. Becky couldn't tell Mom about Fletcher?

Soft steps moved inside the tent, and the outside flap swished. Lexi lurched into the shadows as Fletcher stormed out. His pace quick and decisive, he headed toward the big house.

Quiet sobs inside intensified the ache in Lexi's heart. She couldn't leave Ms. Becky alone.

Lexi knocked on the tent post. "Ms. Becky? Can I come in?"

Sniffles, then a nose blow, and a throat clearing came before Ms. Becky spoke. "Of course, dear. I'm awake."

Red eyes and soggy cheeks outweighed Ms. Becky's brave smile attempt.

The dear lady just lost her best friend. Lexi walked across the room and hugged her. Should she feign ignorance? Better to get it over with. "What are you going to do about Fletcher?"

Ms. Becky frowned and backed away as if burned. "What do you mean?"

"I didn't mean to eavesdrop." The lie tasted bitter. "But I overheard his confession. What are you going to do about it?"

Ms. Becky's face fell, and fresh tears sheened her eyes. "Fletcher's like a brother. He meant well. Perhaps if I'd listened to him more or explained my position better…" She swiped a sleeve across her cheek. "It's my fault, really."

Only a person with Ms. Becky's gentle heart could flip someone else's wrong and take the blame on herself. "No, ma'am. It's not."

The need to comfort a friend battled against the need to convince her to turn Fletcher in. If the guy leaked information to the Imperium to get his own way within the rebellion, who knew how far he'd take the deception? Platoons of Freedom Force could be heading in their direction now.

Yet, Ms. Becky's pain gave Lexi pause. She hated herself for sharpening her agony. "If you won't go to my mother, you're forcing me to." She touched Ms. Becky's shoulder. "Please."

Silence stretched between them. Ms. Becky kept her head bowed and wrung her hands, the war in her mind between loyalties obvious. Lexi squeezed the older woman's shoulder, a reminder that a decision had to be made.

When Ms. Becky looked up, the sorrow in her eyes stabbed pain through Lexi's heart. Ms. Becky nodded. "Let's go talk to your mom."

Dread washed through Lexi. Her feet clunked like lead weights, pulling her into the earth as they trudged toward the main house. Mom would be furious, but would she turn that anger toward the man who betrayed them or take it out on the messenger? Ms. Becky's suffering didn't need to be deepened.

A dust storm sped away from the gate as they reached the front of the compound. Lexi hadn't heard of any missions this morning. Unease skittered down her spine.

On the farmhouse stairs, Ms. Becky applied pressure to Lexi's arm as if she'd grown feeble and needed support. In the command center, Mom, using crutches today, stood with Reeves, Thrym, and other leaders. She pointed out various areas on a schematic of the Imperium's administration building.

Ms. Becky cleared her throat. "Tora, we need to talk."

"Just who I needed to see." Mom waved them both over to join the group. "I didn't realize you'd planned a mission for Fletcher and his team. We could have coordinated."

For a moment, Ms. Becky's step wavered. Then she squared her shoulders and raised her chin. "He's left us—and taken everyone loyal to him."

Now Mom's head jerked up. "What are you talking about?"

Ms. Becky's sucked in a deep breath. "He meant well. I know he did." She held out her hands, a convict pleading mercy. "He said he couldn't stay out of the fight. Told me I needed to get on board."

"What are you telling me, Becky?" Mom advanced on her friend, her expression hardening.

Ms. Becky wobbled backward. "I'm certain he supports the rebellion and wouldn't do anything to harm us."

Eyes flashing, Mom closed the gap between them. "What. Exactly. Has he done?"

Sobs racked Ms. Becky's shoulders. "He was the one who informed on us and knew the attack was coming. Helped them connect with our recruiters."

With a growl, Mom turned her back on Ms. Becky. "Get her out of here. Make sure she doesn't step foot inside this house again."

"No." Ms. Becky struggled to free herself from the men who grabbed her arms and towed her away. "Listen. He won't harm us. He made a mistake."

Mom whirled to face Ms. Becky. "A mistake? You call that a *mistake*? Good men died. He gave the Imperium an opening. They could have wiped us out."

"Don't you see? That's proof he didn't. He only gave them an opportunity to poke at us. His men made sure it went no further."

Lexi never imagined her mother's face could take on such a dark red.

Eyes bulging, Mom jabbed a finger at Ms. Becky. "And now he's taken vehicles and firepower, leaving us crippled. On top of that, we'll have to move camp." She waved at the men flanking Ms. Becky. "Get her out of here before I do something I'll regret."

They dragged her away while she cried and apologized.

While Mom moved on, returning to Thrym's side, Lexi ground her teeth. Her molars grated over forcing Ms. Becky to confess, then clenched down harder at what Fletcher'd done. Mom needed support. Lexi approached the circle of planners.

Mom stopped her with one palm in the air. "Before you take one more step, I need to know where your allegiance lies."

Lexi blinked, her thoughts muddled. "You don't trust me? I brought her here to confess as soon as I figured out what happened."

Her mother gave Lexi her no-nonsense glare. "It's no secret you've supported Ms. Becky's ideas, just like Fletcher claimed. Now it's time to choose. Either you're with me, or you're with *her*."

Every eye in the room settled on her, their stares skittering across her skin like ants. Her friendship with Ms. Becky placed her in the spotlight. If Lexi stuck close to her mother, perhaps she could influence the direction they took.

Across the room, Reeves, his face unreadable, waited for her response as much as the others. If only she could draw him aside, ask his advice.

Could she sway her mother in a less violent direction? Or would Mom pull Lexi deeper into a world of mayhem in the fight for freedom? If she walked away now, she'd never get another invitation to the table.

A sinking sensation settled in her gut. She could see the path forward, but it felt like giving in to everything she'd fought against since coming to the camp. The time to join her mother's side had come. "I'm with you, Mom."

Chapter 20

The absence of Fletcher and those loyal to him left too much elbow room as the remaining rebel leaders gathered to hear Mom's orders. Where her mother normally had two giant sentinels flanking her, now only Thrym stood to her right, her left unguarded.

Lexi struggled to concentrate, her mind drifted to Ms. Becky and the team who left the camp and where Ethan fit in. Mom better lay off. Ms. Becky shouldn't have to pay for Fletcher's treachery any more than Lexi and Reeves should pay for Ethan's.

Someone poked her ribs, and she received Reeves's wink before he refocused on the briefing. If only they could escape this mess for a while, just the two of them—hidden away where no one could find them. His fingers sought hers, brushing lightly against them before interlocking, his body position blocking their connection from view. The soft stroke of his thumb against her palm sent a ripple of pleasure through her. The intimacy of the gesture grew by the second, and her desire to respond, to pull him closer and claim a thousand kisses sent heat to her cheeks.

A crescendo of groans alerted Lexi she'd missed something

important. Best to focus on Mom instead of her husband.

Mom put one hand up, palm out. "I know. None of us want to have to pack up and move, but we have no choice."

More mumbles followed but at a subdued level.

"I want to believe, as I know many of you do, that Fletcher's team would never join the Imperium, but we can't be certain."

"I don't see how we can move all the civilians and equipment fast enough." One man gestured to the computers, vis screens, and drone equipment. "It took us years to bring it all here."

Thrym stepped forward. "You're right. We can't. This camp originally served as a hiding place. Sanctuary for those the Imperium earmarked for termination. We'll leave it the way we found it, serving as Solitude once more."

A shiver ran down Lexi's spine. She waited for someone to argue the point. When no one spoke up, she cleared her throat. "But who will protect them if the Imperium attacks? We can't leave them helpless. We can't abandon them."

Her mother's gaze settled on Lexi, the no-nonsense glare she'd seen so often since arriving at the rebel camp in full force. "As we all know, Ms. Becky has played on both sides of the fence her entire adult life. Her deals with Tempest were the basis on which Fletcher tried to manipulate her. She'll be fine." Mom focused on the man who'd asked the question. "Any of the seniors who can find transportation after we've moved all military assets are welcome to join us."

Lexi's mouth went dry. What about Nana? She'd spent most of her time in the medical tents helping Ms. Becky with the infirm. Mom wouldn't leave Nana behind, would she? Tempted to ask in front of witnesses, Lexi opened her mouth, but Mom's next instructions slammed it shut.

"We're headed to a location only Thrym and I are aware

of. It's higher, mountainous terrain, so we'll use caves in addition to tents at the new camp. Box critical items. Leave anything unnecessary. We're traveling light." She paused until the mumbling quieted again. "Twenty-four hours, people. We move out this time tomorrow."

* * *

Why had Lexi stuffed her duffel so full? She pounced on it again. The clip engaged, capturing the contents from springing back out. Reeves broke down their cot. Their first bed. One of the few items from their "home" they could take with them. "Can you write our name on it or mark it somehow? I want to be certain no one else takes it. I've gotten used to cuddling in that one."

"Someday, we'll do more than cuddle." Reeves gave her an eyebrow waggle. He slid the cot into its travel bag, then pulled her into his arms. "If it means that much to you, I'll be sure it makes it into our new spot." He nuzzled her. "But with you by my side, any bed we end up with will be home."

His lips, warm and inviting, blazed a trail of kisses down her neck.

She snuggled in. "How much longer till we have to leave?"

He pressed a chaste kiss atop her head and chuckled. "Too soon."

She gazed around their temporary home. "Do you think we'll ever come back here?"

"I sure hope not." He hefted his backpack along with the cot bag onto his shoulder. "I'd like to sleep in a real bed after this is all over. One with thick pillows and air-conditioning."

"And private showers, trips to the greenhouse…" Their apartment back in the Reclamation tower beckoned, now more like a dream than a possibility. She could barely remember it. "But… do you really think we'll have that again?"

His gaze traced the tent's perimeter, then landed on her. "All that and more. I can feel it. We'll live the best life possible, and you're going to be stuck with me until we're both old and gray."

"That sounds like my kind of dream."

Reeves opened his backpack. "Yeah, a good dream, but here we are—fleeing again. I'd never have thought Fletcher was our mole." He jammed items in with more thrust than necessary. "I was sure it was Ethan—still can't believe that jerk made me like him so much so fast, then vanished right when you and I were counting on him. I'm sorry, Lex. I let him play me and failed you."

Her mouth dry, she swallowed to work up some saliva. She should confess Reeves wasn't the only one Ethan was playing, but she couldn't bring a word to her mouth.

A hand thumped on the outside of the tent. "Lexi? You here?"

Dad's voice. Shouldn't he be busy packing? "Come on in."

He strode in with confidence—a different man from the one they'd rescued. He'd somehow already filled out, his cheeks fuller, more rounded. His eyes sparkled like an excited child at his birthday party. "I see you two are ready. Very efficient."

Lexi shifted the backpack on her shoulder. "I figured you'd be helping."

He nodded. "Helped a bit, but wanted to run an idea past the two of you since I know you've both been in the leadership meetings. I'm hoping you might support my idea, you know, with your mother."

If he hadn't shared the idea with Mom, then he didn't figure she'd like it. Just like old times. Lexi acting the mediator, the grease between cogs to relieve friction.

Reeves beat her to the response. "What's your thought?"

Rubbing his hands together, her father grinned. "I'm sure Lexi explained to you what my job was in the Imperium?"

Reeves dropped the bag he'd been holding. "Something in security with the drones, right?"

"Yes." Dad beamed. "I performed several jobs, but my favorite was in security. One thing my daughter might not have understood is that I helped maintain the computer systems. Including the ones supporting the drones."

He worked in a variety of roles, filling in wherever needed. She'd never inquired as to the extent of it. "Mom wants to take out the computers with the bomb. That's why she stole the scientist. Did you want to help plan that?"

He brushed a hand through his graying hair. "Not exactly. My approach would be more along the lines of kidnapping rather than destroying."

Reeves's brows furrowed. "You want to steal the Imperium's computers? How could we pull that off? It's the most guarded area of the administration."

Dad's grin broadened, the glow in his eyes brighter. "We don't even need to go there. We can control them all from here." He paused.

Was he waiting for something? Lexi and Reeves continued to stare at him.

"There's a back door in the software. We used it for system testing and debugging… sort of the lazy way of gaining access without all the login procedures. If I hack in through the main security software, I can lock down everything from the air-conditioning to the water systems. They won't even be able to flush a toilet once I've encrypted it."

It sounded too easy. "But with you out of the picture, wouldn't they have changed their processes? Canceled your login?"

He shook his head. "Not necessarily. Network security has gotten lackadaisical over the years. With no foreign enemy and the rebels mostly concerned with kidnapping people the Imperium planned to retire anyway, there hasn't been a break-in attempt for years. When teens showed any inclinations toward hacking, they assigned them to systems design or programming." He crossed his arms. "Besides, maintenance left so many back doors, I'll bet not a single person knows them all."

Reeves rubbed his jaw, his day-old stubble raspy. "As long as you kept critical areas like the medical unit running, we could take over without firing a single shot." After a moment, he nodded. "Yeah, it could work."

A tingle shot through Lexi. This could be the solution they all wanted. Freedom without bloodshed. "Mom would have to go for it. We could force Tempest to relinquish control of the council and release any family members she's hidden away. Once they can vote their conscience, we should find a peaceful resolution."

"Um…" Reeves cleared his throat. "If you're bringing this idea to us instead of Tora, I'm assuming you think she'll reject it. Why would she?"

Valid point. Something wasn't quite right.

Dad tucked his hands into his pockets and ducked his head. A shrug rolled his shoulders. "Your mother and I have what I'll call a philosophical divide on tactics. I broached the subject with her. But she wants a visible, physical overthrow of power no Imperium citizen will forget. She craves validation of the struggle and sacrifices the rebels have suffered to free the masses." He blew out his breath. "Honestly, I think she likes to blow stuff up."

After the explosion her mother triggered when she faked her death, Lexi understood Dad's thought processes. Mom seemed to enjoy the show of power mass deaths provided. No wonder she'd never gotten along with Ms. Becky's kinder, gentler rebellion methods. But Mom would see reason if they forced it upon her. Maybe.

Lexi sucked in her breath and pushed out her words. "I have an idea—a way to put the plan out publicly." If Mom rejected it, she'd need to come up with convincing reasons to save face. "What if we proved to her how well it would work? Not just her, but Thrym and all the leaders? Then it might not be only her decision to make."

Dad's eyes narrowed. "Tell me more."

Reeves grinned, his chest swelling as he caught her in a side hug. "I have no idea where you're going with this, but from that look in your eye, it's going to be good."

Her heart fluttered. When he was at her side, she could accomplish anything. "Here's the plan...."

Chapter 21

Lexi's skin crawled, her teeth clenched. Feigning a casual demeanor had never been a skill she'd mastered, especially when unsettled. And this closed-in setting with its stale air and damp rock floor and walls, now crowded with desks and electronics, didn't offer a calming atmosphere.

In the front of the cave—their new command center—Mom and Thrym huddled behind the skinny scientist while he expounded on his weapon's design features. The brainiac only took a few days to assess what resources would be available at the old military base, cobble together the list of parts, and create the schematics required to build it. Lexi seethed over her mother's treatment of the scientist. She'd coerced him into haste, keeping him from his family until she got what she wanted.

An alarm brought Lexi back to her task. The drone she manned dipped too low to the ground. The shrill sound a reminder to stay focused. Dust storms had grounded the drones for days, but today the winds died down enough to run remote patrols of their new base.

Exhaustion from the move to the mountains threatened her mental acuity. Not to mention, she still had grit in unmentionable places. She missed the showers at their old camp, especially the occasions she'd gotten to use the ones in the house. Heaven… compared to this barren hellscape. Before the Great War, trees covered the mounds where her drone now flew. These days the view contained only boulders surrounded by rocks, all upon a giant hump of stone. At least the sun could power their batteries again, bringing back some semblance of civilization.

Her tearful farewell with Nana added more anxiety. Ms. Becky remained at the camp rather than follow the group across the difficult terrain. She'd refused to believe Fletcher would betray her and insisted they'd be safe. There, Ms. Becky could care for the elderly and infirm. When Nana decided to stay and help, Lexi tried to change her mind, but Nana stood her ground.

Another alarm brought Lexi's attention to the present, and she pulled up on the thumb controls, skimming the surface of the jutting rock it sped toward. A hand on her shoulder drew her focus from the video feed.

Reeves leaned close to her ear. "Don't smash that drone, or they'll never let you fly another one." He moved on, leaving her to focus.

He wasn't wrong. Drones provided critical early warning intel. The farther they moved from the Imperium, the less opportunity to steal replacements. Hers flew solo this morning, and she peeked at her watch, then returned her gaze to the screen. She needed to finish this flight.

Rocks covered the mountain, and few spots looked like they'd provide a soft landing. She couldn't lose this job. Setting her device in hover mode, she lowered it atop a flat rock. A look around verified no one saw.

She focused on her screen. Her view went black. Then an avatar appeared.

Gasps rose across the cave. Every eye focused on the various screens, all showing the same feed.

Her mother scowled. "What's going on, people?"

From the front, a shaky voice spoke up. "We've been hacked. Shutting down in ten."

Lexi schooled her face. On her vis like on everyone else's, the cartoonlike character strode to the upper left of the screen. Then words scrolled across it.

"THIS IS WHAT TRUE CONTROL LOOKS LIKE."

An Imperium map appeared, and red dots popped up one by one in various spots of critical infrastructure for water, sewage, production, security, and more she didn't recognize.

The voice from the front shouted again. "Going down in five."

Vis screens around them flashed red. Then the avatar strode to the other side and pointed at words that scrolled below him.

"YOU CAN SHUT ME OUT, BUT I WILL TAKE DOWN YOUR INFRASTRUCTURE IF YOU DO."

Mom's face mottled red. "Stop!"

A head popped up from behind a bank of computers. "Paused."

Mom ran a hand through her hair. "What damage can they do?"

Everyone scanned the cave, looking for the answer from someone else.

The guy in the front cleared his throat. "Nothing that I can think of, but if they're already in, they'll still be there when I reboot, unless I can find the access point."

Thrym growled and smacked a palm against a desk, rattling

the equipment on it. "If I get my hands on this guy, he's done for."

A strobe flashed across the screens. Then the avatar reappeared and waved to its audience.

"YOUR SYSTEMS WILL NOW RETURN TO FULL FUNCTIONALITY. THIS ENDS THE DEMONSTRATION OF THE POWER OF TECHNOLOGY."

All the screens returned to normal. Lexi's showed the feed from the drone she'd been commanding, a boulder filling the screen. She held her breath and flicked the control, relieved to see it rise again, undamaged.

The cave exploded in a flurry of shouts, her mother's the loudest. "I want to know how they got in, whether they're still connected, and how to block them—and I want it *now*."

Lexi sucked in a deep breath, stood, and faced her mother. "It was me."

Because of the commotion, no one seemed to have heard, so she moved to stand between her mother and Thrym. "Mom."

"Not now, Lexi." Her mother didn't even turn, intent on the screen in front of her.

Visions of her ten-year-old self resurfaced. Except back then, her father, not Mom, had shunted her off to the side. Would she ever be an adult in her parents' view?

She sucked in a breath and shouted above the din. *"It was me!"*

The words echoed against the cavern walls.

Everyone spun to her.

Mom's eyes widened. "You?"

Aphids! Perhaps the outburst hadn't been wise. Prickles stabbed at her skin like a thousand insects feasting at once, the heat rising in her face. "Kind of?" Her heart pounded with every gaze on her, burning through her skin. "Well, not just me. You could say it was a group effort."

When her mother's eyes narrowed, Lexi rushed on. "We needed to prove there's another way. One less violent. No one has to die for us to win this battle."

Thrym's face morphed from angry red to purple, as if he hadn't breathed since Lexi's announcement. He took a menacing step toward her, backing her into her desk. "So *you* took down our systems? What if the Freedom Force is out there right now, planning to take advantage of your little trick?"

Reeves appeared at her side, close enough she could feel his warmth. "Thought of that. Lexi did a perimeter check before we launched the bug."

Grumbling under his breath, Thrym glared at her mother. "I guess we know who 'we' are now."

Her father spoke up from the back, Rumi at his side, arms crossed. "I'm part of that group as well. Probably the one you should be angry with if you plan to blame anyone."

Why'd he have to bring Rumi? For a smart man, he lacked common sense. Mom already operated on a hair trigger and didn't need anything extra to set her off.

Time to pull Mom's attention back to the demonstration's importance. "It doesn't matter who did what. All that matters is we can seize control of the Imperium's systems as easily as we took control of the rebels.'"

Dad stepped forward. "We can lock down communications, utilities, weapons—everything—until they give in to our demands. Make Tempest confess to her control over the council. Free anyone she's holding to allow the council to vote their conscience."

Mom's head tipped sideways. "How much can we realistically control?"

Was that curiosity agleam in her eyes? Had she turned a corner?

He grinned. "The only way they could get any of their systems back online would be to disconnect the central hub, the mainframe, and override the code—if they can find it. But if they do that, it all goes down. Tempest wouldn't even be able to take a shower or flush her toilet. None of them could."

Pride in her husband apparent, Rumi added, "Gunner can hide the code so deep and in so many places it would take years to find it all. We'll have them by their technological throats."

The words were like gas on a fire.

Lexi butted in before her mother discounted the entire plan just to spite her rival. "This can work, Mom. Please. We have to try."

His face having returned to a normal color, Thrym pulled her mother to the side and mumbled. Mom's eyebrows rose, scrunched, then returned to their normal resting position. She nodded, and Thrym stood down. The hint of his smile gave Lexi a queasy sensation.

Dad and Rumi joined Lexi and Reeves in a huddle surrounded by Mom's leadership team. It didn't need to be an us-versus-them situation, but would Mom see it in any other framework?

Lexi held her breath, waiting.

Mom glanced at the screens once more before she spoke. "You've got twenty-four hours to prove you can gain full control. I'll consider it a success if you're able to reverse broadcast and send messages to the whole of the Imperium via the vis screens. And I want them to be without when it happens. No elevators, no drones, no jobs to go to because it's all shut down."

Dad clapped and grinned. "Let's get started."

Hours later, Lexi's vision blurred. She must be going cross-eyed. Her mother had a good point about their vulnerability during their little demonstration. As penance, Lexi kept busy with her drone, flying the edges of their camp over and over.

Reeves slid into a chair beside her. "You skipped your break. Why don't you take one now? I can fly this one for you."

"How's Dad doing? Is he making progress?"

"It's spectacular how fast he's moving. Said he won't even need the full day before he'll be ready." He rubbed a hand across her aching back, his touch reassuring. "Have you seen anything?"

"The usual. Another convoy to the old army base. They've been gone a while now." She set the drone to return mode for maintenance. Reeves could pick up a fresh one. "Not sure what they're after. I thought they'd finished up yesterday."

He put his hand out for the controllers. "Who knows? Thrym's a cautious guy. Likes to have multiple backup plans. I'm sure it's just one of those."

She tipped her monitor to him as he slid the gloves on. "Once they see what Dad can do, Thrym'll change his tune."

"Let's hope so." Reeves leaned over and whispered. "Why don't you see if you can get Rumi to take a walk with you? It might ease the tension."

It didn't take a computer scientist to know what he meant. She stood and stretched.

Mom stood in the middle, consulting with one of Thrym's top men. Every few minutes, she shot a glance to where Dad hunched over a keyboard before a bank of computer and vis screens. Rumi hovered to his right like a personal guard.

Lexi tapped Rumi's shoulder. "Let's get out of here for a few minutes. We can pick up some food and bring it back for the guys."

Rumi hesitated, looking at her husband as if waiting for something. When he said nothing, she stood. "We won't be long, Gunner. Is there anything in particular you'd like?"

"No." Her father didn't look up. "Whatever is fine."

Mom's gaze tracked them to the door and likely would've followed them further if her mother had X-ray vision.

Outside, Lexi breathed in the dry air. "How are you doing? You look as though you were never even sick. Dad too, for that matter."

"We're both good." She kicked a stone out of their path. "Well, actually, Gunner hasn't spent much time with me. Says he needs to 'figure things out,' whatever that means."

Lexi winced at Rumi's hurt voice. It wasn't fair how she lost her first assigned husband, and now her second marriage looked as unsettled as a drone in a tornado. If Mom had been honest in the first place, how much different would all their lives be right now? "That sounds so hard. I'm sorry."

Rumi stopped in the middle of the path. "Are you? I mean… they're your parents. I'm sure you think of me as an intruder."

Though Lexi didn't think Rumi meant the comment as a jab, it struck her in the heart with its sharpened edge. "You've changed so much since I met you. And you didn't deserve how I treated you back then. I'm sorry."

With a nod, Rumi moved on. "Your father has a choice to make. I get that. But I hope, no matter what, you and I can still be friends."

The knife in Lexi's heart twisted. "I'd like that. No matter what."

It wouldn't be long before her father finished. Then they'd make their play against the Imperium and Tempest. If they won and all went home again, what would that new life look like? Would Dad stay married to Rumi? Or would he go back to Mom? The Imperium had never seen this problem before, to Lexi's knowledge, and contemplating it hurt her head.

Better to focus on the pressing issue. They needed to win this war. They could sort out family dynamics afterward.

Chapter 22

L exi failed to hold back a yawn. Even with the infrared, her drone images returned mostly black with subtle gray variations. Not even a raccoon or mouse invaded the rocky terrain. "Remind me, again, why we're doing this in the middle of the night."

Reeves leaned in. "Response time for their cybersecurity team will be slow at this hour. Your dad said he often caught people asleep on the night shift. That doesn't mean we shouldn't be ready."

Her neck popped when she stretched. "I feel their pain. I can barely keep my eyes open."

He snickered. "If it makes you feel any better, Tempest will have to deal with the same sponge bath as you for the foreseeable future should this all work out."

The thought made the early hour more bearable, and she couldn't keep a straight face.

From the front of the cave, her father shouted and pumped his fist into the air. "We're in."

Moving her gaze off her screen, she looked at Reeves's vis monitor. Their rebel symbol, a violet bird in the shape of a Y, overtook the screens. Anyone awake and paying attention in the vicinity of any vis screen would know the hack had begun. Anticipation shivered through Lexi.

Whoops of joy reverberated, but Thrym's voice rumbled like an approaching storm. "Enough. Pay attention to your stations."

Their large central screen exhibited each Imperium tower's schematics, their control centers flickering red dots. Each camera, vis screen, door lock, air-conditioning unit, sewage pump, and any other modern convenience presented as white lights with red connections to the tower's mainframe. It looked like a spider's web covering the building—the arachnid hovering at the bottom, waiting for her prey to become entangled.

Smaller screens around the cave monitored critical areas they wanted to maintain when everything else failed. Though the Imperium had little use for the elderly, they nursed ill children back to health in various medical units. Toilets would go down there, but ventilators would remain on. All operating rooms remained functional, in case they were in use or needed. Lexi had supported her father when he'd insisted on this single point of contention.

With another rumble, Thrym shouted orders. "Status calls. Anyone seeing problems, shout out the system name. We take it down in five...."

Tension kept Lexi's breaths shallow, her spine erect. By now, someone should have noticed if they weren't sleeping on the job. Could her father have missed something? A critical firewall installed since his imprisonment and escape?

"... two... one... Activate!"

Lexi held her breath, took one last look at her lonely drone's view, then returned her gaze to the towers' images. The white lights flickered, then went dark. The red lines faded as though someone had drawn them back into the servers.

The mainframe lights dimmed to yellow, with only enough connectivity to support the lines to the critical areas they'd designated as safety zones. The only convenience left to the majority would be vis screens.

Mom, who'd let Thrym and Dad run the operation thus far, spoke the next order. "Let's send our message."

The bird on the vis screens shrank and floated into the top left corner. A message scrolled below it.

CITIZENS OF THE IMPERIUM: THE TIME FOR TRUTH HAS COME. FEAR CAN NO LONGER RULE OUR WORLD.

UNTIL THE COUNCIL AND ITS LEADERSHIP AGREE TO TRANSPARENCY AND A RETURN TO DEMOCRACY, THE PEOPLE OF THE IMPERIUM WILL GO WITHOUT. THE SAME AS THOSE LIVING IN EXILE.

ONCE THOSE FORCED TO LIVE AND DIE IN THE FAVELA ARE WELCOMED HOME, THE ELDERLY ARE NO LONGER TRANSPORTED TO SOLITUDE, AND THE FORCED MARRIAGE AND MILITARY SERVICE ARE ELIMINATED, THEN YOUR SERVICES WILL BE RESTORED.

STAND UNITED TO REGAIN OUR FREEDOMS.

The message repeated on a loop.

Tempest's wicked smile assailed Lexi's memory. If no one had awakened her yet, they would soon.

They'd left the cameras and microphones in the council chambers live so they could observe when the group met.

All thoughts of sleep vanished the moment her father had stolen their system's controls. She looked through the drone's lens, searching for any signs of movement. Still nothing.

The sun rose before the room where Lexi'd been forced to perjure herself came to life. With the only light coming from windows, shadows hid the corners. The first disheveled council member, escorted by a Freedom Force guard, slumped in and took her seat at the enormous table. Others trickled in, each looking as if the military had pulled them out of their beds and forced them into their clothing. Some sported misaligned buttons on their shirts.

After the last member took their seat, Tempest floated in like it was business as usual, her military uniform pressed and flawless. She gave the cameras a rude gesture, then gazed around the table, making eye contact with each leader.

Tempest began her speech, but there was no audio. Odd. The room had microphones tucked everywhere for vis productions.

"Is it just me?" Lexi asked. "Or are all the microphones dead?"

A voice from the front of the cave hollered back. "One second…"

Tempest's voice boomed into the room until someone reduced the volume. "Sorry about that."

Everyone focused on Tempest. "Our security forces are already well on their way to restoring systems. We knew the day would come when the rebels would attack the innocents of the Imperium. While none of us relish this proof of their malfeasance, our citizens must see how vile our enemy can be."

Reactions varied. A few council members leaned into Tempest's words, nodding their agreement like good puppets. Others shifted their gazes from person to person as if looking for the correct reaction. One sat ramrod straight, lips pursed, and jaw set.

Tempest continued. "The Imperium is strong, and its people are our backbone. We will never capitulate to blackmail." She pointed to the vis screen and the rebels' message. "Those who sow discord among our people will be rooted out, and our union will grow stronger with every dawn."

Her message sent, she rose and led the parade of council members from the chamber. The room fell into silence as their footsteps faded.

Lexi tried to read the others' reactions. Reeves rubbed a palm across his cheek, the scratch of his early morning stubble audible. Thrym stood, arms crossed and statue still, except for his jaw. His cheek muscles moved as he appeared to chew on what he'd heard.

Her mother sank back in her chair, linked her hands behind her head, then blew out a breath. "It's a start. They need to stew in their problems. Miss those everyday luxuries. They'll be back. I'm confident."

Thrips and aphids, the alternative was too horrible to contemplate. If this failed… Lexi shuddered.

A whoop sounded from the far right. The programmer who'd helped her father raised a fist. "You gotta see this. I was searching through the camera feeds. You won't believe what I found."

Her father stood. "Put it on the main screen."

"It's difficult to see, but with the camera's power light, you can just make it out."

The enormous image in the front switched from the rebels' message to a darkened stairwell, the steps visible in the dim lighting. But the programmer narrowed the lens's focus, and

Lexi's heart flipped in her chest. The spray-painted image of a bird. The rebels' symbol.

Thrym let out a low whistle. "Looks like we've got a new generation of rebels on the loose."

Her mother's face broke out in a grin. "People are fed up. Tempest went too far. I'd be angry too if I had a young teen right now." She took in the cave, capturing the attention of as many as she could. "This is it. I can taste victory."

* * *

Lack of sleep and too much time hunched over her drone controls left Lexi cranky. How long would the Imperium hold out? Camera feeds during the day showed citizens in a state of unrest. Lines had formed in various places. People holding empty bowls, buckets, and bottles in search of water. More of the rebellion's symbols popped up as the day wore on.

Since night had fallen, she returned to scouting the area between their new camp and the Imperium, flying out as far as the drone could. She'd also traced portions of the path between their current location and their old base, wishing Nana would change her mind and join them.

Reeves returned from a break, pausing behind her to rub the ache from her shoulders. "Anything interesting?"

With a shake of her head, she patted his hand. "Mind-numbingly quiet."

He chuckled, slid into the seat beside her, and picked up his drone controls. "Quiet is good."

An alert brought her attention back to her screen. The canvas of muted grays and blacks from the infrared scanner had changed. In the distance, a flare of heat turned a section bright white with yellow bursts.

She moved the drone toward the source, a press of her thumb giving it a burst of speed. As the area grew larger, she froze, nausea rising into her throat. It couldn't be. They wouldn't… "Nana."

Reeves crowded in to see her view. "What is it?"

Words wouldn't come. She jabbed a finger at her screen, her mouth dry as the surrounding desert. "Look."

"Shoot. Not good." He jumped to his feet. "Thrym, Tora, you need to see this."

The sleepy room came to life, and people gathered to see the view from Lexi's drone. Thrym slapped her desk, causing the screen to jump. "I knew Tempest wouldn't give up easily. We're one step ahead of her, though."

Mom hustled from the front of the cave. "What is it?"

Thrym frowned. "They've attacked our old base. Heat signatures show multiple fires."

Rather than growing hotter, the colors morphed as they shrank. The white from the explosions cooled to hot yellow, then orange and red. The heat of the attack waned, but the temperatures transferred from their former camp to Lexi's body as anger welled inside of her. "I have to go. Nana needs us."

She yanked at the gloves, ignoring the jumble of the video as her drone obeyed the commands it perceived from her movements.

Already freed from his controls, Reeves clasped her shaking fingers. His blue eyes glistened while he stripped off her gloves. "We'll go together. But we have to wait. They probably bombed the camp remotely, but we can't be certain the Freedom Force isn't on the move." He pulled her in tight. "The moment Thrym gives the all clear, we'll be on our way."

Her mother joined them. "Reeves, take Lexi for a walk. We'll talk when she's calm."

Lexi leaned on her husband, her legs sturdy as a mud pie. The air in the cave was too thick to inhale. The moment they stepped into the night, she gulped in deep breaths. Nana couldn't be gone. Ms. Becky either. Lexi had to get to them.

She found herself braced against a boulder with Reeves rubbing her hands between his. Was she cold? She must be as his were so very warm.

His gaze captured her attention. Why had she never realized his eyes were like the bluest lake from the archive pictures? Back in the beforetime, when families frolicked around the waters instead of avoiding their polluted banks.

His lips kept moving, and she had to concentrate to understand. "You're okay, Lex. We're going to be okay."

"No." The word came out calm, like how the wind died down just after a dust storm spent its rage. "It wasn't supposed to be like this. It's a nonviolent solution. No one gets hurt. We made sure of it."

His headshake slow, he towed her into the haven of his arms. "We can only limit ourselves. You can never truly restrain someone else. Control is a myth people have believed for generations."

Then the tears came, and he rubbed soothing circles over her back while she soaked his shirt. They held each other. By the time she'd run dry, the sun shone, lighting the world around them.

They had to go back to their old base. Had to know for sure what she knew in her heart. No one could have survived that much destructive power.

On the off chance Ms. Becky's invisible friend existed, Lexi lifted a silent prayer upward. *If it's possible, let Nana and Ms. Becky be alive when we get there.*

Chapter 23

When Lexi and Reeves returned to the command center, Thrym had already assembled a team. Rumi waited in the lead UTV, her mouth set in a grim line. She caught Lexi's attention. "Let's go. I'm not waiting any longer. My brother…"

How could Lexi have forgotten Zane and his family? Their baby. A chill skittered down her spine. She slid into the front passenger seat beside Rumi and patted her shaking arm. "We'll find them."

Reeves crawled into the back seat. "Might as well head out. Looks like we're traveling light. Just them to help." He pointed to a second UTV with four men behind them, then into the sky. "And, of course, them."

Lexi tracked two drones overhead, an escort and a lookout. She looked back to the second UTV where the two men in the back wore the gloves for the drones. Portable monitors strapped to the front seats gave them visibility. They'd get a bird's-eye view. Smart.

Footsteps crunched over gravel. Her mother joined them. "Sorry I'm late. I had to ensure we're set here. Chances are good the attack was the Imperium's attempt to distract us."

Tears welled in her red-rimmed eyes, and she gripped Lexi's shoulder. "Part of me wishes you'd stay here. I don't want you to have to see…" Her voice broke, forcing her to pause and clear her throat. "You need to understand no one could have survived that attack—*no one*."

Mom's unnatural concern hurt more than if she'd been flippant. Nana, Ms. Becky, Zane, and his family—all gone. Annihilated in retribution.

Lexi sucked in a deep breath in search of any remaining fortitude. "I need to know for certain."

A tear slipped down Mom's cheek, and she swiped it away.

Maybe her concern was genuine?

Then her expression shifted as if she'd forbidden the sorrow another moment. Returned to war mode, she crossed her arms and widened her stance. "Your father asked me to send his love. He's staying behind to monitor the systems. He needs to keep one step ahead of the programmers trying to lock him back out."

Rumi tapped the accelerator. The vehicle lurched. "We need to get going."

Mom glared at Rumi, then took the last seat.

They headed down the mountain, unable to talk because of the jarring ride over rocky terrain. Once they reached the bottom, the ground evened out, but the desire to converse seemed to have bounced out of everyone by then.

The sun had almost reached its zenith when they arrived at the smoldering camp. An unfamiliar stench hung in the air, and Lexi tasted it with each breath. She swallowed back the bile in her throat.

Though the gate remained closed, they skirted it via a sizeable gap of fallen fence. A bomb strike on a nearby tent had blasted the area, pushing shreds of canvas through the fence.

What had been their headquarters, the old farmhouse, lay in ruins. One wall still stood, but the other three crumbled into the middle, their charred remains a blackened skeleton. On the cement steps lay a corpse someone had draped with a blanket.

Rumi drove forward but slowed the vehicle to a crawl as they passed tents in various states of destruction. Some were nothing but blackened poles. Others had collapsed but not burned.

A few dwellings survived, but where were the people? Someone had covered the bodies. Lexi's heart hammered in her chest. Nana could have done this kindness—providing dignity for the deceased.

Her nose burned. The stench of charred flesh mingled with the acrid scent of burned wood and plastic.

The remnants of the medical tent came into view, and Rumi braked at what used to be the entrance. "Whoa."

Lexi focused on a walker, blackened and misshapen, poking up from the ground. A reminder of why some stayed behind when the rebels moved—the immobile and infirm. Once again, the Imperium's lack of empathy and devaluation of life was on full display. But the rebels also abandoned them to their fate. Were they any better? "I can't believe anyone survived."

A whir above her head reminded Lexi of their drone companions. They circled overhead—the operators taking in the camp's entirety. What she'd give for that same view, to see the extent of the damage in a few frames.

"Tora. Lexi." A woman waved and limped toward them.

"Nana!" Lexi jumped out of the UTV and ran to her

grandmother, her heart pounding. "You're all right!"

They crashed into each other, and she caught Nana in a crushing embrace, tears streaming down both of their faces. Mom joined them in the huddle.

Lexi released Nana, the older woman wobbled on her feet, so Lexi steadied her. "You're hurt."

Nana grimaced. "It's just a bruise. I took a tumble."

Soot smeared her face and clothes, but no blood indicated deeper injuries.

"We need to get you to a doctor."

"No. I'm fine." She patted Lexi's hand. "But we've got people who need medical attention."

Concern shadowed Reeves's face. "We didn't think anyone could have survived."

By then, Rumi had driven the UTV closer, and Reeves eased Nana into the vehicle. "Rest here. I still can't believe you're alive."

She rubbed her injured leg. "If not for Ms. Becky, I wouldn't be." Her voice broke, and she swallowed before continuing. "She's in the greenhouse."

Reeves climbed into the UTV bed, and they all piled in and took off. The path worn into the earth was now an obstacle course of debris. The destruction lessened as they drew closer to the greenhouse. Walking wounded cared for those unable to move. A supply tent, its contents stacked outside as if someone had disemboweled it, served as the new medical center.

Nana led them inside, one arm wrapped around Reeves's for support. Ms. Becky lay on a cot, the first in a row of bloodied wounded. A bandage, soaked in soot and crimson, looped around her forehead.

Lexi kneeled beside her friend and brushed a hand across

her pale cheek. The coolness of her skin sent a shiver racing through Lexi's spine. "We're going to get you treatment. Just hold on."

A gentle hand settled on Lexi's back, and Nana joined her, knees popping as she lowered herself. "She knew they'd target the medical tent. The moment of the first explosion, she told us to evacuate as many as we could." Her hand covered Ms. Becky's. "They didn't give us much time. Clumsy me—tripped over my own two feet and landed hard. She helped me up and got me out before the bomb hit. Shielded me from the blast with her body."

Tears slid down Nana's cheeks, and Lexi pulled her into a side hug, searching for words of comfort. "Typical. She always put others first."

"The best way to find peace is to stop looking out for yourself and start looking out for others." Nana bowed her head. "At least that's what she believed."

Reeves cleared his throat. "I think she's gone."

Lexi swiped her eyes to clear her vision and felt for a pulse. Nothing.

Mom repeated the gesture, then shook her head in confirmation.

* * *

By the time they returned to their mountain base, Lexi felt like a rag hung out to dry. It had taken multiple trips with others helping to bring the survivors to the base. Fewer than fifty of the hundred who'd stayed behind survived.

Miraculously, Zane sustained only minor injuries after

flying debris hit his back as he helped evacuate the medical tent. His wife had been working in the greenhouse and their daughter had been with her. They'd escaped uninjured. Miracle or dumb luck? Lexi knew what Ms. Becky would have said. Perhaps her prayer had meant something.

They'd buried Ms. Becky in sight of the greenhouse where she'd spent so much time. Someday, Lexi would return to leave a more permanent marker on the grave. The impromptu marker she'd created with the backside of a plastic sign wasn't dignified enough to be permanent. People needed to know where someone filled with so much love rested.

Dad met Lexi and Reeves at the mouth of the cave and hugged her, starting a fresh wave of tears. Lexi must have cried an ocean's worth already. How could she have any left?

He held her, as if bearing in her sorrow. When her mother joined them, Dad released Lexi. "Tora, I'm certain you're exhausted. But you're needed inside."

Her mother's shoulders sagged under the weight of the day, but she nodded and strode into the cave entrance. The rest of them trudged behind.

Inside, Mom joined Thrym before the main vis screen. It displayed drone footage of the destruction of the old camp. Her father's voice came from the vis speakers. "This is what our government does. It disposes of the weak and any who would choose freedom from their rule."

Having spent the entire day sifting through the wreckage, the images took Lexi back, as if she were seeing it all fresh. Her stomach knotted—such a tragedy. A hand settled on her back. Once again, Reeves shored up her reserves, his strength seeping into her.

Dad pointed at the main screen. "We've been feeding drone

footage of the base camp into the Imperium's vis systems. Everyone knows the council attacked and killed people who were supposedly safe in Solitude." He went to his keyboard and tapped in commands. "And the people are responding."

Another series of scenes flashed on the main screen. Citizens clogged hallways, lobbies, offices, and any place they could shove their signs in front of cameras. They'd had enough, and their messages were clear.

End control.

Freedom to choose.

Bring back democracy.

A strange sensation skittered across Lexi's skin. Something akin to weightlessness. This could be it—what they'd fought and some died for. "What is the Freedom Force doing?"

"So far, they're protecting the Administration building." He tapped in more commands. The scene changed to the council room. A sign propped in front of Tempest's chair read "Council meeting at 6:00," but the room remained empty.

"Obviously, they want us to listen in when that gathering starts, which is why we needed you inside, Tora. That's in forty-five minutes."

While they waited for the meeting, Lexi munched on a protein bar and watched the city cameras' feed. The new rebellion's symbol showed up everywhere. People wore it like a badge of honor painted on signs, doors, and even faces. Teens, with hair dyed violet like the symbol, stood out like berries in the rooftop gardens. There now had to be too many for the Imperium to quell. They couldn't jail them all. Could they?

Her father hollered. "Doors are opening."

All screens in the cave synchronized to show the council

chambers. The Freedom Force guards came in first, opened the huge wooden doors, and stood at attention as the council members filed in. If Lexi hadn't known better, she'd have thought the video feed showed some ancient ritual as they all walked in synchronized steps, faces somber.

They came in two at a time and took their seats, starting with the two beside the head chair. With the last places claimed, except for Tempest's, the secretary who followed the leader around scurried to the head chair, removed the sign, then rushed out of the room.

Corvinus Vale, the councilman whose family the rebels rescued, stood and cleared his throat. "This meeting of the Imperium Council is now called to order. Bring in the accused."

A shudder ran through Lexi when guards escorted Tempest in, her hands bound. Tempest's sneer emphasized her unkempt clothing and hair. When she stood at the podium Lexi had spoken from, she shook off the guards' hold and faced the council, her head erect and shoulders back. "You have no right—"

"Tempest Malachy," Corvinus interrupted, "the Council of the Imperium accuses you of treason against the Imperium and against humanity. Additional charges include false imprisonment, murder, and falsifying evidence and testimony to this council—all for personal gain and aggrandizement. How do you plead?"

Her nostrils flared, and she moved from behind the podium. When a guard stopped her, she returned to the microphone and glared at her accuser. "I'm no more guilty than each of you."

The room rippled, gazes darting and council members

resituating themselves in their chairs as if they couldn't find a comfortable position.

Corvinus continued. "Your trial will begin in one week, and we will assign you legal representation." He signaled to the guards, who pulled her out the door while she screamed profanities.

Once the doors closed, he faced the main camera. "We ask the rebel leadership of Y to meet with the council in this room in two days. The time for reconciliation has come. Join us to restore our city to one of freedom and democracy." He gestured first to those on his right, then left. "All who would personally guarantee the safe passage of the rebels, please stand."

Some sprang to their feet as if their seats ejected them. Others took their time. Eventually, all rose.

Once they all stood, he gazed into the camera again. "Meeting adjourned."

As the council filed out, a few smiles broke out around the cave, but no one looked as excited as Lexi felt.

Thrym stood beside her mother, arms crossed, glower set deep. "It's a trick. One last attempt to pull us in and take us down. Don't believe a word of it."

Lexi froze. She wanted to argue, but what if he was right?

Reeves stepped forward. "I believe them." He spoke to her mother. "If you don't want to go, send me. I'll be our ambassador."

The thought of Reeves going in alone—if it was a trap—set Lexi's heart racing. "No—"

Mom raised a hand to silence the protests popping up. "I'm going." That hand pointed at Thrym. "With or without you."

Chapter 24

Both of Lexi's parents argued against her participation, but she'd insisted. She'd go, invitation or no. She needed to see this through to its conclusion, either way.

The handgun, tucked in a holster at the small of her back, was a concession to Reeves. Twin sheaths of blades clung to her hips—her weapons of choice.

Thrym took on the role of an armory pack mule, slinging ammo belts over his shoulders, fastening grenades to his belt, holstering a handgun on each hip, and carrying an assault rifle. Beside him, the others looked more like they were gearing up for a day of gardening.

Their foursome left the rebel forces secure at the base. Thrym remained steadfast at Mom's side, as always, while Reeves refused to let Lexi go into danger without him. A team stationed just outside the city provided a drone escort, ready to provide backup firepower.

Corvinus met them in the Favela at the base of the Administration towers. Two guards flanked him, their weapons trained downward, but ready. A sharp wave of cologne trailed him, its cloying sweetness burning Lexi's nose. "Welcome."

He gave his polished political smile. "We're pleased you've accepted our invitation."

He gestured toward the weapon Thrym cradled, his finger hovering close to the trigger. "Those aren't necessary."

Thrym lifted the edge of a bag strapped to his waist, exposing enough C-4 to end the discussion. He grinned. "You've got unnecessary backup, and we've got a matching set. Let's agree to move forward."

Mom waved for him to close the flap. "Any of us can trigger the bomb. For all you know, it's on a dead man's switch. So let's not quibble."

With a nod to his guards, Corvinus headed inside, his men leading the way.

Nerves on edge, Lexi, Reeves by her side, followed her mother and Thrym into the council chambers. All four walked with measured steps. If ever Lexi wished she had eyes on the back of her head, today would be the day.

Corvinus gestured them in. "We're prepared to negotiate a peaceful resolution." The grand table had two open chairs, but Corvinus took the one Tempest previously inhabited and left his former seat empty.

His broad smile would have calmed Lexi if not for the other council members' tense postures. Fingers tapped on the semicircular tabletop, and feet bobbed beneath it. Nervous sweat scented the air. Where the podium previously stood, a table with four chairs faced the larger group.

A woman, Samara according to her nameplate, sat ramrod stiff with arms crossed. "It's inappropriate to bring weapons into this chamber. As you can see, none of us are armed."

Mom pointed to the guards at the door. "They leave the room, and we'll set our arms down."

The woman opened and closed her mouth several times, but she said nothing.

Corvinus came to her rescue. "Gentlemen"—he waved toward the guards—"would you be so kind as to wait outside the doors? I'm certain we'll be fine."

They paused a beat, looked at each other, then complied. The door clicked shut behind them, and all eyes turned to their rebel group.

Thrym grumbled low in his throat when Mom took her seat and laid her rifle on the flat surface. She motioned for them to do the same.

Lexi and Reeves complied, but Thrym stood stubbornly behind her.

"Thrym." Mom mumbled under her breath, loud enough for Lexi to hear. "You're not helping."

He clattered the remaining chair from the table, flipped it to face the door, sat, and laid his weapon at his feet.

Mom let out a slow breath. "Close enough."

A smile twitched at Reeves's lips, and Lexi had to suck her lips into her mouth to school her face. Thrym's stubborn refusal to leave their backs unguarded settled her angst.

Corvinus cleared his throat. "Thank you for your willingness to talk."

Was he serious about a peaceful solution or simply appearing to care? He spent as much time staring into the camera as he did at them. Her father's broadcast of this meeting meant the council, and its decisions, were out there for the citizens to see. The whole of the Imperium would judge them by what they all said and did today.

If she didn't know better, her mother's relaxed posture might've fooled her. But the tension in her eyes told a different story.

With a nod, Mom responded. "Future generations will view today as a turning point in the Imperium's history. It's the responsibility of all who sit in this room to turn this meeting into a tsunami of change for the good of our citizens. A day to return freedom of choice to our people. A day to remove the blinders this council has used to hide the truth of Solitude."

Samara's face reddened. She stabbed a finger onto the table. "This council had no knowledge of Tempest's nefarious dealings with Solitude. We've brought our former leader up for judgment. I take no responsibility for her actions."

Mom's spine stiffened. "I find it hard to believe this entire council can plead ignorance of everything Tempest did." Ice glazed her voice. "Since you put no controls in place to prevent her actions, you all are culpable for the deaths of thousands."

The room erupted in protests and side discussions. Would Mom signal they should leave before things got ugly?

A bang silenced them.

Lexi looked at Corvinus, expecting to see a gavel or some such thing in his hand, but he gaped like the rest.

A rapid succession of booms echoed through the room. They originated from beyond the doors.

Gunshots.

The rebels jumped from their chairs and grabbed their weapons. Thrym flipped the table on its side and used it as a shield, their guns pointed at the doorway.

A cacophony of violence closed in on the chamber.

Lexi shifted. Across from her, the council members had ducked behind chairs or anything else to shield themselves. One group of four struggled to turn their massive table on its side, but bolts held it in position.

An explosion blew the doors inward. Pain erupted in her chest and head as the blast hurled the table into them and launched them across the room.

Her ears rang, and the room tilted as if the entire building swayed. Debris littered the floor and coated her skin. She pushed herself onto her elbow and blinked to decipher her world.

Soldiers… entered the room.

She needed to move. Where had Reeves gone? Mom? Dizzy nausea rolled over her with her second attempt to rise. The copper taste of blood added to the misery.

Rotating onto her stomach, she forced herself to her hands and knees. Reeves's face came into focus, just feet from her, his arm draped over his head at an odd angle.

No. He couldn't be…

Her heart pounded in her throat. The rhythm quickened with every inch she crawled closer.

Muffled shouts came from the opening that once served as the chamber door. Men rushed in, a giant in the lead.

Fletcher.

"Everybody up! Hands on your heads!" His voice was barely audible, but his beet-red face got the point across.

She tried to speak, wave him off. They didn't need to be rescued.

Then she remembered. He wasn't one of theirs anymore. But he wasn't Imperium either. Her muddled brain couldn't fit the puzzle pieces together.

He planted himself in the entrance while his men moved behind the debris-littered council table and hauled council members to their feet one by one.

The blast had thrown her mother and Thrym in the opposite

direction of Reeves and herself. Thrym remained on the floor, unmoving.

How had his explosives not gone off? This building and everyone in the room should be a pile of rubble with a cloud of pink mist throughout.

They plucked his weapons from his body and cast them aside.

Another of Fletcher's men hauled her mother upright, her legs stumbling to catch up.

He wasn't here to help.

Lexi had to get to Reeves.

With a burst of effort, she stumbled to reach him, but a powerful hand grabbed her shirt from behind and yanked her up so violently her world blurred. As her vision cleared, Ethan's face snapped into focus. His lips formed a disapproving frown. "I don't want you hurt, Rebel Heart, so behave."

The muffled words sent a shiver down her spine.

She forced down the urge to slap him. Instead, she laced her fingers behind her neck, palms pressing hard against her skin to ground herself.

Her gaze found Reeves, and her breath caught in her throat.

His arm twitched, and his low groan broke the stillness.

Her chest loosened, and a shaky exhale slipped past her lips. He was alive!

Hands up in surrender, Mom stepped toward Fletcher. "What are you doing? We've got the council right where we wanted them. Tempest is going to pay for her crimes, and they're negotiating."

His eyes bulged, and he jabbed his gun at her. "How can you be so blind? They're sacrificing Tempest to save themselves. They all need to go."

A scream drew Lexi's attention. The council members now stood at gunpoint near their overturned chairs. If she were judge and juror, the guilt on their faces would put them all behind bars for the rest of their lives—or worse.

Corvinus, his face slack, stared at his feet.

Mom took another step and shook her head. "Now isn't the time to point fingers. This is our moment to change the system while everyone is ready. I know you didn't always agree with Ms. Becky. I didn't either. But she got a few things right. This isn't what she'd have wanted for you. Violence was never her way."

"When did you become a bleeding heart?" He jabbed a finger at the cowering council members. "These demons don't deserve any mercy. I saw what they did to our old camp." His voice broke, and he sucked in a breath, his lip trembling. "Saw her grave."

His focus moved from Mom to Corvinus. He raised his automatic rifle, rested the butt on his shoulder, and poised his finger on the trigger. "He'll pay for her life with his own."

Lexi's mouth went dry, and her hands trembled. Fletcher's actions could end the fragile peace before it bloomed. "Remember what Ms. Becky wanted. Peace..."

Fletcher swung his gun in her direction. "Finish that sentence, and it'll be your last."

Lexi froze, along with the beating of her heart.

"No!" Mom's calm façade shattered, her eyes wide, hands spread toward Fletcher. "You're our friend. We've always been a team." She spread her hands toward the room and spoke to his men. "We can be one again. But only if you put your guns away."

His rifle swung once again, redirecting toward Mom along

with his glare. "Becky tried peace for years. Couldn't convince her it wouldn't work—but I knew. Knew they'd kill her, eventually. She wouldn't listen. Violence is their native tongue." He waved the gun barrel toward Corvinus. "Now, how do you like it when the gun's pointed at you?"

Sweat glistened on Corvinus's now twitching face. His mouth opened, but no words came out.

The rebel behind Corvinus shoved him in the back. "Time we gave the council a taste of their own blood. If I recall, they favor firing squads."

Corvinus dropped to his knees.

The rebel yanked him back up and dragged him into the center of the room. The other rebel followed suit until all the council stood side by side in a line of quaking terror.

Tears streaked down Samara's face as she clung to her neighbor.

The stench of urine burned Lexi's nose—Corvinus's panic evident for the cameras and audiences across the Imperium as a dark stain spread down the length of his pants.

She had to do something. Fletcher, Ethan, and two more. Four against four, or it would be if Thrym and Reeves rejoined. Even if they didn't, it seemed unfathomable that Ethan or Fletcher would injure either herself or Mom.

What about Thrym? The eye Lexi could see looked like a lizard's slit partly open to let the light in. What were the odds he'd been feigning unconsciousness?

God, if you're really there and listening, now would be the time to do something to help us.

Hands up, she took a hesitant step toward Fletcher, drawing his aim once again. Even if Thrym couldn't help, if she eased in closer, she'd kick Fletcher's kneecap. Distract him so her mother could attack.

Together, they could take him down. "Don't do this. Please. We're better than them."

Thrym moaned, drawing the room's attention. Fletcher frowned at him, then waved for his men. "Cover him."

Lexi took advantage of Fletcher's momentary distraction and charged, head low, toward his knees.

Her world broke into pandemonium with her mother's scream. "Fletcher, no!"

Pain smacked her when someone crashed into her side, throwing her to the floor in tandem with the explosion of a gun.

Spots danced in her vision after her head cracked against the unyielding marble floor.

"Down!"

"Now!"

"Freeze!"

Women screamed and men grunted.

The whoosh of movement around her left her feeling like her body floated in the air. She opened her eyes, and the ceiling spun above her.

Get up. Help Mom.

Lexi rolled to her side. Her ribs ached. A trickle of warmth slid down her cheek. Her vision cleared enough to take in Reeves.

His face sported a new bruise, but he'd planted one knee on Ethan's back, pinning him to the ground.

Ethan squirmed and caught her gaze. "Get this idiot off me. He'll never be worthy of you, Rebel Heart. I'm the one fighting to make your cause come true and set us free to be together."

The council members must have jumped in to help with

three or four of them on each of Fletcher's other two men.

Pain shot through her as she scanned the rest of the room.

Thrym stood over Fletcher's prone body.

A scream pierced the air. It escaped her throat.

Next to Fletcher lay her mother, her unseeing eyes pointed at Lexi, and one lifeless hand stretched out toward her on the ground.

Reeves, having secured and bound Ethan, stepped up behind Lexi. "It's over."

Over. Mom had won her lifelong battle.

But what had Lexi lost? Winning wasn't supposed to feel like this.

She leaned back into Reeves's support and let him lead her from the room. More than ready to let the leaders deal with the aftermath.

Chapter 25

The sky's gray overcast fit both the day and Lexi's mood. Reeves on her left and her father on her right, she stood before the fresh mound covering her mother's grave.

Rather than lay her to rest within the Imperium, Lexi wanted to remember her mother as the brave woman she'd taught Lexi to be—wild and free. On sunny days, the greenhouse's shadow would shade Mom and Ms. Becky, side by side once again.

Reeves squeezed her shoulder. "I love the words you chose for the markers. They're perfect."

Finalizing the epitaph weighed on her heart, as if putting it in writing made her loss more permanent. Stupid childish thought.

When Lexi waved her hand over the stone, it activated a hidden speaker, and Lexi's own voice then uttered the words: "Here lies Tora Verity. A fierce spirit, a fearless leader, a mother, and a friend who gave all."

Reeves then activated the motion sensor for the stone beside her mother's and again, Lexi's voice spoke: "Here lies our dear friend, Ms. Becky. Faithful to the end, she walked the path of compassion."

"Maybe I should have used a more formal introduction?"

"No, she was always Ms. Becky to everyone who loved her."

Over the past two days, Lexi feared she might drown in the never-ending tears. But today her eyes remained as dry as the skies. Would more tears come along with the expected afternoon downpour?

Dad's face drooped. He'd loved Mom in his own way. He leaned in and whispered. "We can't miss the voting tonight, and we need to get back before it storms. Do you want a few moments alone?"

Her eyes grew damp, and her voice failed. Perhaps they wouldn't be able to beat the rain after all.

With a last squeeze, Reeves kissed her cheek. "I'll be over by the UTV. If you need me, just wave."

Then she stood alone. Though the rest of her family waited behind her, the hole in her universe left by the ones in front of her seemed unendurable. Yet both women would insist she push forward.

The thought dropped her to her knees. She grabbed a handful of the fresh-turned earth and squeezed. "I love you, Mom. I wish we'd had time to make things right between us. Ms. Becky's right here with you to keep you company." A sob escaped, and she swallowed it back. "I'll come back as often as I can to visit, but I knew you'd want to be out here, not cooped up in the Imperium." The back of her free hand swiped at her leaky eyes. "You shouldn't have done it… stepped in front of that bullet for me. But I'm going to live the rest of my life making sure your sacrifice means something."

Below Ms. Becky's marker, the mound had already receded a bit into the ground as if the earth were absorbing a loved one back into its womb. "Take care of Mom for me, just like you took care of everyone you met."

Lexi stood and brushed the dirt from her palms and pant legs. "Just so you know, we won. No—*you* won. Now rest in peace."

** * **

The tension in the council room sizzled across Lexi's skin, rebels occupied half of the chairs while the original council members gave them nervous glances from the other half.

Thrym and Corvinus stood shoulder to shoulder at the head of the huge council table, the single seat of power pushed back until one of them could claim it.

Lexi's seat beside her father, in the room where she'd sat with her mother days ago, brought waves of flashbacks. Her hands trembled at the memory of her mother's open, lifeless eyes.

She wouldn't let the world forget her mother's heroism. Nor would her father.

A bell sounded, and her father stood. "The voting window has expired, as per our agreement." He looked first at Thrym, then at Corvinus. "A reminder that all in this chamber agreed to let the citizens vote for Tempest's replacement as a temporary arrangement until both sides can present plans to move the Imperium forward. Thus, the leader chosen today will serve for one year, during which this combined council will manage the Imperium."

If only everyone didn't look so angry. Could the fragile peace hold?

Thrym's stiff posture and nervous hands showed he had

no clue what to do with them if they didn't wield weapons. Crossed arms, lack of eye contact, and the tap of fingers on tables and feet on hard floors set the room abuzz.

The large vis came alive in one corner, and her father directed the group's attention to it. "Each of the towers' servers are finalizing the tallies for their respective citizens."

The screen flashed with numbers as six groups of Imperium votes sped through the calculations. Individual opinions merged seamlessly with those of their neighbors as the computer tallied the votes. A final decision that reflected the will of the masses. One they'd all agreed to abide by.

On one side of the tally board, the deep-purple bird symbolizing the rebel leader Thrym stood in stark contrast to the official gold seal of the Imperium council representing Corvinus.

Reclamation's count completed first, Thrym winning the popular vote with a wide margin. Lexi almost felt embarrassed for Corvinus. *Almost.*

The Growers and Production results came in simultaneously, with Thrym claiming victory again, though by a tighter margin.

Corvinus appeared to shrink with each loss, his shoulders drooping. But when the Freedom Force building delivered a strong win in his favor, he straightened, standing taller and regaining some confidence. With the Administration building narrowly siding with Corvinus, the outcome loomed uncertain.

Only one building remained—Maintenance.

Lexi's heart leaped in her chest when it returned a strong vote for Thrym, and the overall total showed a wide enough margin that no one could doubt the citizens of the Imperium demanded change.

Thrym extended a beefy hand toward Corvinus, who flinched as if bracing for a blow. Thrym left his hand out, knitting his eyebrows.

Corvinus's cheeks flushed as he accepted the gesture of peace.

Power had shifted from the old guard to the new, yet the mood remained split. On one side of the giant curved table, tension simmered, while on the other, smiles, hearty shoulder slaps, and handshakes spread in celebration.

Corvinus retook his former council seat. "My congratulations to the winner. I'll continue to serve the Imperium in my capacity as a council member."

Still standing beside the seat he'd won, Thrym cleared his throat, picked up a tablet, flicked on the screen, and read. "Thank you to the citizens of the Imperium for placing your trust in me. I will do my best to deliver the change you've shown you want." He glanced around the room, then back at the tablet, hesitating. With a faint sigh, he set the device down and leaned forward, his thick knuckles braced on the tabletop.

"Let's be honest." Vulnerability edged his steady voice. "I'm more at home in a strategy room than a boardroom. Most of our people want peace—no more death, no more destruction on either side. That's not my strength, but I know some good people who can help us get there—together."

His gaze shifted to Lexi, Reeves, and her father, nodding at each of them in turn. They had a monumental task ahead, and it would take every person in the room working together to succeed.

Thrym stood straighter, his presence commanding yet

tinged with unease, as if still adjusting to the weight of his new role.

* * *

Lexi's Administration uniform itched, the stiff fabric chafing at her neckline like an accusation. "I swear, someone must have put extra starch in this to make me look as nervous as I feel."

She tugged at the collar in a futile attempt to loosen it. The urge to rip it off increased with each passing moment. Her hands trembled as she tried to fasten the last button. "I know I have to testify, but the thought that my words might put someone in front of a firing squad"—her voice faltered, her jaw tightening—"sets my teeth on edge. Even if it is Tempest."

The rebels under Fletcher, including Ethan, awaited individual trials in the same prison that held Tempest. Lexi would never know what Ethan's true motivations were, but at least, she'd been able to discuss the whole thing openly with Reeves.

Reeves stepped up behind her, his reflection appearing in the mirror and stealing her breath. It had been so long since they'd had a quiet moment together, and the way the overhead lights caught his eyes—like a pristine blue lake untouched by the poison of war—made her chest ache.

He slipped his arms around her waist, eased her against him, and rested his chin on her shoulder. His warm smile softened the edges of her fraying nerves as his gaze met hers in the glass.

"You're beautiful," he murmured, his voice steady with quiet conviction.

Now, more than ever, she wished she could stay here, wrapped in his arms, away from the world's demands. But today's task was about honoring Ms. Becky and Mom, and she owed them that much. Taking a deep breath, she straightened her shoulders. "This is it—the last of the big chores to close the chapter on the Imperium's old ways. Once Tempest's trial is done, people will settle into the new ways. Don't you think?"

Reeves brushed a kiss against her neck, lingering before letting her go. His touch was a promise, a reminder their battle was nearly over. After crossing the room, he opened the bedroom door, his smile both tired and hopeful.

"People already have." He clasped her hand as she passed. "I heard two seventeen-year-olds rejected their marriage assignments. Said they wanted to wait. Can you believe it?"

Lexi paused, her eyes meeting his. The smallest of laughs escaped, more from relief than humor. "Yeah"—she scooted out the door—"I can."

She could. If she'd had the choice back then, she'd have done the same—fought for control over her own future and body. But, then again, if she had, she might never have met Reeves. A chill tingled down her spine, her heart tightening. Despite everything, she couldn't imagine giving up the love they were building amid so much chaos.

The doorbell buzzed, cutting through the quiet, and Reeves moved to answer it.

Her father stood there, his grin uncharacteristically broad. Beside him, Rumi clung to his arm, her fingers laced through his as though she were holding onto an anchor.

Lexi gawked—Rumi's eyes were bright and clear. Free of the manic twitch Dr. Ichtacka's experimental drugs induced. Her shy smile, once buried under layers of trauma and manipulation, had returned, softening her features and making her look almost like a kid entering a new neighborhood for the first time.

Reeves stepped back to let them in.

Dad pulled Lexi into a warm hug, his tension palpable. "We've got news." He drew back and gripped her shoulders. "No trial today, after all."

Lexi blinked, racing to process the shift.

Rumi shrugged, a flicker of her warrior personality edging her wry grin. "Tempest decided to talk after all. She must know she'll face a firing squad, but wants to delay the inevitable by naming names."

"Sweet seedlings, they better not give her too much time. She's had enough chance to say her piece." Lexi's voice cracked. Rumi and Dad didn't seem as upset as they should be. Lexi's chest tightened. "I thought today was the day we'd get it over with."

Rumi's grin stretched wide, her edge replaced with something softer—hope. "It'll end soon enough, but she might have company in the defenders' box." She hugged Lexi before letting her go. "She'll pay for what she's done."

She allowed herself a moment to breathe, to let reality settle in. But even as the relief relaxed her, a bittersweet ache clenched her chest. If only her mother and Ms. Becky had lived to see this day. They deserved to stand here with them, to celebrate the end of the reign of terror they had endured and fought against.

The old Imperium was gone, toppled by their collective effort. The silence stretched. One era of oppression had closed, and a new one of hope had begun—building something better. Something worthy of the struggle they'd endured and the people they'd lost.

Her mother. Ms. Becky. Their memories anchored Lexi, their strength guiding her forward. She straightened her spine and gave a determined nod. "Let's make sure our losses mean something."

Epilogue

"Wake up, sleepyhead." Reeves brushed his lips across Lexi's bare shoulder, then poked her in the ribs for good measure.

She swatted away his hand. "I don't wanna."

He huffed in her ear and snuggled her into his arms, her favorite place to be. "Well, you could always skip your first day on the job and waste it here with me. Everyone will understand."

When he put it that way, she had only one option. She sighed, swung her legs out of bed, then set her feet on the cold bamboo floor of their Administration apartment.

After the tents with cots and uneven ground underfoot, their new abode still felt pretentious. Excessive, even. "Once we're past the opening ceremony, I'll be fine. Right? Tell me I'll be fine."

The love in his eyes warmed her as much as his grin. "Lexi Verity Scheffer—daughter of the war hero, Tora Verity—tell me a tiny speech isn't sending shudders of panic through you."

"Of course not." She stood and pulled a fluffy beige robe around her shoulders. "Er... what if we switch places? You give the speech, and I'll—"

"No way. I'd trip all over my tongue."

A pillow thudded against her shoulder.

She picked it up and threw it back.

He dodged. "I wish I could be there."

"And I wish I could be there for your big day too." She sidled up to him, wrapped her arms around his neck, and kissed him. "Assistant chief of security. I'm so proud of you."

His straight white teeth practically glowed in the early morning light streaming in through the window. "The job offer had more to do with my history with the new chief. If I can just keep Thrym from growling at the newbies and scaring them all off, we'll be fine."

"Dismantling the Freedom Force is no small undertaking. So, we'd both better get moving before we're late."

She opened the bedroom door into the living area. The sizzle from the frypan emitted a salty whiff of bacon. Nana stood at their stove, already dressed for the day in her white administration top. Instead of the matching white pants, she wore a purple shade reminiscent of the greenhouse lilacs. "It's about time you two got up. I thought I'd have to eat this bacon by myself."

Lexi placed a hand over her middle. The aroma of such a rare treat normally made her mouth water. Today, her stomach lurched. "It's so sweet of you to celebrate, but you shouldn't have splurged. I'm so excited I doubt I could eat a bite."

Reeves came up and snatched a piece of bacon off the plate. "I'll eat her share if she doesn't want it. Thanks, Nana."

Nana pointed toward the bathroom. "You'd better hurry and get ready. Being late isn't the way to start your first day. Especially as the new director of Reconciliation."

After a quick cleanup, they all headed to the administration's work tower. As they crossed the bridge, Lexi revisited the day it all started for her. The spray-painted rebellion symbol and the test she'd tanked to avoid the life of an engineer. Now she willingly walked across the bridge, not as a student, but as a leader in a newborn government finding its way while its people watched.

They slipped into the first open elevator and hit the buttons for the seventh and tenth floors. When the door slid open, Reeves leaned down and kissed the top of her head. "This is my stop. Have a good day. I can't wait to hear about it tonight."

She squeezed his hand before releasing him. "You too."

After the doors opened again, she exited the elevator, Nana close behind. Lexi gave her grandmother a side hug before heading down the long hallway. "I wish Mom and Ms. Becky were with us today. They would have loved this."

Nana walked beside her, smiling at those they passed. "They'd both be so proud of you, just like I am."

"Isn't it wonderful the way people now dress?" Lexi waved toward those around her. Though they still wore the designated shirts of their assigned jobs, a vibrant array of pants colors reflected newfound individuality. A new way of thinking had taken hold of the Imperium's people, and today should bring a new generation of problem solvers together.

They reached the door. A freshly hung plaque gleamed beside it: Department for Resource Equity and Compassion. Lexi gripped the knob and turned. "Here we are."

The chamber inside thrummed. A woman approached Lexi, a tablet held at the ready. "Mrs. Scheffer, I'm honored to meet you. I'm your executive assistant, Mart." Brown hair swung over her shoulders as she shook Lexi's hand, then smiled at

Nana. "And, Mrs. Smith, so pleased to welcome you."

Heat rushed to Lexi's cheeks. "Please. Call me Lexi."

Mart nodded, then tapped on her tablet. "I'll show you to your office. You'll be addressing your team in the main conference room in fifteen minutes."

The view from her window displayed how far they had to go. Below, the Favela had bloomed with people who'd come out of hiding. Long lines formed with those looking for food, clothing, and, some even hoped, housing. She'd tackle those lines as one of the agency's first initiatives.

But first, her speech needed to rally them together. *This is for you, Ms. Becky.*

Though she had eaten nothing yet, her stomach roiled like a volcano on the brink of eruption. Public speaking wasn't her favorite activity, and the trauma of her forced "interviews" with Tempest further soured her natural distaste for it. If only she could say what needed to be said without a group of people staring at her.

Mart popped her head in the doorway, the neon green of her pants too bright for morning. "Five minutes, Mrs. Scheffer. I mean, Lexi."

Lexi followed Mart through a maze of cubicles to an open space lined with tables and chairs. When the people milling about saw her enter, a swarm of movement ensued until everyone had found a seat. Now, all watched her.

No pressure.

Lexi sucked in a deep breath and blew it out before she stepped up to the podium. "For those of you who don't know me, I'm Lexi Verity Scheffer, and I'm honored to work with you all in this new endeavor." Except for the quiet shuffle of people resituating themselves, they remained silent. "I wish you all could have met Ms. Becky. She taught me more about compassion than anyone I've ever met. Her life inspires our new motto: 'Peace through selflessness.'

"Our purpose is to develop systems to ensure our society can care for our elderly without overburdening our younger generation. Together, we will redefine resource allocation as a shared responsibility.

"You will all become advocates for sustainable systems such as community-supported housing and shared caregiving networks. Never again will someone die just because they've reached an age society deems untenable. From now on, grandparents will live to impart their wisdom to the next generation. No longer will we cast anyone away."

Heads nodded encouragement.

Her shoulders relaxed. "And most importantly, our team will support research into healthier aging. Everyone deserves the best food, healthcare, and work that provides enough exercise to promote stronger bodies instead of hours sitting behind a screen or over decaying garbage on an assembly line to the detriment of our minds and muscles."

Nana fiddled with the necklace Lexi and Reeves had given her to celebrate her birthday. A cross like the one Lexi found on her first day in Reclamation. Nana recently shared some stories she'd learned as a child. Legends the Imperium worked so hard to obliterate.

Lexi refocused on the audience and cleared her throat. "Not only that, but we'll also provide opportunities for all people to learn the beliefs of our ancestors. We will no longer fear the exploration of spiritual realms. People will be free to pray, study, and believe as they wish. Open discussion will be a hallmark of this organization—starting today."

Her gaze roamed, connecting with as many of the people as she could in the brief pause. "Together, we'll reclaim this city for our children and our children's children."

The group broke out in applause. Heat surged to her face when some of them stood.

Compared to her mother and Ms. Becky, she'd done nothing to deserve accolades. But she could represent them. She could continue with the mission they'd begun. Ensure no one got left behind.

When she returned to the apartment, her legs ached from walking and standing all day. Everyone wanted to speak with her, to tell her about lost loved ones they wished they'd known better.

Having Nana in her life after everything that had happened was what Ms. Becky would have called a blessing, but tonight, Lexi was grateful Nana decided to visit Dad and Rumi for supper. An evening alone with Reeves was exactly what she needed.

Silence filled the apartment. Maybe she'd beaten him home. But no, the basket of flowering strawberry plants, with ripening berries, on the kitchen counter proved someone had been there. She sniffed the fragrant leaves and earthy undertones. Extravagant, but beautiful. And tonight... appropriate.

Reeves emerged from their bedroom, already changed out of his uniform and into a pair of shorts and a T-shirt. He gestured to the plants. "I hope I remembered your favorite."

She joined him on the couch and kissed him. "They're perfect. Thank you."

"How'd your first day go?"

She slipped off her shoes and wiggled her toes, ecstatic

to free them from their bonds as well. "You were right. Amazing is the perfect word to describe it. Everyone seems so determined to find ways to make sure every citizen gets what they need. We're already planning to build two new wings off the residential tower. First dibs on the apartments will go to the homeless. They plan to name them in honor of my mom"—her voice cracked, and she swallowed hard—"and Ms. Becky."

"Would Nana move out if she could get her own place?" He massaged her shoulder with one hand. "She's welcome to stay as long as she likes. I know you enjoy having her close by."

"I know we just moved in here, but I thought we might like one of the new apartments. They're planning for them to be multigenerational homes, perfect for grandparents to live with their children and grandchildren like some did before the Great War."

"Hmm." His voice rumbled on her neck as he leaned in. "That sounds wonderful. Maybe someday we'll have a little one of our own, and I'd love for the little guy to know his great-nana."

She ran a hand down his arm, then took his hand in hers. "Or maybe it'll be a girl. Strong like her grandma and noble like Ms. Becky."

"And like her mama." He kissed her, drawing her closer.

Her stomach growled so loud he pulled away and stared at her middle.

With a laugh, she stood and headed toward the kitchen. "Today was such a rush. I haven't eaten yet. Let's grab a bite, then finish that thought."

He followed her into the kitchen. "You haven't spoken to your dad or Rumi today, have you?"

"No. Why do you ask? Is everything okay?"

"Well, I wasn't supposed to say anything, so you need to look surprised when Rumi shares the news." He gathered her hands into his. "You're going to have a sibling. Rumi's expecting."

A shiver ran down Lexi's spine. Dr. Ichtacka's experiments. His attempts at making super soldiers. The new government put an end to his work, but what about those who'd already taken the regimen? Would the baby be all right? "But what about the drugs she took? Do the doctors know about them?"

Reeves smoothed her hair. "They know, and they're keeping a close eye. Since she'd been drug free for quite some time before conception, they think there will be no lasting effects for her or the baby."

Lexi tried to accept the good news and ignore the tension in her gut. Rumi would have her chance at motherhood, and, as Lexi's mother always wanted, Lexi would no longer be an only child. "What a gift. Sweet seedlings, now we gotta make the New Imperium a city worthy of raising this next generation."

He pulled her in close, his heart beating in time with her own. "We will. I'm sure of it."

The End

About the Author

You can connect with me on:

🌐 https://angeladshelton.com

🐦 https://x.com/AngelaDShelton

📘 https://www.facebook.com/AngelaDShelton.Author

Subscribe to my newsletter:

✉ https://bookhip.com/DVWFRXR

Also by Angela D. Shelton

Snippets of Love - Free Short Stories
https://dl.bookfunnel.com/lhewji0hqg
Escape into *Snippets of Love*, a collection of charming short stories filled with faith, hope, and unexpected second chances. Whether it's a rekindled romance, a surprise Christmas miracle, or a twist of fate that changes everything, these heartfelt tales will warm your heart and remind you that love always finds a way.

Free download for you at: https://BookHip.com/HRALZNH or on my website.